JOHNNIE IN MIAMI

DS Whitaker

This is a work of fiction. Names, characters, businesses, places, events, locales, and incidents are the products of the author's imagination or used in a fictitious and satirical manner. Any resemblance to actual persons, living or dead, or actual events is purely coincidental. Certain long-standing institutions, agencies, and public offices are mentioned, but the characters involved and their actions are wholly imaginary. The opinions expressed are those of the characters and should not be confused with the authors. Also, please do not feed wildlife or remove them from their natural habitat.

ISBN: 978-1-954794-02-3 (EB)
ISBN: 978-1-954794-03-0 (TP)
LOC:

Author photo by Diana Lang
Cover Design by DS Whitaker

To Tim for his love and support

Note to readers: This book centers on a character in deep mental distress and describes thoughts of suicide and an attempted suicide. Although my books are largely intended to be comedic, the treatment of mental illness is a serious subject and one I have personal experience with. The characters' opinions and biases are intended to open the discussion around mental illness. Often society attaches stigma to this topic; I think we can do better. It has a positive ending; I promise.

This probably goes without saying, but while Johnnie's struggles are at the center of the series, most of the other characters have anger issues, feel inadequacies, or live with dark secrets. My message is: everyone has some kind of past trauma or insecurity. We are all just doing the best we can. And wouldn't it be great if we could all be there for each other in the process.

DS Whitaker

PROLOGUE

Under the moonlight, Stumpy scrambled to the top of the white cooler chest beside the old man they called Cud. He reached out with his green, taloned foot to get his attention.

[Are you okay?] asked the short-tailed iguana.

The man with the short white hair didn't act like his old friend, but his breath had the same smell of melons.

Cud, with a beach towel around his shoulders, muttered to the air above, with shouts interspersed.

It didn't seem right. [What is wrong?]

His human friend made no eye contact.

Stumpy bobbed up and down, remembering the times in the evening when they danced on the glittering sand after the man's swim in the ocean.

[Dance with me! Look at me! Be my friend!]

Instead, his companion curled up in a ball on top of his broken boogie board and cried. Stumpy knew cries. And sadness. Cud hadn't leaked water from his eyes like this in many seasons.

Did he do something wrong? Did the Iguana King bring sorrow?

Stumpy wandered away, crossed the beach, and climbed his favorite tall palm tree. At the top, he gazed across the dark bay. The warm night air tickled his dorsal crests.

Where was his other pal, Johnnie? His friend with the brown boots seemed busy in the mornings lately. And he forgot cheese puffs for three days in a row.

Things were changing. Changing in not good ways.

The Iguana King cannot be sad.

Stumpy shut his eyes and tried to think of happier times. But it was not to be. His companion in the mangroves simpered and moaned, piercing the smooth breeze with melancholy. Birds jostled at these screams and flew away.

His home on the beach—once full of fun and treats and smiles—only brought waves of fear and worry.

It was now a very bad, very sad place.

And he missed his friends.

Chapter 1

"Quiz Show Challenge is starting soon." Greta scraped remnants of spaghetti and bread-crusts from her plate into the trash bin. She left their plates and utensils on the counter.

Johnnie pulled down Greta's Murphy bed. In a coordinated manner, like they had done all week, she did her part and positioned the television to face it.

He enjoyed their new routine, but he couldn't look away from the mess in the tiny kitchenette. The red sauce oozed off the forks onto the counter. *Like a crime scene.* "Should we wash the dishes first?" He used the 'royal we', knowing that he was actually offering to wash all the dishes, but it seemed more diplomatic phrased in the plural.

She grinned, grabbed the remote, jogged past him, and dove onto the mattress. "No, leave them! I just want to cuddle and watch the show."

He couldn't argue. Still, he enjoyed doing dishes and the orderliness of a clean counter. Greta's small apartment didn't have a dishwasher.

Johnnie placed the pillows neatly on the bed, then strode seven steps to the sink. "I don't mind…"

As he picked up the sponge from the sink, she leapt up from her reclining position, came up behind him and wrapped her arms are around his waist. "Marine, I'm giving you an order. Leave them." Greta pulled him away from the kitchen counter, back across the short distance. With her attention to the television, she said, "Look, it's college night."

The pimple-faced teenagers on the screen described their academic and personal achievements to the host. The kid from Princeton explained he spoke five languages and volunteered with an orphanage in Yemen last year.

Johnnie scoffed. "Jumping Jesus, really? Yemen? That's bullshit. I'm rooting for the one from Miami-Dade College." Miami was the perceived underdog compared to Princeton and Stanford.

"Shhh." Greta sat cross-legged, her torso leaning forward slightly, her eyes glued to the screen. "They're announcing the categories."

Johnnie slid his body behind hers, brushed her long red hair to the side, and rubbed her shoulders.

He paid only passing attention to the categories as the announcer called them out: U.S. Presidents; Foods that begin with P; Anatomy; Dog Breeds; Literature; and World Conquerors.

"Oooh. Conquerors," Greta crooned. "Did I tell you I moved on from William the Conqueror and now I'm reading about Attila the Hun?"

Johnnie admired her neck and her birthmark that looked like a bright pink three-leaf clover. "Yeah?"

With extreme focus, she called out the correct answers to the first three clues. "What are Dachshunds?" "Who was James Monroe?" "What are pistachios?" With every question, she twitched her thumb like pressing an imaginary button. With every validated answer, she clenched her fist and whispered, "Yes!" He chuckled inwardly at her enthusiasm.

The host gave the next clue, "The largest bone in the human body."

Greta looked down at herself and huffed.

The answer rolled off his tongue. "Femur." Part of him did not know how he recalled the word. But he knew he'd broken his during the incursion five years ago. It had taken several months for him to heal fully and walk again.

The announcer confirmed it was femur.

"You got one!" Greta kissed him on the cheek.

"Had to happen at some point, I guess," Johnnie said with a smile. He didn't take her reaction as an insult, because he *never* got a correct answer. Even when he thought he knew certain facts, he couldn't retrieve the information quickly. Which meant watching this show was an exercise in futility. But Greta loved the show and that's all that mattered.

They continued watching. He took off his park uniform, folded it, and placed his stack of clothes on the high-backed wood chair next to his side of the bed, leaving him in his chambray blue boxers and white tank undershirt.

Unfortunately, Greta was still fully dressed in her green shorts and t-shirt that sported a graphic of Pluto, with a slogan beneath insisting it was a planet after all.

The floor-to-ceiling white shelving unit across the room was packed with books except for a single spine-width vacant slot. He glanced at her nightstand, where the thirty-year-old hardcover book about female orgasm had remained since reviewing it on their second night together. After a discussion of his medical issues, they leafed through the tome, identifying all the variations—in the name of science—and assigned a code name for each sexual position. The names were intentionally silly and fun; but now he wondered if they would kill any romantic mood.

In his head, he began the countdown to the first commercial break. *A few more questions...*

When the presenter announced they would be right back after a word from their sponsors, Johnnie crept his fingers under the bottom of her shirt. But she pounced like a cat, twisting and tackling him precisely on cue as the first commercial came on the screen. He loved their game of messing around during breaks. To him, it was the only reason to watch the show.

They were still in a courtship phase and while he could never get a sustained erection, the heavy petting over their clothes and underwear excited him, opening up a world of romantic intimacy that had been closed for years.

She smelled so good. Maybe they had waited long enough. *Fortune favored the bold...*

He continued to debate internally as they kissed through the rest of the commercial break. When the show returned, Greta untangled herself from his embrace and reset her attention to the screen, transfixed like a cat watching a laser pointer. He renewed his patience for a few more minutes and tried to think of other dog breeds beginning with D, but could only think of Dobermans. He called out Doberman for two of the clues, but was wrong twice.

When the second commercial break approached, he wasn't sure if it was too soon.

They kissed again, but it was difficult to keep an amorous mindset while listening to an ad about lubricated catheters. When the next commercial discussed exciting low-cost burial insurance options, he couldn't stand it anymore. He reached for the remote, turned off the television, then dropped the remote on the floor. "Greta, I think I love you and I think we should..."

She gasped. "I think I love you too."

"I think we should do it."

Her eyes widened. "Are you sure? You wanted to wait…" She batted her long eyelashes, teasing him. But in the next moment, before he could explain his reasoning, she fished the straps of her bra through her shirt sleeves and unhitched the back clasp.

Greta pushed him down. She wiggled out of her clothes and reached for his pelvis.

But he knew an attempt in that area would only lead to frustration. He glanced his eyes to the tome on her nightstand and whispered, "Can we try the Bart Simpson?"

She nodded and shimmied over, assuming a conducive position. "Take your time."

As much as he wanted this next step, it had been over five years, and this endeavor would be more awkward than seductive. His fears evaporated quickly with her very specific verbal instructions, mixed with some geeky sex talk where she called him Attila and someone called Cyrus the Great.

Her current fascination with world conquerors was obvious, although it messed with his concentration. But since the mental role-playing made her happy, he tried not to laugh. Soon, her banter—in terms of discussing historic barbarians—ceased and her breath turned heavy. Signs he was on the right track.

In what he considered a short time, Greta moaned and spasmed, indicating success. "Mmm." She leaned to the side, tucking her knees toward her mid-section. He nestled next to her and draped his arm across her hip. She reached for the elastic of his boxers. "Do you want me to…?"

"No." He brushed a stray lock of hair from her eyes. "Maybe another time. I'm sorry I can't…"

Greta snugged the sheet up to her chin. "No, don't worry. That was amazing! Maybe we can add the Monty Python next time. Hey, on the bright side, at least I don't have to go on birth control again. The pill gave me such bad side effects."

He knew all about side effects. A thought overcame him as he kissed the back of her hand. Without thinking, he asked, "Do you want to have kids? I mean, not now…but eventually?"

She flipped to her other side to face him. Squinting, she asked, "Do you?"

His mind raced. After his life-altering injuries five years ago and the months he'd spent in the hospital, he had simply been concerned with repairing himself and becoming a whole person again. With his moods and poor memory, fatherhood would be ludicrous. *And what could he possibly teach a kid? Nothing.*

"No, I...um. I guess I never thought about it." *Change the subject*, his brain screamed. But he blurted out, "But I bet you would be a great mom."

She grinned. "Aw. Thanks."

He stared at the ceiling. "I would be the *worst* dad."

"Why?"

"Come on. You *know* why."

She ran her finger across his sparsely-haired chest. "Well, I don't think anyone ever feels *prepared* to have kids."

He sighed. *Any child raised by Greta would be so incredibly smart and happy*, he thought. In his heart, he knew he should never be a dad. Period. Because he would live in constant terror of yelling at them or leaving them in a supermarket or forgetting to feed them, or a number of horrors.

If Greta wanted kids, then he would be doing her a disservice to maintain their relationship.

He sat up and swung his feet on to the floor. "I should go."

"No. What? Why?"

Johnnie collected his clothes from the chair. He unfolded his shirt and put his arm through the sleeve. "I...you...I need to think."

"Johnnie Crosswell, you can't make love to me and leave two minutes later. It's bad manners." She sat up and crossed her arms. "Now get back here."

Even with her messy red hair, no makeup, and pouty face, she was still so sexy. He detected her scent on his fingers as he buttoned his shirt. *Why was he leaving again?* He scratched the scar above his right ear. *Oh, right...honesty.* "I don't want kids. You deserve someone better."

"We've only been together twelve days."

He wasn't sure of the math and counted to himself. She was likely counting the days since he returned from his shipwreck.

She huffed, "I'm going out on a limb here, but maybe we can decide marriage and kids later? Like, I don't know, after a couple of *years*?"

Deflated, he sat back down next to her, not meeting her gaze. Greta was in her mid-thirties, ten years younger than himself. She still had time to have children if she wanted to. "I don't want to hurt you or mess up your life."

"I won't let you mess up my life." She scooted up behind him and put her arms around his waist, resting her chin on his shoulder. In a sultry voice, she said, "Now, I command you to stay. Pretend I'm Genghis Khan. You will do my bidding."

"Okay, Genghis," he chuckled. *Yes, the famous librarian, Genghis Hobbs.*

She kissed his earlobe. "Hey, did you know he poured molten silver into his enemies' eyes? Badass, right?"

He appreciated her attempt to change the subject. Since they were having an honest conversation, he continued on. "I'm going to ask Doctor Phillips about changing my meds. To help with…you know."

"Are you sure?" She kissed his neck.

Johnnie felt her warm breath and her bare bosom against his shoulder blades. Truthfully, he dreaded changing medication. But the benefit could be so worth it. "Oh, I'm sure." He twisted, pulled her legs towards him, and nuzzled her belly.

"Oooh, Captain Johnnie. Yes! Arrr, matey! Hoist the mizzen in me dungbie, ye scallywag."

Johnnie belly laughed. They had met at the library last month when he was researching pirate lore for a story he was writing. Thankfully, Greta's previous obsession with famous pirates was waning. Their first night together, she revealed her pirate fantasy, complete with her own pirate lass costume. At least he didn't have to wear the goofy eyepatch anymore when they were messing around. He didn't want to tell her how it gave him headaches afterward.

However, her current fascination with legendary world conquerors worried him. She casually mentioned something yesterday about how sexy he would look in a fur vest and Viking hat. He honestly hoped she was kidding. Wearing fur in a tropical zone like St. John could be unbearable and far from sexy.

Johnnie shook off that thought. *Concentrate.* Repetition was good for memory. And now he knew what to do.

She arched her back to release the bunched-up sheet and shove it out of his path.

He was enjoying the Bart Simpson very much. And Greta seemed to like it, too. But he wanted to try *everything*. Including the Dewey Decimal System and the Hello Kitty.

Preferably, without wearing Viking horns.

* * *

Dottie—alone as usual in her one-bedroom Cruz Bay cottage—had just finished her microwave dinner and poured herself a white wine spritzer with a dash of lemon soda and extra ice cubes. She turned on the television. Her green silk slip stuck to her back from perspiration; her ceiling fan provided only minor relief from the humid night air. She listened to the local news while scrolling through real estate listings on her phone.

She longed for a larger place with air conditioning, or a home located high on a hilltop with refreshing cross-breezes. A far cry from her current rental. Situated on a barren patch of dirt behind an automotive shop, her home had stunning views of dented rusty cars and stacks of tires. But it was private, had survived the last hurricane intact, and included a reliable high-speed internet connection. Plus, it was located within walking-distance to the grocery store and her workplace, the legislature annex building.

On her phone, she came across a listing for a four-million-dollar estate with an infinity pool on St. Thomas. Far beyond her reach, but she flipped through the images anyway.

Her phone rang. She checked the incoming number: *Bahamas.*

"Oh, for goodness' sake." It had to be a telemarketer; likely the same time-share company that had been pestering her for the last four years. All because she attended one seminar to receive a free bread maker. She hit 'decline'.

She sipped her wine and scrolled through more home listings until a news story came up on the television about a vehicle accident. A resident had discovered an abandoned SUV at the bottom of a ravine, close to the eco-resort. Interestingly, the driver could not be located. She wiggled her nose in thought. "Huh?"

Her phone showed a voicemail, and she hit play, assuming it would tell her about some very exciting credit opportunity. Instead, a very panicked-sounding young man with a British accent, Jackson Loughton, asked her to call back, saying it was *very* important. And important was her *favorite* subject.

Dottie put down her drink and called him back. "Good evening, Jackson. Sorry, I thought you were a spammer. How are you doing, sweetie?"

"Ms. McPherson, thanks for calling me back. I hope I didn't catch you at a bad time?"

"Of course not. Again, please call me Dottie. What can I do for you?" She switched off the television and put the phone on speaker. Absentmindedly, she unfastened her dainty turquoise earrings.

"I was hesitant to call, but I'm concerned for my grandfather. He was supposed to call me days ago. Have you seen or heard from him? You were so kind to help him find a new apartment last month. Do you know if he's moved in?"

She had no idea, and she prided her whole existence on knowing *everything*. Maybe she was losing her touch. Her best friend, Gertie, had recently been in a whirlwind romance with Jackson's grandfather Cudlow, the homeless recluse billionaire.

"Hmm, now that you mention it, I haven't heard from Cudlow or Gertie."

Consulting the calendar on her phone, Dottie worked out that Gertie had left town over twelve days ago. Dottie smacked her forehead. She'd been so consumed lately trying to pry information about her boss Robin's new love life, she'd completely lost track of Gertie. "When did their cruise end?

"Seven days ago. He said they planned to marry on the ship and would later return to St. John to gather Ms. Brown's belongings before coming here to Nassau. I tried calling them both many times."

"Wait. Hold the front door! They got married?!" Her own shouts startled her.

"That's what he said. Perhaps they went away on an extended honeymoon? I don't want to interfere, but I just need to know if he is all right."

How did she not know about the wedding? "I'll look into it and call you back. Give me a few minutes."

"Thank you, Dottie."

"Anything for you, sugar. Bye." The gears in her brain went into overdrive.

Dottie loved a mystery. But at that moment, she was furious. The last time she spoke with Gertie, her friend had insisted she planned on breaking up with Cudlow, only meeting him in Panama to say a last goodbye.

She called Gertie's home phone.

"Hello?"

Dot skipped the pleasantries. "You got MARRIED?"

Gertie's voice was monotone, her words measured as if she had just woken up. "Hi, Dot. No. It's a long story."

"I bet it is. You should have told me! But what happened to Cudlow? Is he with you? Jackson called me. He's worried sick."

Gertie let out a long sigh. "Cudlow said he was going back to the beach. Johnnie checked on him. He said Cudlow is fine."

"What the hell happened? And why weren't you at church last weekend?"

"I can't."

"Can't what?"

"Can't get into it. I just can't."

Dottie turned on her charms. "Aw, sweetie. You can tell Doctor Dottie."

"No. I'm not letting you blab my life to *everyone* on the entire island anymore. I'm tired. Goodnight, Dottie."

Dot's mouth gaped. "I promise—"

"Bye."

"Wait—"

Gertie hung up.

Maybe she deserved that, she thought. Still, she needed to get to the bottom of things. She dialed Johnnie.

After a few rings, he picked up. "Hello?"

He sounded out of breath. Like he was exercising or something possibly sexier. Her boss, Robin, mentioned her brother had a new girlfriend. *Good for him!*

"Johnnie, it's Dottie. Where is Cudlow? How is he?"

"Oh! Yeah, Dot. Um…" Johnnie sounded like he was stumbling around or moving furniture. "I saw him this morning. He's back at the beach."

"But HOW is he?"

"Yeah, I…I mean, he's physically fine, I think. He's got a weird look in his eyes. Talking strange. Like down on love. I guess it didn't work out with Gertie. I feel bad for him but he'll get better with a little time."

"Weird look? I need more."

"It's hard to describe. Like he's looking straight through you. But he seems calm."

"Did Gertie tell you they almost got married?"

There was a brief silence on Johnnie's end. "What? No."

"Jackson said they planned to wed on the cruise ship. But I just spoke to Gertie and she said they didn't. And that can't be good."

This was a new record. Gertie was right. She couldn't keep any secret to herself. Still, she continued, "Jackson is worried sick. Why is Cudlow living on the damned beach again? We were working on getting him a condo. I mean, what if Cud had a mental breakdown? He could be suicidal for all we know."

"Nah, he didn't seem *that* bad."

"Johnnie, you've known him the longest, but living on the beach is not sane."

"He's been living there for ten years."

"Exactly. He needs help."

Johnnie sighed. "I don't know what to do."

"I'll talk to Jackson. Thanks, Johnnie." She ended the call.

Dottie needed to see the situation for herself. Her next call was to Officer Arturo Bell.

"Artie, it's Auntie Dot."

"Good evening, Dot. How are you?"

"Artie, do you know where Cudlow stays on the beach?"

"Wait, I thought he moved back to the Bahamas? Or living with Gertie?"

"He's back on the beach. I spoke with Johnnie."

After a pause, he said, "Oh no."

"Exactly. His grandson called me. I need to check on him. Now, where do I look?"

After some muffled conversation in the background, Arturo came back on the line. "I'll pick you up in ten minutes."

"Thanks." She finished the rest of her wine, shook her head to clear her thoughts, and put her phone down. She shoved her feet into her sandals, threw an oversized Bob Marley T-shirt over her slip, and grabbed her purse. Her hair was in a bandana and she didn't have any makeup on. A far cry from her usually polished appearance, but Artie was like family and in the dark of night, no one would be around to judge her.

Out the door, waiting in front of her small bungalow, she paced back and forth, contemplating the worst and mumbling toward the moon high in the night sky. She hadn't known Cudlow long, but he was a sweet man who had been important to her best friend, Gertie. Johnnie was presumably Cud's best friend. Now, neither Gertie nor Johnnie seemed to care about Cud living on the public beach again, which, by her math, placed the responsibility on herself.

A few minutes later, Arturo rolled up to her house in a police cruiser. No flashing lights, but the sight of the vehicle gave her pause.

Was she making a mountain out of a molehill? Being a big nosy-body?

Arturo was in uniform. He rolled down his window and smiled. "Hello Dot, hop in."

She walked around and opened the passenger door. "Is this all right? I mean, if you had heard Jackson, the panic in his voice…I just need to clear this up."

"No worries. Happy to oblige." He flashed his white teeth in a broad smile; the smile she recognized well. She'd known him from the time he was a teenager. Unofficially, she was his Aunt Dot, while in reality, she was only a decade older and got her moniker as his mom's best friend. She recalled the frequent block parties, with skinny Artie playing stick ball with other teens in the street, while she and Bernice watched from the front porch, gossiping and enjoying cool lemonade beneath the shade.

"I don't want to make a fuss." She got in the car and put on her seat belt.

"Right." He arched his brow in a manner that showed he wasn't buying any of this. "So, what's the story this time?"

She considered telling Artie about Gertie and Cudlow's cancelled wedding. But restrained herself. Gertie had called her out too strongly and She couldn't give her the satisfaction of being completely right.

"No story. Cudlow's grandson, Jackson, just wanted me to check up on him. That's all." She shrugged and smiled sweetly.

"Hmm-mm." He murmured under his breath and turned the wheel, heading toward the street.

Dottie held her tongue. She ached to ask how his new romance with her boss, Senator Robin Crosswell, was going, because Robin held her cards close, despite her many attempts to glean the smallest detail. And her curiosity burned because the other women at church had asked her and she had *nothing*.

Once parked at the Hawksnest Beach parking lot, Arturo led her to the western portion of the beach, near the rocks. "It's just through here." He switched his flashlight on.

She followed him between and under branches for a few feet until a small clearing came into view. Arturo aimed his flashlight at the center.

A white-haired beast with wide, wild eyes and gangly limbs screamed. "Go away, foul humans! The Iguana King and I demand it! Leave our house!"

A dusty looking mature iguana with a truncated tail sat on the cooler next to Cudlow.

Arturo put down his flashlight. "Mr. Loughton? We just wanted to check on you. May I approach?"

Cudlow, in a dirty t-shirt and with disheveled hair, pointed to the sky. "No! Leave us alone. We are fine. We are happy! You can't make us leave. Stumpy is upset. We are useful."

Oh shit. Dottie felt the blood drain from her face. Cudlow was out of his blessed mind. And he looked a bit thinner than the last time she'd seen him. Dot wasn't sure what she would say to Jackson. But *something* needed to be done. She pulled on Arturo's arm. "We need to talk. Come on."

They walked back to the beach. "He isn't looking good, Artie."

"He isn't breaking any laws. But he should be checked out by a doctor."

"I'm calling Jackson." She dialed the number and put him on speaker.

Jackson answered after the first ring. "Hello, Ms. McPher...I mean, Dottie. What did you find out?"

"Honey, I'm so sorry. He's living like a vagrant again at Hawksnest Beach. I'm here with Officer Arturo Bell and we both agree he doesn't look so good."

Arturo said, "Hello, Jackson. I'm limited with regard to what I can do here legally. Unless you can get a court order. I'm happy to check on him every so often in the meantime. But you should act quickly."

"What is he saying for himself?"

"He's talking crazy," Dottie said, "like in the third person, and he's with an iguana. Acting like they're the same person. Hard to describe."

"An iguana? Stumpy?"

"You know him?"

"It's a long story. I'll charter a flight and be there by in the morning. Thank you for finding him."

Dot said, "Call me when you get in. See you soon." She ended the call and turned to Artie. "What do we do now?"

"I have to get back to the station. There isn't anything for us to do right now."

She looked toward Cud's nest. It pained her to leave a human being in these conditions. A thought came to her. "I have an idea. Let me try something." Dottie didn't wait for Arturo's approval and walked back through the branches.

Cud stared off into space. The iguana was gone.

"Cudlow?" She snapped her fingers. *No response.* "Hey, honey, it's me, Dottie? Remember? Do you want to get some waffles? Are you hungry? I have that good syrup you liked."

Cudlow's head turned in slow motion, like a sloth robot. "Waffles?"

"Yes, sweetie. Lots of waffles. How about some orange juice? Whatever you like, honey."

Cud stood and dusted himself off. His cheeks were sallow and eye sockets dark. He called out, "Stumpy! Waffles! Did you hear? Come back! Yum time!" Cud broke into a jog through the bushes parallel to the beach.

Dottie shook her head. This was *not* what she hoped would happen. She jogged after him.

Arturo called out from the beach, "Dottie! Are you all right? What's happening?"

Dot chased Cud for several minutes and plead with him to forget the iguana. When she caught up to him, back at his nest, Cud hissed, "He goes where I go. We don't need your crummy two-faced waffles. Leave us alone! Go!"

Arturo took Dottie aside. "We can't chase him all night. Let him rest. Jackson will be here in the morning."

"I guess you're right." She fought back tears. Cud's mental decline and physical state reminded her of her own mom who had passed from Alzheimer's. "Arturo, we need to help him. Promise me."

"I promise. Come on. Let him be."

They got back in the police car and they drove back to Cruz Bay.

She stared out the window, lost in her thoughts.

How could Gertie allow Cudlow to get to this state? Did she not care anymore? And why did Johnnie think Cud was fine? They should both be ashamed.

But now she knew one thing.

She'd be back at daybreak, armed with a stack of waffles and fresh-squeezed orange juice.

Chapter 2

Johnnie checked the clock again. Restlessness and overthinking had gotten the better of him over the last hour. Unfortunately, the sun wouldn't be up for some time.

Greta was asleep and had wound the top sheet around herself like a burrito during the night, leaving him awake with not an inch of cover.

Johnnie watched the rise and fall of her breathing, wondering how long their romance would last. This left him to consider his last failed relationship—his marriage to Darla. Which then led to flashbacks of his time in the hospital. Nobody ever expects to wake up in traction, not recognizing their own spouse and not being able to speak in complete sentences. It was only later, after the first month, when he could digest what had occurred and begin to communicate.

Darla had visited every day. She brought him pictures of their past life, used flash cards to help him with the alphabet, or sometimes they just listened to music or watched television. He couldn't recall exactly how many surgeries he'd had, but there were several.

And now, five years later, his time in the Miami VA hospital was a blur, except for the vague memories of Darla holding his hand, how she expertly discussed his medications and treatment with all the doctors and nurses, and the way she always said goodbye with three kisses on his cheek.

Unfortunately, he had more vivid memories of the time after the hospital discharged him. His nightmares, paranoid delusions, and heavy drinking had made their marriage a hell on earth. Sure, he wasn't right in the head at the time, but that was no excuse. In hindsight, his constant shouting with frustration and suicidal behavior must have terrified Darla. He understood why she divorced him.

Now, lying in the dark in Greta's studio apartment, he considered writing Darla an apology. Not that Darla would care after all this time and it wouldn't exonerate him, but it felt like the correct thing to do.

Greta turned in her sleep, breaking him from his pity party.

A swath of sheet became untangled during her movements and he snugged his body to spoon her and fit his torso under the sparse linen. With his arm around her waist, he kissed the back of her neck.

She whispered groggily, "What time is it?"

"Early."

"Hmm." She intertwined her fingers with his.

He gave her hand a squeeze and rested his cheek on the side of her neck. Within a few minutes, her breathing slowed and her fingers went limp.

Pleased she'd fallen back asleep, he was now fully awake and could find no other solution than to get up and head home to shower, have some coffee, and switch out his Park Service uniform.

He quietly extricated himself from the bed, got dressed, exited like a mouse, and locked the front door with the extra key she had given him on their second night together.

Clutching the key like a prize, he jogged down the steps to his red Piaggio Fly scooter, otherwise known as The Flying Pig.

He hadn't slept at his own apartment in Calabash Boom in over a week. His thoughts whipsawed to the idea of them combining their rents to get a bigger place together. Surely, it made sense from a financial standpoint.

With a sigh, he pushed the idea out of his head. It was clearly too early in their relationship for that.

As he drove east around the island in near darkness, he still daydreamed that someday they could be together forever.

* * *

Johnnie arrived at Hawksnest Beach at six in the morning. The sun was coming up, creating a glow behind the hills to the southeast. He parked his scooter and walked to the tool shed. The text messages on his phone included the latest list of chores from Kemper, his boss. An electrician was meeting him at Maho Bay at nine. Kemper added a smile emoji to the end of the list.

Off to his left, two people sat at a picnic table in the early morning shade provided by the pavilion's roof. This struck him as odd, since it was rare to see visitors this early in the morning.

He removed the padlock from the tool shed and took out his rake. A female voice from the direction of the pavilion said, "Good morning, Johnnie. Come join us."

It was Dottie, his sister Robin's administrative assistant. As he approached the table, it became evident that the person with her was Cudlow, but he was wrapped in a fluffy, clean blanket. He noticed the 'clean' aspect of the blanket because it was the opposite of the dirty, discarded beach towels that his eccentric friend had collected over time. A plate of half-eaten waffles lay in front of Cud; plus some type of beverage in an insulated tumbler.

"Good morning, Dot. Hey, Cud." He stood at the end of the table and waved to his white-haired buddy. Not receiving even a flash of recognition, he turned his attention to Dot. "What brings you here this morning, Dot?"

With narrowed eyes, Dot slammed her palm on the table, revealing a perfect manicure with white sparkle polish. She hissed, "I expected more from you."

"I don't understand." He had no clue what she was referring to. "Why are you looking at me like that?"

She gestured to the bench across from them. "Sit."

Johnnie followed orders and sat. The waffles, big with puffy squares, not like the frozen toaster kind, looked sumptuous, sitting on a blue plate at the center of the table. He reached…

She swatted his hand away. "Those are *not* yours."

"Geez. What's going on?" He sat on his hands.

"Cudlow needs help. How could you not see this?"

Johnnie regarded Cud, who seemed enthralled chewing his waffle, holding it with two hands. His friend seemed child-like, licking the golden square twice before each small bite.

"What kind of help?"

Dottie whispered, "Mental help."

"I'm not a doctor. I can't help him with that."

"Does Gertie know?"

"She asked me to check on him when she got home. I did. I see him every morning. He isn't so different from before. Maybe more spaced out. I mean, if he talked about hurting himself, yeah, I'd call someone."

Dot shook her head. "Something bad happened on that cruise. I think it broke him."

"He just needs time."

"Oh, so *now* you're a doctor?"

"No, I mean, sometimes people take a bad turn but it's temporary."

Dottie checked her phone. "Jackson is arriving soon. He just texted; he's in Red Hook, taking the ferry over."

"You called Jackson?"

Cudlow woke from his stupor. "Jackson? Who's Jackson?"

A thousand needles of terror stabbed Johnnie's spine. *Maybe Dot was right.* "Cud, look at me."

Cud looked his way.

"Who am I?"

"Johnnie."

He sighed with relief. *So far, so good.* "Who is this lady?"

"I don't know. A very nice waffle-maker?"

Not remotely the right answer. Cudlow had met Dottie a month prior, during the planning session of how to neutralize the killer named Thomas Smith. "Do you remember your grandson?" He crossed his fingers and held his breath.

Cud stared blankly. "Stumpy doesn't have a grandson. Do you? Stumpy? Where are you? Do you want a waffle? Come boy!" He craned his neck, looking for the iguana. "I need to find him!" Cud dropped the waffle and leapt away from the picnic bench. He ran toward the water, his arms outstretched, swinging his gaze. "Stumpy!" Cud stared at the tops of the palm trees. "Where are you?" He ran some more and moved from view.

Dottie held her head. "Goddamnit." She crossed herself. "Lord O'Mercy, it took me half an hour to get him to come to the table. See what you've done?"

"I'm sorry. I guess I didn't realize." A wave of remorse washed over him. The last few days he'd been so busy with chores at work and focused on spending time with Greta in the evenings, he'd neglected Cud. Perhaps he was selfish. "What can I do to help?"

"Jackson will be here soon enough. He might need to commit Cudlow to an institution; or at least get power of attorney to force him into a hospital for evaluation and treatment."

"No! *Commit him?*"

"There may be no other choice. He looks so thin."

"Now that you mention it, I don't recall him going on his fruit scavenges lately."

"Is that what he normally ate?"

"Sometimes with his fruit sales, he would buy beef jerky or candy bars. Sometimes I offer him an extra sandwich or granola bars."

Dottie seemed pensive, holding her head and closing her eyes.

Johnnie glanced at his watch. If he was going to meet the electrician on time, he had to get to work. "Sorry, Dot. I have to start my chores. Call me later, okay?" He got up from the table and walked down to the waterline with his rake.

Thirty seconds later, Dottie called out, "Yes, you go on ahead." She muttered something.

From the distance, he thought she called him a rat-bastard.

He knew he deserved that. If it weren't for his bank stunt two months ago, helping to solve that murder, Cudlow would have never gotten his makeover and met his landlord, Gertie. Cud's romance with Gertie, or now lack thereof, seemed the cause of this pronounced downward spiral.

Johnnie recalled things Cud had said on his return to St. John: "Stumpy says women are trouble" and "Stumpy says love is an artificial construct that deludes the mind." At the time, he figured his friend was just being silly. But now he knew Cud's problems were much more serious.

He pulled out his cell phone and called his coworker, Ranger Merv.

Merv answered, "Good morning, John." His tone seemed a little frosty. This was odd because Merv was usually upbeat, spouting gross or off-color jokes, or bragging about how many push-ups he did that morning.

"Good morning. I have some work to do at Maho Beach this morning. When you swing by Hawksnest Beach, could you check on my friend Cudlow?"

"Why, what's wrong?"

"He might be insane."

"Ha! I could have told you that. Who lives on a beach when they are a billionaire?"

"Merv, I'm serious. He's in a bad way. His grandson is coming to get him. Just check on him if you can."

"Sure. Hey, since I have you on the phone, I heard a rumor that our boss-lady Kemper has a crush on someone."

"Congratulations."

"No, that's the thing. I haven't made any progress. The rumor is she likes *you*."

"What? No, that's dumb."

"Why is that dumb?"

Kemper was one of the nicest, most caring people he'd ever known, but he never thought of her like that. Maybe dumb was too strong a word. He deflected. "Besides, I have a girlfriend."

"You *do*?"

Johnnie didn't appreciate the sound of pure incredulity in Merv's voice. "Yeah, not that it's any of your business."

"Damn, way to go! Wow! Look at you, Casanova. Are you doing the nasty?" Merv's voice was now the jovial mocking tone he was accustomed to. "Who's the lucky lady? Is it Mandy, the bartender at the Yellow Parrot? I saw her wink at you last time we got together for brewskies."

"No. You don't know her."

"What about that woman who paddle-boards around here? I've seen how you stare at her. Isn't she like six-feet tall? I mean, otherwise, she's fine as hell. Did she break up with that long-haired idiot?"

Merv was referring to the Goddess. A mysterious woman who glided through Hawksnest Bay most mornings like an ancient Greek deity and just as mythical. For years, Johnnie had been fascinated with her from afar. He had nicknamed her boyfriend Fabio because of the hair-style resemblance. "Fuck no. Jumping Jesus. Don't be a dick. I have to go."

Merv laughed. "Bye, Johnnie-boy."

He ended the call and pocketed his phone.

Out of the corner of his eye, Cudlow raced into view, in his birthday suit, running into the surf, yelling, "We are useful!" Cud's ribs had no fat on them. His elbows and knees appeared so bony.

He hoped Jackson would be here soon.

It was clear now that Cud belonged in a hospital.

He'd failed his friend, confirming his belief that he was in no shape to care for anybody.

Stumpy climbed down from his usual palm tree and sauntered over to him. [Johnnie! Good morning!]

"Hey Stumpy." He continued to gaze at his lunatic friend in the surf. [Yum time?]

"Sorry, I forgot."

[You forget a lot lately.]

"Yeah, I'm sorry."

The iguana blinked at him and rested his front foot on Johnnie's boot. [Cud makes me sad.]

Johnnie looked down at Stumpy. "I know."

Tears formed in Johnnie's eyes as he watched Cud exit the water several yards away and sit cross-legged on the surf's edge, facing the ocean, scooping sand and forming it into the shape of an iguana. Cud spoke to the sand creature and muttered, "See, Stumpy, we don't need anyone else."

Johnnie whispered back to Stumpy, "Yes, I'm very sad, too."

* * *

Jackson's flight touched down on St. Thomas and he took a taxi east across the island to the Red Hook ferry.

He had packed little. Just a change of clothes in a nylon backpack. As he waited for the ferry to cross over to St. John, he called Felicity, the company's lawyer.

She picked up right away. "Good morning, Jackson."

"I should be there in a half hour. What did you find out?"

"You'll need a doctor's report before you can petition the courts."

"But what if I can't convince him to see a doctor?"

"Unless he breaks a law or is an obvious danger to himself or others, the chances of getting medical guardianship are slim."

"I understand." Jackson shifted his weight from side to side. "I'm so worried. I wish I understood what happened."

"Will you be visiting Ms. Brown?"

"Yes, if I can. But first I need to see Pawpaw. Maybe it isn't as bad as Ms. McPherson indicated. One can hope."

"Let me know what I can do."

"Yes, of course. Thank you, Felicity."

The ferry opened its gangplank, and he got in the queue. A thought popped into his head…something Dottie had said. "He's living like a vagrant *again*." Which meant it was possible his grandfather had lied to him for years. He had to learn the truth. Looking up the phone number, he called the East End Eco-Lodge.

A woman answered, "Eco-Lodge, Good morning, how may I direct your call?"

"Good morning. I'd like to talk to the manager."

"May I ask what this is regarding?"

"One of your long-time residents." He boarded the ferry and climbed the back stairs to the top deck.

"I'm sorry…long-time?"

"My grandfather, last name Loughton, has lived at your facility for the last ten years."

"I'm sorry, sir. You may have us mistaken with another lodge? We're a hotel. We don't have permanent residents."

Jackson sighed. "Over the last ten years, have you had any guests that stayed months at a time?"

"No, sir. I've worked here for the last five years. I'm not aware of anyone meeting that description."

Jackson closed his eyes and moaned quietly to himself. Steeling his emotions, he replied, "I'm sorry to have troubled you."

"No trouble, sir. Have a nice day."

"Same to you. Goodbye." Jackson ended the call and put his phone in his pocket. He gripped the railing, staring at the waves, and wondered why Pawpaw would lie to him so blatantly all these years.

The ferry shuddered as it pulled away from the dock. A seagull flew overhead and landed on the railing four-feet to his right and cawed at him.

In his frustration, he waved his arms at the filthy bird. "Get out of here."

He found an empty bench and sat. The hum of the ferry's engines, plus the strong wave-action, sent vibrations up through his spine. The sun overhead was cooking his hair and forehead and he realized he should have brought a hat. *But who can think of hats and sunscreen when packing for an emergency trip to retrieve their mentally unstable Grandpaw?*

All the signs were there. The calls from public payphones. Pawpaw had never talked about his lodging. In fact, he rarely called except on holidays. When his grandfather asked him to take over the company, his life had changed; attending endless meetings that rarely allowed free time. And in the evenings, he chose to decompress through video games and television. But he should have made time to visit. To see how and where his grandfather was living. Cudlow always seemed so upbeat on the phone. *How was he supposed to have suspected his true state?*

It was clear to Jackson what needed to happen. Pawpaw was coming home to the Bahamas. Come hell or high water. He would keep an eye on his grandfather to ensure his health and wellbeing. If he needed to go to court, he would use every legal and monetary resource at his disposal.

And never let his grandfather out of his sight again.

* * *

Jackson, driving a yellow Jeep he'd rented, pulled into the Hawksnest Beach parking lot at nine fifteen. He dialed Dottie. "I'm here."

She said, "I see you. Come to the pavilion."

A petite, dark-skinned woman waved from fifty feet away.

Jackson walked up; she met him half-way. Dottie wore cream culottes with a yellow silk blouse and white espadrilles. Around her neck, three delicate gold chains; a tiny gold cross dangled from one of them. She extended her arms and hugged him.

"Oh, sweetie. I'm so sorry. How was your trip?" Below her steeply arched brows, her eyes conveyed concern; her demeanor and voice gave off an air of authority and competence.

"The flight was fine. Where is he?"

"I don't know."

What now? "You said he was here!"

"He was. I brought him breakfast, and he was calm. But then he got agitated, went for a swim, made a sand iguana and then disappeared."

"Oh, bollocks."

Dottie rubbed his shoulder. "I'm sure he'll be back. Come. I'll show you where he's been living."

He followed her down the beach and through the vegetation.

The sight before him was incredible. A circular cleared area, with a scuffed boogie board with ragged edges, a hard-sided cooler with a broken lid for a side table. Disgusting dirty beach towels, a rusted camp stove, and a mound of random flip-flops. A tattered, moldy tarp folded up with a craggy rock on top to keep it from blowing away. Several discarded water bottles.

Jackson didn't say a word; he couldn't speak. He opened the cooler gingerly, trying not to touch the animal dung on top. He hoped it contained food and water—hoping Pawpaw was feeding himself at a bare minimum. Sadly, it was empty.

Dottie took a step back, her arms folded; she stared at the ground.

He turned to her. "I'm seen enough." Jackson strode past her and retraced his steps.

Back at the pavilion, he sat at the picnic table and rubbed his eyes.

Dottie joined him, still silent.

"Where does he go during the day?"

"I'm sorry. I wish I knew. Perhaps Johnnie…"

"I need to talk to Miss Brown."

"Are you sure?"

"Do you know how to get there?"

"Yes. I'll drive."

A few minutes later, riding in Dottie's white Toyota pickup truck, they traveled through Calabash Boom along winding roads. Halfway up the hillside, at a mailbox with hand-painted flowers and vines, she turned onto a gravel driveway. A modest ranch-style house, sporting faded yellow siding and kelly green shutters, came into view.

Dottie pointed to the left to a square, white, cinder-block structure. "That converted garage is where Johnnie lives. But he won't be home until after three-thirty."

Jackson fixed his gaze on the main house. The curtains were drawn. It looked abandoned.

Dottie whispered, "Should I come in with you?"

He exited the truck and waved at her to join him. He wasn't sure what he would say to Gertie and needed backup.

Jackson rang the doorbell. He didn't discern any chimes through the door. He hit the bell again, pressing it with force, as if that would make a difference. Then he knocked. [Rap Rap Rap] After waiting a minute, he banged with his fist. [Bang Bang Bang Bang]

A groggy looking woman—medium height, dark skin with no makeup, wearing a terry robe with her hair in a silk wrap—opened the door. He recognized her from her impromptu visit to his house in the Bahamas weeks ago, but this time, she appeared a shell of that former woman.

Dottie said to Gertie, "What's wrong with you?"

Gertie said in a near whisper, "Jackson, why are you here?"

He couldn't contain his anger any longer. "WHAT DID YOU DO TO HIM?"

Gertie gestured for them to enter. "Come in. Have a seat."

Jackson said, "I don't want to sit. I want answers."

Dottie said, "I'll check the fridge…y'all look hungry," and she walked straight ahead to the kitchen.

Gertie whispered, "I'll tell you whatever you want to know. Just stop shouting."

"Are you hung-over Gertie?" Dottie asked.

"No. I just don't sleep well."

He didn't care about Gertie's sleep habits. "Tell me what happened! Did you break his heart? Have you seen where he's been living?"

Gertie pulled out a chair from the dining table to his right and sat facing them. With a stony expression that conveyed sorrow and devastation, she met Jackson's eyes and said, "I care about him more than you know. During our vows, he called me Freddy. I was upset. I ran. What was I supposed to do?"

Jackson's mind flashed back to a time three weeks earlier when Pawpaw was working in his study. How he walked in to see him holding the wedding picture with Grandmaw Winnifred and was talking to it. Asking her forgiveness, telling her about his new love, Gertrude. And how he asked Freddy's blessing to move on—saying he hoped to marry Gertie. What stuck most in his mind, though, was Pawpaw asking Grandmaw's spirit to *release him from his purgatory*, whatever that meant.

He had thought it sweet and sentimental at the time. But there was a slight mania in his tone...*a likely warning sign.*

Jackson shook his head. "He was under such strain with the business. Maybe he pushed himself too hard. You know he did it all for you."

Gertie stared at the terracotta floor tiles, sitting sideways, her arm draped across the back of her chair. She looked up with a perplexed squint. "What are you talking about?"

How could she not know? Jackson took a deep breath. "The only reason he bought that awful land development company was to save you from that murderer Thomas Smith."

"Hold on...Cudlow did *what*?"

Dottie's head popped out from behind the refrigerator door; she held a layer cake in her hands and placed it on the counter, and nudged the fridge door closed with her knee. "Mmm, hmm. That's right. I read about that." She dipped her finger in the frosting and sampled it.

Instinctively, Jackson joined Dottie near the kitchen counter, as if the cake had a sudden strange hold over his amygdala. "He spent hundreds of millions to protect you from that killer Smith and you hated him for it." He stabbed his fingers into the cake and stuffed a wad in his mouth. Partially out of spite, but mostly because he didn't have breakfast. The chocolate frosting was heaven on his tongue. At any other time, with such a sweet reward, his mood would have improved. Still, his anger at Gertie stuck in his throat.

Gertie threw up her hands. With a new fire behind her eyes, she said, "After Smith escaped, Cudlow gave me ten million dollars and ran away. What was I supposed to make of that?" She slapped the table with her palms and gave him a look of defiance.

He intended to yell, but it came out as a mumble as he chewed. "You could have thanked him." Some frosting fell onto his light blue polo shirt. He didn't care.

Gertie's nostrils flared as she erupted from her seat. "Was I supposed to marry him to preserve his sanity? When he thinks I'm his dead wife? Would you marry someone who did that?" Gertie waved her hand in dismissal. "You all need to leave."

"Oh, so it's like *that*, now?" Dottie put her hand on her hip. "Gertie, I know you can be a bitch sometimes, but this…takes the cake." She shoved the cake plate across the counter and it toppled over the edge, landing on the floor icing-side down. The ceramic plate hit the tile floor, where the edge chipped but the plate survived.

Despite Dottie's theatrics, Jackson knew Gertie had made a fair point. He wondered if he shared the blame as well. Cudlow was his grandfather and he should have looked out for him. This *wasn't* entirely on Gertie. Jackson inspected his chocolate-covered fingers and instantly felt ashamed. Arguing with Gertie wouldn't solve anything, and he needed to search for Cudlow. He took a calming breath and said, "Sorry for the mess. If you see him, please call me." He wiped his hand on his knee-length black linen shorts and dropped his business card on the dining table, and headed for the door.

Dottie followed. Before she closed the door, Dot yelled, "Well, I'm NOT sorry. Hmpf."

She muttered as she got into the driver's seat of her truck. "Waste of a good cake."

He got in the passenger side. "Where can we look?"

Dottie shook her head. "Wish I knew. We can ask Johnnie." Glancing at her watch, she added, "He should still be at Maho Bay." She handed him her phone. "You text him."

Jackson nodded. As they traveled the winding lane down the hillside, Dottie seemed to be lost in thought, driving with her shoulders hunched forward.

He texted Johnnie and waited. To break the tension, he asked, "Do you know whatever happened to that Smith fellow?"

Dottie relaxed into the seatback. From his vantage point, he detected what appeared to be a wry smile. She waggled her butt. "Not that I know for sure, but don't worry. I'd bet we'll never see him again."

Chapter 3

Ranger Merv parked his white government long-bed pickup in the 'Park Service Only' marked spot at Hawksnest Beach. It was close to 9:30, which meant Johnnie would have finished his chores and moved on to the next beach. Which *also* meant he would have Stumpy to himself.

With a baggie of dried apricots in his pocket, he hoped today's haul would come through. Perhaps it was his imagination, but the iguana seemed sad and listless. Somewhat less interested in their usual game of trading treasure for treats. An iguana with depression made no sense. Sure, Stumpy was smarter than the other iguanas, but still just a dumb reptile.

He leaned against the support post of the pavilion and shook the baggie, tucking it under one arm to disguise it.

Normally, Stumpy would greet him the moment he entered the beach. *Where was he?*

Did Crosswell run off with him again?

He let out a low whistle.

The aging, short-tailed iguana sauntered towards the pavilion and looked up at him. Unlike other times, Stumpy wasn't craning his neck and manically jawing at the air with excitement.

"Get!" He took out an apricot and held it between his fingers to reinforce the command.

Stumpy turned and sauntered back under the brush.

While he waited, his phone chirped. A text from Ranger Taylor: "Parrot tonight? And some dessert?"

Her request was code for beers at the Yellow Parrot Bar in Cruz Bay after dark, followed by a quickie behind the dumpster in the alley. Taylor was a freak, always wanted him to lick her face while they did the nasty. As much as he wanted out of their fuck-buddy arrangement, he kept finding himself meeting up with her.

Admittedly, he found himself doing many unhealthy and immoral things over the last few years, never learning his lesson despite his self-loathing. Gambling and sex were his Achilles heels. The thrill of the win or the conquest. He knew it only reflected his own sense of inadequacy. But he couldn't stop.

Merv texted back, "Maybe." His own code meaning he'd most likely meet up with her, even if he didn't want to admit it to himself.

Not that Taylor would feel stood up if he didn't show. She had a couple of other guys on the hook that could fill in. Word had it that the ferry driver, Jupiter, and the owner of the Yellow Parrot, Earl, were some of her steadies. She'd hinted at offering him a threesome, but it wasn't his style. As it was, no one knew about their sordid relationship and he intended to keep it that way. If his supervisor, Kemper, ever found out, he'd have no chance of winning her love.

Stumpy waddled back with something metallic and round in his mouth. He bent to take it. *Just a quarter.*

The iguana had the right idea, but it wasn't enough.

He tore an apricot in half and dropped it to the ground. After Stumpy finished chewing, Merv called again, "Get!"

His leathery friend remained in place and stared up at him. [Treat?]

"No. Get!"

Stumpy blinked at him twice and moseyed off again.

Merv sighed. The process was taking too long.

A hairy man in a speedo walked up to him. "Ranger, I lost my car keys. Has anyone reported finding any keys?"

He recited the company line by heart, "There is a Lost and Found at the Visitor Center at Cruz Bay. You can call and ask for Candace. She may be able to help you."

"But I just lost them. They were under a beach towel five minutes ago."

"Did you ask any of the other visitors? Did you check the restroom?"

"Um, no."

"You should ask around. If you still can't find them, call the Lost and Found at the Visitor Center."

"Seriously? You are no help at all."

"Sorry you feel that way."

Speedo man stalked off.

Merv fanned his face with his flat hat and fit it back on his head.

Stumpy returned with another shiny object. He crouched to inspect it.

A thin gold band with a dainty gold flower on top; a tiny blue stone at the center. Very pretty. Probably not worth more than a couple hundred at the pawnshop. Still, better than the quarter.

"Good!" He pocketed the ring and threw two apricots on the ground.

As the iguana noshed, Merv wondered about the man's keys. And he wondered if he had to be such a dick to the guy.

He went to the tool shed and picked out a metal rake. Sometimes a little scraping along the sand would turn up keys if they became buried. Merv brought the rake to the man.

"Sir, I can help you look."

Speedo guy's eyes widened. "Hey, wouldn't you know it? My wife put them in our lunch bag and didn't tell me. But thanks. You know, you had me going there. Thought you were a raging asshole. Excuse my French."

Merv laughed. "Well, you wouldn't be the first to think that. Glad you found your keys. Have a nice day now." He tipped his hat.

The man in the tiny bathing suit gave him a wave. "Thanks. You, too."

Merv walked down the shoreline, admiring the happy visitors and wondering how he could be so miserable around so much scenic beauty. He knew it came down to all his terrible personal choices. *Why couldn't he fly straight and be a man worthy to win Kemper's heart?* His mother raised him better than this.

He leaned against a palm tree and gazed at the water.

If Crosswell could overcome his doofus anxieties and find a nice girlfriend, maybe he could become a better person too. On his phone, he googled, 'Gamblers Anonymous USVI'. It wasn't easy to stay anonymous on a small island like St. John, which is the reason he'd never attended a meeting. *Maybe he could try St. Thomas?*

At the edge of his vision, he noticed two kids, a boy and a girl, building a campfire by the rocks on the west end. *Time to go back to work.*

As he approached, the pre-teen instigators hid the lighter and scattered the leaves and twigs they had piled up.

Merv donned his most authoritative tone and pulled his hat down to shade his eyes. "You know fires are prohibited, correct?"

The girl nodded.

He examined the detritus. The rain overnight had luckily made the wood and leaves too damp to ignite. "Give it to me."

"Give you what?" the boy asked.

"The lighter."

The girl handed it over, her eyes wide with fear. "Are we in trouble?"

He inspected the lighter. It was old, with some rust spots around the wheel, but might be gold-plated. It had an insignia: the letters TCB with a lightning bolt.

Weird.

"I'm giving you a warning. Don't let there be a next time."

The kids looked at each other and ran away into the surf to splash around.

Lighters were certainly collectible. This one might clean up and bring him some good money.

He grinned.

Maybe his luck was changing.

* * *

After Jackson and Dottie left, Gertie ignored the lump of brown cake on the kitchen floor and went to her bathroom to splash water on her face. The woman in the mirror looked awful, with deep circles under her eyes and puffy eyelids.

She had gotten her original wish to break clean from Cudlow. Yet, she was grieving as she'd lost a friend and lover. Although she continued to wonder if he was ever truly hers, given how he kept calling her Freddy. Now she wished she had kept some of the millions he bestowed, allowing her to travel. To be anywhere but here. To distract herself with new places and people. Maybe visit her cousin Lisa and apologize in person for how she badly she had behaved in Paris.

Gertie looked out her back window. The vegetable garden was still in shambles. *But what did it matter?* Nothing mattered anymore. The pit in her stomach prevented sleep or any enjoyment of her previous hobbies. The cross-stitch next to her bedside remained untouched for days. All her hobbies were too quiet, allowing self-reflection she didn't want now.

As she gazed out the window, she saw a figure approach her garden.

Cudlow!

But he looked less like a human being and more like that Golem creature in the Hobbit movies. *Where was the dashing, well-spoken, lucid man she nearly wed a week ago?* He knelt at her garden, smelling the pink roses, and seemed to be muttering.

She opened the window a crack to listen.

"We can be useful. We are useful. Freddy still loves me. She loves me."

Gertie froze. She left the bathroom and located her phone on the kitchen counter. With Jackson's business card in hand, she dialed him.

He answered on the second ring. "Hello, Jackson Loughton."

"Jackson, it's Gertie. He's here." She realized she was whispering.

"Ms. Brown? Sorry, I can't hear with all these bleeding potholes. What's that?"

In the background, Dottie raised her voice, complaining about chickens in the road.

After waiting a of couple seconds—allowing for the background rumbling and Dottie's exclamations to subside—Gertie cleared her throat. "Cudlow's here. In my yard. In the garden out back…hold on." She strode to the bathroom window, but ducked so Cud wouldn't see her. She glanced out, confirming he was still there. "Yes, he's here."

"We're on our way. Sit tight." To Dottie, he said, "Turn around. He's at Gertie's house."

"Yes, see you soon." She hung up.

What to do? Should she talk to him? Make sure he stays put? Or would she be inviting more trouble for both of them?

She decided to talk to him. To learn for herself how mad Cudlow was. Gertie took off her headscarf, changed out of her pajamas into her billowy orange dress, and put on her sneakers. She went out the front door to approach him cautiously from around the side of the house instead of using the rear kitchen door.

Quiet as a mouse. Don't scare him…

She rounded the corner. He was sitting cross-legged in the dirt. Alarmed, she noticed he was pulling both weeds and plants. *Not her heirloom tomatoes!*

"Stop!" In her distress, she yelled, but quickly realized her mistake.

Cudlow bounded up and dashed to her left, toward the rear of Johnnie's garage apartment.

"No! Wait! Come back." She ran to intercept him, but he sped around the building. Gertie could hear him mumbling to himself, meaning he hadn't gone far.

A distraction might help. That was how she managed unruly seven-year-olds when she was a public-school teacher.

Gertie sat in the center of the garden. She spoke to her large garden gnome in the center. "Hello, little gnome, do you want to help me in the garden?"

In a squeaky voice, she pantomimed the gnome's voice. "Yes, Miss Gertie. I love plants."

"I do too, Gnomey. Look, we can put the plants back in the ground where they can grow big and strong. You try."

Gertie peered toward the garage. Cudlow was peeking around the corner, his eyes wide, like a child's.

She continued her playacting with the gnome.

Cudlow came into the open, a few steps toward the garden.

Gertie sang, "The itsy-bitsy spider went up the water spout..." She bounced the pointy-headed figurine up and down, like a tiny dance.

Cudlow sat on the ground, twenty-feet away, transfixed by her play.

She waved him over. In a sing-song voice, she said, "Do you want to play? Help me with the garden?"

"We are useful?"

"Yes! You certainly are! Help me! It's fun." She patted the soil. "Do you want to water the plants? Plants like water. Water is...useful."

He nodded and came closer.

"Do you see the hose there? Can you spray the plants?"

Cudlow went to the hose reel and unwound a few feet of it. The end had a spray nozzle.

Gertie dusted soil from her dress and joined him. "Let's see. Use the gentle setting. Like a light rain."

She adjusted the spray dial for him. Cudlow watered the rows of plants as Gertie stood by his side. He smiled, revealing his sweet dimples. A face she loved, but now it seemed to belong to a different person.

"Good," she said. After a minute, she asked, "Do you remember me?"

He shook his head. "I don't know."

She placed her hand on his shoulder. "That's okay. Do you know who you are?"

He aimed the hose at the sky, creating a rainbow with the mist. "I don't know."

"What should I call you?"

He furrowed his brow. "Useful?"

She pursed her lips. "Like a name, like Joe or Gary. Or…Cudlow?" She held her breath. *Did she push too far? Mentioning his real name?*

Cudlow said, "Call me Gnomey. I like Gnomey." He dropped the hose, still spewing water, and dashed to retrieve the garden gnome, which was now slick with mud. He cradled it and then plopped down in the wet dirt, mimicking Gertie's pretend dance with the object. Cudlow began singing the nursery rhyme, *"London Bridge is Falling Down."*

Gertie hung her head. At least Cudlow was calm and in good spirits. But he looked so malnourished.

She went to her kitchen's rear door. "Gnomey, would you like some eggs and toast? Come in."

Cudlow looked up and stopped singing. "Can I bring Gnomey?"

She smiled, "Yes, of course. Both Gnomeys are welcome. Do you want cookies and milk too?"

Cudlow rose, holding the gnome. "He likes cookies." He followed her into the kitchen.

"Have a seat at the table." She pulled four cookies from her cupboard and poured him a glass of milk. After placing them on the table in front of him, she said, "I'll be right back."

She went out the front door and closed it behind her. Gertie looked down the road for Dottie's white pickup, shifting her weight from foot to foot. Using her mental focus to will the vehicle to appear.

With Cudlow now secure, her armor crumbled; she wiped away tears. *How could he have disintegrated like this so quickly?* He was fine just days ago. Part of her was relieved they didn't get married. The other part felt responsible for his decline.

One thing was certain, he needed professional help.

Cudlow appeared at the front door. "Gnomey wants more milk."

She rubbed her face and turned on a smile to mask her sadness. "Coming! I'll get the milk."

Gertie walked back inside and locked the door behind her.

Now she understood why Dottie was so angry with her.

Cudlow had truly gone off the deep end.

* * *

Johnnie finished his work day and eagerly drove his scooter east towards Calabash Boom for a quick stop home to pick up a book and a change of clothes before heading to Greta's.

When he arrived, he saw Dottie's pickup parked on the driveway next to Gertie's car.

He took off his helmet, tucked it under his arm, and headed to his apartment. As he put the key in the lock, he heard a young man's familiar British accent.

"John, could you join us?"

It was Jackson, standing behind him.

Johnnie scratched the scar between his neck and shoulder. "Jackson, hey." The last time he'd seen Cudlow's grandson was at the Loughton mansion in the Bahamas. After the shipwreck last month, Johnnie and his new friend Mo—a jolly former cruise ship director slash political refugee—spent a few days with Jackson, mostly playing video games to decompress. "How's Mo?"

Jackson gave him a weary glance. "Mo's fine. He's heading up the company's new Nature World theme park project. But that is irrelevant. We need your help."

"What's going on?"

"Cudlow is here. We're discussing next steps."

His eyes went wide. "He's here?"

"Yes, inside. He's in a bad way."

Johnnie nodded and followed Jackson. The scene inside Gertie's living room seemed familiar, with Gertie, Dottie and Cud sitting at the dining table, with desserts and cold cuts on platters in front of them. But Cudlow looked so small, like a fragile bird.

He pulled up a chair and waved to Cud. "Hey, buddy."

Gertie whispered, "He's calling himself Gnomey."

"What? Why?"

She rubbed her temples. "My fault. Don't ask."

Jackson sat at the head of the table and interlaced his fingers. "I need to get Pawpaw to a hospital. Our family lawyer, Felicity, is working on the paperwork, but unless he does something illegal, the process could take too long. And I don't want to put him in restraints."

Gertie said, "Cudlow won't get in the car with Jackson. We tried. It took an hour to calm him down."

Johnnie asked, "So now what?"

Dottie pointed at him. "We want *you* to try."

"Try what?"

Gertie said, "We hope maybe he'll go with you."

Jackson chewed on his thumbnail. "John, I have a helicopter waiting at the car ferry dock to take us to the airport on St. Thomas. I just need your help to get him there. I can't have him running away again."

"I'll try." Johnnie got up and walked around the table to kneel next to Cud's chair. "Hey, Cud. Do you want to go to the beach? We can see Stumpy. Feed him some cheese puffs. Maybe go for a swim? You like swims."

Cudlow said, "Stumpy? Where is he?"

"He's at Hawksnest Beach, remember? He's waiting for us. Come on. Do you want to ride with me on the scooter?"

Cud nodded.

An audible exhale rose from the others.

Johnnie extended his hand. "Come on. Take my hand. It will be fun. Like the old times." Cud's hand felt like bones, his skin cold. His friend's breath was foul, like he hadn't brushed his teeth in a week, which was probably the case. He guided Cud to the front door, then mouthed to Jackson, "We'll meet you there."

Outside, they shuffled together toward his scooter. Johnnie took the extra helmet out of his seat compartment and handed it to Cud. "Do you remember how to put this on?"

"We are useful?"

"Yes, Cudlow. Very." He helped Cud fasten the chin strap. "Good. Come, you hold on to me, tight, okay?"

Cudlow got on the seat behind John.

"Stumpy will be happy to see you." Johnnie turned the key to start the engine. "Wave goodbye!" He waved to the three standing in the doorway; standing like statues, their faces conveying a mix of hope, anticipation, and dread.

As he made a slow turn in the driveway, Cudlow let go of Johnnie and scrambled off the seat while in motion. "We can't forget Gnomey!" He stumbled on the loose stone, yet righted himself and ran toward Gertie's door.

The trio by the door groaned. Dottie smacked her head. She went inside and emerged with the fiberglass garden sculpture. She handed it to Cudlow. "Here you go, sweetie."

He held it lovingly like a baby and cooed, "You are coming with me."

Dottie patted Cudlow on the shoulder. "You go with Johnnie now. Have fun."

Once on the road, Cud held onto Johnnie with one arm while cradling the gnome with the other. His friend seemed at peace, but Johnnie's heart was racing, pounding against his breastbone. He wondered if he could get Cud all the way around the island and to the dock in one piece. As they turned onto Centerline Road, Dottie and Jackson passed them in her pickup. He gave a thumbs up sign. *All was going well.*

As the turn for Hawksnest beach came into view, he held his breath and continued straight, hoping Cudlow wouldn't notice. It was hard to tell what Cudlow was seeing and thinking during the ride.

Cud yelled, "You passed it! Stumpy! We need him!" He hit Johnnie's helmet with the garden gnome. [whack] "Stop!" [whack] "Go back!"

He pulled to a stop in the road. Not a wise choice ever. "Stop hitting me! Okay, we'll go back."

Cudlow got off the scooter and ran in the middle of the road, back down the hill to the beach parking lot.

Johnnie turned his scooter around and followed, planning to get ahead of Cudlow. "Cud, get off the road! It isn't safe!"

A stake truck barreled towards them, clearly exceeding the speed limit, straight at Cud.

"Shit!" Johnnie sped up and swerved ahead of Cud. The truck was right there. Johnnie's life flashed in front of him. Something about his third-grade teacher laughing at his story about a hamster who solved crimes; plus, his wedding to Darla; then his arrest in Miami. Instinctively, he jumped off the scooter and rolled to the side, sending the Flying Pig into a death spiral under the truck's front wheels.

The truck driver swerved, but still hit the front tire of the scooter with a metallic screech. He braked and came to a jarring stop in the opposite lane. But Cud was safe, having climbed over the stone knee-wall; he was off the road and gone again.

Johnnie panted and blinked. *Yes, he was alive.* Sitting up, he gingerly inspected his injuries. His knee was scraped and bloody, with a deep gash three inches long. Next, he extended his leg to test whether it was broken.

But he was lucky; the injury was superficial. *No broken femur.* Next, he removed his helmet and noticed long black streaks where he skidded on the pavement. His right bicep received the brunt of the road rash, with pebbles of asphalt embedded. He brushed off the largest black nuggets. As he learned to breathe again, relief came, knowing he was still in one piece.

As he pushed off from the ground, ready to get up and find Cud, a crushing pain like the shock of a lightning bolt sent him backwards. He crumpled into a ball on his side, clasping his right shoulder, which was clearly dislocated.

The truck driver glared at him from behind the windshield. He honked and drove around him, continuing on as if nothing happened.

His mangled scooter was hard up against the rock wall, pieces of plastic and red metal scattered across the pavement. *When would he ever learn to stop charging oncoming traffic?*

Despite the pain, his immediate priorities were clear.

Get off the fucking road.

Confirm he was indeed alive and not a ghost.

Inspect for additional injuries.

Call Jackson.

Then worry about Cud.

Chapter 4

Johnnie sat with Cudlow at the picnic pavilion at Hawksnest. The sunset streaked red across the sky to the west and long deep shadows fell across the parking lot behind them.

Stumpy waddled up and looked at them.

"Hey," Johnnie said.

Cudlow beamed at the iguana. "Stumpy! We were useful today. What did you do? Meet my friend Gnomey." He picked up the gnome sitting on the bench beside him and made it do a nod and sway. In a squeaky voice, he said, "I'm Gnomey. Nice to meet you, Stumpy. We can be friends. And see each other every day."

Stumpy cocked his head sideways, staring at Johnnie. *[Cudlow is acting strange.]*

Johnnie gave him a nod to indicate, '*I know.*'

Cudlow said, "We had cookies before. And some other nice food from a nice lady." He directed his attention away from Stumpy and said to Johnnie, "Did you feed Stumpy today?"

Johnnie saw a hint of reason and lucidity in Cud's eyes. "No. Not if you mean cheese puffs. But he's an iguana. He has food all around him."

Cud said in an even tone, but with a hint of questioning, "I used to give him fruit."

"Yes. Yes, you did."

Cud shook his head. "I don't know what I'm doing." Despite this statement, there was a knowing in his expression. As if he objectively understood his recent behavior was off.

Johnnie froze. His friend was back. "Do you remember Jackson?"

The former glossiness in Cud's eyes was replaced with focused recognition. With a furrowed brow, he grimaced. "He's such a good kid. I should go home. I can't explain it. There's an ache behind my eyes. Ears ringing…"

"You haven't been yourself lately."

A far away gaze crossed Cud's face, like he was thinking. Johnnie thought he would say something else, but instead, he lay his head on his arms on the table and closed his eyes.

Poor Cud looked so exhausted. In seconds, deep breaths of sleep rose from his friend. John wanted to place his hand on Cud's shoulder to comfort him, but knew that might unsettle him. *No*, Johnnie thought, *Cud needed rest*. He'd let his friend nap until Jackson arrived, which would be a matter of minutes, anyway.

As he sat there, afraid to make a noise, Johnnie took a nap as well. He mimicked Cud and laid his head on his arms on the table.

What seemed to be a long time later, Johnnie woke to the whisper of his name.

"John?"

He looked around and noticed the sun was in the same position, low in the sky, meaning perhaps only a minute or two had passed since he'd fallen asleep. Cud was still out.

Jackson said, "Shh." He motioned with a wave, asking John to follow.

Away from the pavilion, Jackson asked, "What happened?"

Johnnie showed his bloody arm and knee. "We had a close call with a truck."

"Are you all right?"

"I'll be fine. You won't believe it, but Cud came back. He might not be completely insane."

"What do you mean?" Jackson glanced at his watch.

"He was speaking normally. Just for a minute before he fell asleep. This changes *everything*."

"So, what are you saying?"

"Please don't send him to an institution."

"I'm sorry, it isn't up to you. You should have seen him today. He's completely bonkers. I've never been so scared."

"I know. I'm scared, too. But I tell you, just now, he knew who you were. He said…" Already Johnnie had forgotten the exact phrase. "I can't remember exactly, but he knows things aren't right. And believe me, that is HUGE."

"You've seen how he is. Let me ask you, what happened with the truck? Did Pawpaw do something to cause the accident?"

Johnnie's heart sank. Jackson had a point. Cud could have gotten them *both* killed. "Yes, he was hitting me and then jumped off the scooter. I know he's not well. But he's IN THERE. Do you know what I'm saying?"

"We need to get going. The pilot can't wait all day. I'm going to wake him." Jackson walked across the sand, back to the pavilion.

Alarm seized Johnnie's brain. His own experience told him that mental hospitals were terrible, convinced that nothing meaningful could be achieved through group therapy, and that the meds were more for control than healing. He couldn't let Cud rot in one of those places.

He ran after Jackson, which was more of a hobble. His knee had seized up, but he disregarded the pain. "No! You can't. DON'T!"

Jackson shook his head and didn't break his stride. "He's my responsibility. Not yours. Now bugger off."

Johnnie grabbed Jackson's arm and pulled him roughly. A big mistake. Johnnie doubled over and fell to the sand, his dislocated shoulder on fire from the jolt. "Oww." He pressed his arm against its socket, trying to halt the pain. "Fuck, fuck, FUCK!"

Jackson turned, "Are you all right?"

Through gritted teeth, he hissed, "Never better."

"John, you know I adore Pawpaw. I'm simply gutted at the idea of sending him to hospital. But it's only until he gets better. He needs bloody doctors! Surely, you see. He'll have the best care. I must handle this." Jackson continued his stride toward Cud.

Johnnie gripped his shoulder with his opposite hand, hoping he didn't need a doctor himself. In his heart of hearts, he knew Jackson was sincere and probably right. But he still hated the idea with his entire existence. Like a petulant child, he planted his butt on the sand, content to watch from a distance, like viewing an outdoor movie, to see what would happen next when Jackson woke Cud.

His vindication was swift. After Jackson gently tapped his grandfather on the shoulder, Cud's eyes flew open like a scared animal. He reared back, scanned the area, and yelled, "Who are you?" In mere seconds, Cud was on the move, running into the mangroves toward his nest.

Jackson gave chase. They both disappeared. Birds chattered at the disturbance. He heard more distant yells. With them both using British accents, he had a tough time telling them apart, except one seemed to plead and the other angry. It was probably Cud who yelled something about Stumpy.

Cudlow burst from the tree-line and raced across the beach near the water's edge, heading west like he was doing a hundred-yard dash, knees high, arms pumping. A few seconds later, Jackson, with leaves and sand in his usually perfectly smooth hair, jogged towards Johnnie. "Which way did he go?" His regularly translucent complexion was fire-engine red and puffy.

He pointed.

Jackson began walking, out of breath. As his heavy steps sunk into the soft sand, he swung his head back toward Johnnie. "A little help?"

"Oh, I thought you said you could handle this."

He took a couple deep breaths, then sneered, "Don't be a twat."

"Hey, you owe me a new scooter."

Jackson rolled his eyes and grimaced, "Bollocks." He took another deep breath before resuming his jog.

Johnnie called out, "He turned right at the rocks."

This was going to take a while. He pulled out his phone and called Greta. She answered on the second ring.

"Hey you. Dinner is getting cold."

"I'm sorry, but I have an emergency. And a slight accident. I don't think I'm coming over tonight."

"What happened?"

"Cudlow has gone insane and is currently being chased by his grandson. Plus a truck flattened my scooter. I'm bleeding and my shoulder is dislocated. But I'll live."

"Oh, that's awful! Can I do anything?"

Suddenly, he didn't care about his injuries or his scooter. Because a new thought crossed his mind. "Well, I have this idea. If I took Cud to my psychiatrist in Miami, would you come with me?"

"Wait, did you say *Miami*?"

"Um, yes."

Greta squealed. "Do you KNOW what is happening this weekend in Miami?"

He had no clue. Before he could ask, she explained.

"The American Library Association conference! I've been browsing the agenda for months, praying I could go. Miss Teller wouldn't pay for it. But if we could split the cost of the hotel…"

"Hold on. It's just an idea. I don't know if Jackson will go for it."

"No, we HAVE to go. Promise me! Did you know that Obama and Tina Fey are speaking? Please? I have goosebumps."

"Hold on. Let me see what I can work out. I'll call you later."

He could hear the smile in her voice. "I love you."

Johnnie grinned. It still felt weird hearing someone say that to him, but it was the good weird that made his ears tingle. In that moment, he basked in her words, feeling like a normal human being—with a real human relationship—and not at all like the miscreant angry loner he'd been over the last five years. "I love you, too, Ms. Khan."

Greta chuckled.

"Bye." He ended the call.

Back at the pavilion, Dottie and Jackson had cornered Cud between them. A chaotic scene accompanied by alternating bits of pleading and panicked nonsense words.

Johnnie got up from the sand, slowly like an old man, dusted the sand from his bloody knee—sand that made his wound sting—and hobbled over to join them. "What's going on?"

Dottie whispered, "He won't go without Stumpy."

"Ha!"

She narrowed her eyes. "It's not funny."

"It *kind of* is." He sat at the table, which was now the front row for this odd standoff.

Cudlow clenched his fists, his face red and breaths labored. "We are USEFUL!"

Dottie said, "Yes, yes, you are, sweetie. We just want you to come with us. To a nice place."

Jackson said, "Yes, a very nice place. There will be cookies. And…you can bring Gnomey."

Cud said, "I don't want Gnomey. I AM Gnomey. I want STUMPY!"

Dottie clapped her palm to her forehead. "Why, honey. Why Stumpy?"

Cud's face turned a shade redder. "Stumpy doesn't GO AWAY!"

She put her hand out low, her words near a whisper, "I know you love Stumpy, but he'll be here when you get back."

Cud yelled, "LIAR!"

Johnnie beat his hands on the table like a drumroll to get their attention. When they all turned their heads his way, he announced, "Cud, Stumpy loves to travel. And I'll come with you. Would you go with me AND Stumpy on an airplane to a fun place? There will be lots of good food and cookies."

Cud nodded. "Stumpy and I go together?"

"Absolutely. Remember, he went with me on a boat last month? He wants to try an airplane. That sounds like fun, right? We can soar above the clouds." Johnnie walked up to Cud and put his good arm around his friend's shoulder. "AND...I hear they serve Stroopwafels on airplanes. Totally yummy. What do you say?"

Cudlow broke into a grin and shimmied his hips. "Okay dokie."

Jackson turned to Johnnie. Still out of breath from the chase and holding his side, he gasped, "You would do that? Go with us?"

"Not exactly. I want to try this MY way."

"Oh, for goodness...what do you mean?"

Cud broke from Johnnie's embrace and shouted, "Stumpy! We need to pack our things. Come, boy! Did you hear? An adventure in the sky! Yum time! Where are you?"

Jackson sighed and threw up his hands. "Really?" He said this more to the Gods than to Dottie or Johnnie.

Johnnie glared at Jackson. "Look, I have a proposal. I want to take Cud to my psychiatrist in Miami. She's amazing. One of the best. Give me a week. After that, you can cart Cud away in chains." He didn't really mean that, but he wanted to emphasize his point.

The setting sun cast dark shadows that blanketed the beach. Cud's happy yells in the distance seemed amplified in the still night air. He was muttering something about packing up his sea glass collection and his flip-flops.

"John," Jackson stared off toward his grandfather's voice and slicked back his damp bangs from his heated forehead, "Fine. You have one week. And I'm going with you."

* * *

Ranger Merv arrived on the beach after dark, this time in civilian clothes. Most of the visitors were gone. Just two cars in the parking lot. A man and woman walked along the surf. Another woman sat on a beach blanket, apparently stargazing and noshing on a sandwich.

He checked his phone. Another message from Bisbee, only more specific; this time naming which bones he would break.

Where was he going to get ten large in 24 hours? The rest of his debt, a hundred and forty-two grand, was still a problem, but not an *immediate* one. With Stumpy gone all those days recently, he'd gotten behind. His training program for the other iguanas wasn't going well at all. None of them understood 'fetch'. *Dumb as rocks.*

Merv touched the underside of his jaw where Bisbee had held the knife. The blade didn't break the skin, but the man with a cross tattoo on his forehead had pressed the metal so hard, Merv's mandible was bruised.

He looked up at the tall palms. *No Stumpy.* When Stumpy was away a couple of weeks ago, Merv tried a metal detector to find the iguana's stash. But he couldn't do that openly, as it was against park regulations.

He called out, "Yum time."

The woman stargazing must have heard him, because she craned her neck to stare at him.

Merv called out, "I'm not talking to you."

He waited in place. Still no sign of his green partner in crime.

His phone buzzed. Merv gazed at the sky, wishing '*Please don't be Bisbee*'. He grimaced, took a deep breath, and read the text message. Johnnie had copied him on a text to their boss Kemper, asking if he could take off another week for a vacation in Miami. And like last time, Johnnie gave almost no advance notice, wanting to leave immediately.

"Where does that guy get off?" he thought. Kemper let Johnnie get away with too much. Leave slips were supposed to be put in at least a month ahead of time.

Panic gripped him. *What if Johnnie took Stumpy again?* The weirdo brought the wild iguana on his last jaunt; which left Merv without his usual extra income from jewelry and wallets Stumpy stole from unsuspecting beach-goers.

He needed to find out and typed a reply:

"Have fun. Are you going with our green friend?"

Merv stared at the words. His question was ridiculous. Surely Johnnie wouldn't do it again. *What grown man travels with a non-domesticated reptile?*

He scratched his tall forehead and hit send anyway.

A few seconds later, Johnnie replied:

> "It won't be fun. I'm taking Cud to a doctor in Miami. He wouldn't leave without Stumpy. He's with us now. Sorry for the short notice."

"Mother—." Merv wound up his arm to throw his phone. Instead, he boxed with the air, pumping his fists in a frenzy. *Shit-balls!*

Think, think.

He typed furiously:

> "Regulation Title 36, Part 2, Subsection 2 says you can't take wildlife."

Merv wanted to cite the monetary fine, but didn't have time to look it up. He added:

> "Kemper, tell him."

He waited, trying to control his breathing. *Come on, come on…*

Finally, a text from Kemper. It merely said,

> "Best wishes to Cudlow. Please be back by July 14th."

"FUUUUUCK!"

The woman on the beach yelled, "Shut up! I'm on vacation here!"

"No! You shut up!" The moment he said that, he knew it sounded bad. He couldn't have a meltdown or argue with a park guest, even off-duty. What he needed was a plan.

Time for extreme measures.

Merv texted Kemper, but without adding Johnnie to the thread.

> "Boss, I was going to take off a couple of days this weekend. Could you put me down for annual leave?"

He added the dates, then crossed his fingers and rocked back and forth waiting for her reply.

Kemper wrote back. "Sure."

Yes! He wiggled his shoulders. Now he had to scrape up some money for a cheap flight to Miami, figure out how to track Johnnie and steal an iguana. He searched travel sites on his phone for a last-minute airfare deal. An off-brand airline had a ninety-nine dollar-deal from San Juan. He selected a one-way ticket. Next, he found another bargain for the first segment between St. Thomas and Puerto Rico that used a coupon code. Finding flights that lined up wasn't easy. It meant he had to leave on the last ferry in less than two hours.

Merv jogged back to his car.

Ranger Taylor stood feet apart, arms crossed, in the center of the path where it met the parking lot.

"Oh, it's you," she said.

"Hey, Taylor. What brings you here?"

"Someone called. Did you see a tall white guy screaming and cursing?"

"Oh," he had to think fast. "Yeah, he left already."

Her shoulders slumped. "Ha, thought we had another live one. Well, I'm going home. Want to join me?"

He'd been dodging her texts since Monday. It was wrong of him to have slept with her that time—three weeks ago, when they went out as a group to watch televised soccer at the Yellow Parrot. But when his attempts to ingratiate himself with Kemper were met with indifference, his ego needed the boost of a one-night stand.

And it was doubly wrong for him to go along with Taylor's *fuck buddy* agreement. Sure, it sounded fun and without consequences at the time, but in practice...well, that was another story. Plus, she kept asking him to lick her face during the deed, which was not his idea of sexy.

"Yeah, Taylor," he wrung his hands, "I'm gonna be away for a few days. In fact, I need to go pack. Maybe when I get back? Okay?"

She smiled and licked her lips, "Sure, big guy." She snapped her fingers at him, "Call me." And she was gone.

Now he was dodging two people. Bisbee wanted the money tomorrow by noon.

If he was lucky, and he hoped he was, he'd already be in Miami by then.

While he was there, he'd put a few choice bets on some pony and greyhound races. He usually did well on those. But the sure bet was getting Stumpy and putting him to work, possibly on South Beach, where the rich celebrities lounged.

He *had* to return with ten large.

Or he wouldn't come back at all.

Chapter 5

Dr. Louella Phillips rolled her elongated and low-profile racing wheelchair towards the thirty-story modern apartment building in Miami she called home. Fresh from a forty-five-minute workout at Bayfront Park, beads of sweat dripped down her forehead. The armpits of her T-shirt were visibly damp. With temperatures in the mid-eighties, the heat radiating off the sidewalks—plus the stifling effect of the surrounding residential towers—baked her skin. The ornamental rows of tall palms offered almost no refuge from the sun.

She checked her Timex Ironman watch. *Just enough time for a quick shower before her next video appointment.*

Approaching the front door, she hit the handicapped access button on the stanchion, timing her roll to enter the lobby at a steady rate of speed.

She was not prepared for the sight in front of her.

One of her patients, Johnnie Crosswell, and a group of strangers, stood a circle in the center of the lobby and stared at her. Her girlfriend, Ann, was also present, dressed for an assignment with her camera bag slung over her shoulder. Ann was conversing with the doorman on the side. Which meant this complete debacle was likely ruining both of their workdays.

Ann broke off her talk with the doorman and approached. "I'm sorry. I didn't know if I should let them up. I have a photoshoot at the Vizcaya Museum in twenty minutes. Johnnie said he had an appointment?"

Lou used her teeth to unlatch the Velcro of her gloves. After she tucked her gloves into the elastic of her waistband, she rubbed the sweat from her eyes and whispered to Ann, "I didn't invite him here. Who is he with?"

Ann winced. "I'm not sure. Supposedly, the old man is an insane homeless man? John wants to you to switch his appointment to take his friend instead. That didn't sound right. But Johnnie refused to leave."

Lou took a deep breath. "Don't worry, babe. I'll take care of it. You go back up."

Ann kissed Lou on the top of her head. "I'll be upstairs. Yell if you need anything."

Lou waited for Ann to get on the elevator before she addressed Johnnie's band of presumed misfits. She unzipped the pack on the back of her wheelchair and retrieved a white hand towel to dab the moisture from her face and neck.

Johnnie walked up. "Dr. Phillips, I know I should have called first, but this is an emergency."

She studied his face. He didn't seem manic. *A good sign.* Although showing up unannounced was a new one. She tread carefully. "What *kind* of emergency?"

The young man of the troupe threw his hands in the air. "Johnnie, why did I let you talk me into this? I thought you said you cleared this with your therapist?" He walked up and extended his hand. "Dr. Phillips, my apologies, we've obviously ambushed you, which was not our intention." He shot a glowering look at John. "We should leave. Can we call and make a proper appointment?"

She shook his hand. The young man—probably in his mid-twenties with thick brown hair and ears that stuck out a bit but not freakishly—seemed sincere...and sane. But looks could be deceiving. "And *you* are?"

"I'm Jackson." He gestured to the old man. "This is my grandfather. The one we are concerned for."

The man with the white hair and gaunt face looked agitated, scanning the room like a threatened ferret. He cradled a molded-plastic garden gnome with one arm. A woman with red hair held his other hand, trying to keep his attention and whispering to him softly.

Lou shook her head. "I'm sorry, Jackson, I'm having trouble getting my bearings. Excuse my French, but I'm sweating my balls off. First, I'm going to take a shower and get some liquids. You stay here. Everyone else needs to leave. Give me a few minutes to get presentable, and I'll call the front desk to send you up. Perhaps you can fill me in from the beginning. Deal?"

Jackson nodded. "Yes. Thank you so much, doctor. Again, I'm terribly sorry for the intrusion."

Johnnie said, "I'm sorry, too."

She cut him a stern look. "I'll deal with you later, understand?"

Off to the side, the old man yelled, "Stumpy! We forgot him!"

The redheaded woman with Johnnie's group patted the old man's arm. "Stumpy is napping at the house, remember? He said he was tired from the flight. Plus, you have Gnomey." She reached into her handbag. "Do you want another cookie?"

Lou wanted to ask about the man's plastic garden friend, but really needed that cool shower. She said to Jackson, "Give me fifteen," and rolled towards the elevator.

Behind her, she heard Jackson tell Johnnie, "Go to the house. Wait for me there. And don't let him out of your sight for one second."

Days like this made her question her decision to become a psychiatrist. There was a reason she preferred video sessions. And Johnnie had made some very questionable choices in the past, but this was a blatant disregard for her boundaries. Still, the fear in Johnnie's eyes seemed genuine, and the old man seemed so sweet yet frail, making her inclined to help.

She just hoped this surprise wouldn't devolve into weird stalking. She'd been there before. Moving again would be a total bitch.

* * *

A few minutes later, Jackson rode the elevator to the twenty-eighth floor and looked for apartment 2801. He rang the doorbell. The woman with the crew cut and shoulder tattoo, whom he'd met minutes ago in the lobby, greeted him at the door. Ann gave him a wide smile. "Hello. She's in her office."

He entered and took in the surroundings. Modern décor, rounded support columns, and ocean-facing glass doors with a long balcony. Sleek chrome end tables, an open-concept kitchen with white lacquer cabinets and dark granite countertops. The floors were white oak. Very little furniture, but given the need for wheelchair access, it made sense. Modern abstract paintings in cobalt blue covered the white walls.

Ann's camera bag was on the counter, and he felt a wave of remorse. "I'm sorry to take you away from your work."

"It's okay. I texted the clients. They were running late as well. Can I get you something to drink before I head out?"

"I'll take a glass of water if it's not too much trouble."

She went behind the island and picked out a tall glass from the upper cabinet. "How do you know Johnnie?" she asked casually.

"He's a friend of grandfather's. Thank you for being so understanding. You could have rightfully tossed us to the curb."

"Where are you from?" She handed him the glass.

"I was raised in London until I was eighteen. Now I live on Grand Bahama." The ice-cold glass in his hand felt refreshing. He downed the contents, satisfying a thirst he didn't know he had.

"Well, she's in her office, the door to the right."

"Thank you." He smiled, handed Ann the empty glass, and went to the office. The door was ajar, but he still knocked. "Doctor Phillips?"

Seated on a more typical wheelchair than the one before, situated behind a glass-topped desk to his left, she waved him in. "Have a seat, Jackson."

He took a seat on the only other chair in the room, made of leather and chrome similar in size to her own chair. Her office had no windows but was brightly lit by a brass mid-century chandelier that looked like Sputnik. Scanning, he noticed thin pile beige carpet on the floor and a wall with black and white travel photographs artfully hung behind her. He wondered if Ann had taken them. One photo of a tiger in a mountain setting caught his interest, reminding him of the company's latest project to build a nature-themed amusement park. A project that demanded his attention, as evidenced by the multitude of emails and texts he received from the office since he'd arrived in Miami.

Jackson cleared his throat. "Thank you for seeing me. I'm sure you are awash with questions."

Dr. Phillips was no longer in her workout gear, but her face was still beet red, contrasting with the crisp white of her cotton wrap dress. Her hair still wet and slicked back from her face. She opened a folder, holding a pen perched for taking notes. "Yes, you could say that. Please, start at the beginning."

"Honestly, I'm at a loss myself. Pawpaw's problems go back quite far."

"What is your grandfather's name? His age?"

"Cudlow. Cudlow Loughton. He's seventy-five."

"I think I've heard that name. Wait...isn't he...?"

"The investment mogul? Yes. Or was. I only discovered recently he's been living as a vagrant on a beach for the last ten years."

"Homeless? Let me guess...on St. John?"

"Precisely. He's been deceiving to me for a decade. He led me to believe he was living at an eco-resort. Roughing it, comparatively, but not…well, how to put it…not insane."

"And Johnnie is his friend?"

"Yes. I would say they are very good friends."

"And the woman?"

"Johnnie's girlfriend, Greta."

Her eyes widened, as if he had said something strange, but she quickly composed herself. "How is your grandfather's overall health? Do you have his medical history?"

Jackson sunk his head. "He's lost a lot of weight in the last month. Grandfather came home to Nassau in early June, working on new business deals. Other than working too hard, he seemed fine. But he's had a bit of a heartbreak recently. He planned to re-marry, about two weeks ago, to Johnnie's landlady, Ms. Brown. Something happened…she left him at the altar. I think this is the cause of his downturn."

"I see. But does he have a doctor? Someone who might have records of his bloodwork, history of illnesses, surgeries, vaccinations, medications, allergies?"

"I'm afraid he's a mystery to me. His former internist passed away a few years back. Before Grandmaw Winnie died, he was in excellent health. As far as I know, his annual physicals were all stellar. But I imagine, if he's lived on a beach all these years since, he likely hasn't gone to a doctor…"

She exhaled. "I'll need to get a full medical workup; it's the first step for all my new patients. Given his lack of records, I'm inclined to order a comprehensive battery of tests, but it could take a couple of days. I have admitting privileges at Princewood Hospital. With your permission, I'd like him to stay at least two days to get them all completed right away."

"Yes, yes, absolutely."

"Is there anything else you can tell me about his current condition?"

"He gets very agitated. Angry but not violent. He wouldn't leave St. John without a blasted iguana named Stumpy. Plus, as you saw, he has bonded with that silly garden gnome. He seems like a child who won't go anywhere without his favorite stuffy." Tears welled, despite his efforts to remain calm. "I love him very much. I'd be eternally grateful for anything you can do to help him."

She handed him a blank patient information form. "Please fill this out to the best of your ability. I'll make some calls to get the process started."

He scanned it. "I'll try."

The doctor located an empty clipboard from the credenza behind her desk and handed it to Jackson, along with a pen. "Does your grandfather have medical insurance?"

Jackson shook his head. "No. But money isn't an issue." He began filling in the information at the top. *The easy stuff.*

"I see. Make sure you provide your full contact information. Do you have medical power of attorney or guardianship? Many patients in your grandfather's state don't go voluntarily."

"Our family lawyer is working on it. But without a diagnosis, we can't get our case in front of a judge."

She clucked her tongue. "Yes. I can write a letter. A temporary guardianship or health care surrogacy to determine his capacity would be the first step. Jot down some bullets of the behaviors you've witnessed and any concerns for his health and safety and let me know whom I should address the letter to."

"Thank you, Doctor Phillips." Jackson chewed on his fingernail as he lifted the pen from the paper. "He's not a U.S. citizen, so I don't have a social security number for him." He grimaced, "Maybe this would be simpler back home…"

"Jackson, please call me Lou. I'm not a miracle worker and this could be a long road. I will try to get to the bottom of your grandfather's problems, but at the same time, all we can do is take one step at a time and temper our expectations. Do you understand what I'm saying?"

"You're saying he might not get better."

She clasped her hands together in front of her. "It is a distinct possibility. Let me be clear: I'm not saying there is no hope. Sometimes people go through periods of short-term crisis—many times helped with medication—living normal lives once stabilized. But as the saying goes, hope for the best and prepare for the worst."

He nodded and returned to writing, finding it hard to read the small print through watery eyes.

"Jackson, I'm going to go into the living room to make some calls. Are you all right here?"

He nodded again.

Lou rolled her wheelchair away from the desk and left the room and closed the door.

Jackson reviewed the page. *Allergies? Surgeries?* No idea. *Weight?* Unknown. *Smoking?* No. *Family history of heart disease?* He shook his head.

What was the point? He didn't even know Pawpaw's blood type.

Part of him felt tempted to call his dad to locate answers. But his father had been champing at the bit to challenge grandfather's will. If Pawpaw died and dad knew of his insanity, he could challenge all Cud's decisions in the courts and wrest control of the company and all the family money.

Perhaps it was unfair for father to be cut out of the will completely. But he remembered the fight on the night Grandmaw Winnie died. How dad shouted such awful things. The raw hate in father's eyes.

But if dad could answer key medical questions, it might be worth going against his grandfather's wishes.

He took out his cell phone and called.

A gruff voice on the other end said, "Elson Loughton."

"Dad, it's Jackson."

"Ha! Well, looky there. What do you want, traitor?"

Jackson squeezed his eyes shut. *The name calling had begun…* "Dad, I don't want to get into it. I'm filling out a medical form…for myself…and I need some medical history."

"What's wrong with you, boy?"

"Nothing. Just a routine exam. Did anyone in our family have heart disease? Thyroid issues? Blood disorders?"

"How's your grandfather? Still living like a hermit? Or did the old bastard finally pass away?"

"Dad, can you just answer my questions?"

"Your mother would have a fit if she knew I was talking with you. You chose your side. Broke our hearts."

"Dad, I didn't call to start a fuss."

"Well, you made your bed. Now lie in it." The line went dead.

Jackson shouted, "Fuck you, ya wanker!"

He looked around the room and gathered his composure. He should have known better.

His upper lip quivered as he checked off the boxes for "Don't know" next to the list of conditions. He mustn't cry. Must stay strong. Get through the day and then tackle the next. *Carry on,* as they say.

Jackson finished the form, rubbed his face, stood up straight, and opened the door.

"Doctor…Lou? It's ready."

* * *

Johnnie, Greta and Cud took a taxi back to the home Jackson had rented for their stay. The white stucco, Spanish-style house was massive and private, with a gate and privacy hedge surrounding the property. With Cud's constant outbursts, it made sense to stay away from hotels and public places. The McMansion had six bedrooms and five bathrooms. More than enough space for the four-some. The backyard was gorgeous, with a pristine rectangular pool, manicured Zoysia grass and fragrant purple clematis vines covering the trellis over the patio.

They escorted Cud inside, who still held Gnomey, and locked the door, turning the top bolt for good measure. As Cud wandered to the kitchen, Johnnie whispered to Greta, "What do we do now?"

She pursed her lips. "We should get groceries if we plan to stay."

"Right." He scratched his neck. "Good idea."

"We could have them delivered."

Noises erupted from the kitchen, like pots and pans.

Johnnie ran toward the sound. "Jumping Johosephat… Cud!"

Cudlow had opened all the cabinets and pulled out every pot and pan. Johnnie grabbed a couple to put back, but Cud's fingers were in the cutlery drawer next, scooping up forks; he dropped them on the floor as well, with a musical clatter. The gnome was on the counter.

He lowered his voice. "Cud, what are you doing?"

Cudlow closed the drawer. "Can I have a glass of water?"

Johnnie smiled. "Sure. Let me help." He found a glass in an upper cabinet and filled it with tap water. "Here you go."

Cudlow took a sip, then spat the water on the floor. "I want juice."

Greta came in. "Oh boy. I'll find a mop."

Johnnie took the glass out of Cud's hands. "What kind of juice? We're making a grocery list. What kinds of food and drinks do you want?"

Cudlow gave a blank stare. "I don't know. I'm very sleepy." He shambled out of the room toward the den.

Johnnie followed him.

Cud curled up on the sofa and closed his eyes.

"Cud?" he asked. "Are you okay?"

Cud didn't respond. But his breathing appeared steady from the rise and fall of his chest. Johnnie thought it best to let him sleep. He joined Greta in the kitchen, who was wiping up water from the floor with paper towels.

"What is he doing?" she asked, still crouching.

"I think he's asleep."

"Thank goodness. After all his yelling on the flight, I need a nap myself."

"I'm going to unpack."

Greta rose from the floor and threw the soaked paper towel into the trash. "Good idea."

Johnnie and Greta headed to the bedroom they had picked out earlier. It was one of the smaller ones, but had French doors leading to the backyard.

He opened his khaki green duffel bag and arranged the contents on the bed in precise piles. After his last debacle using black garbage bags as luggage, Gertie reminded him that his green duffel was under his bed. He put his folded clothes into the bottom two drawers of the white dresser.

Greta grabbed his diary. "What's this?"

Johnnie's jaw fell open. *What could he tell her? That it contained all his innermost thoughts and fears?* He hadn't told her about his diary. In fact, with all the nights he'd spent at her apartment, he hadn't written in his diary in days. "Just a notebook. For writing ideas." Not exactly a fib, but far from the whole truth.

"Can I read it?" She opened the front cover.

He pounced to take it from her hands. "It's private. Sorry." He tucked the book into the top drawer of his nightstand.

"That's okay." She lounged on her side of bed, on the swath free of Johnnie's piles, and placed an extra pillow behind her head. "Hey, do you think we should rent scooters to get around? We may want to split up. The librarian conference is a few miles away."

"Sure. I miss the Flying Pig."

She frowned. "Have you decided what you'll get when you get back to St. John? You'll need a vehicle for work."

He scooped up his toothbrush, toothpaste and comb and walked them into the adjoining bathroom. "I haven't decided yet. Might get a compact car." Johnnie washed his face with warm water and brushed his teeth. He'd forgotten deodorant and his razor. Still, he considered the toothbrush a victory.

When he returned to the bedroom, Greta was asleep. *Out cold.* He wondered if there was a carbon monoxide leak. Admittedly, it had already been a long day, at least emotionally. Coaxing Cud onto the plane was worse than herding cats into a rainstorm. The flight itself wasn't long, but Cud's whimpering had set his teeth on edge.

Johnnie put away his remaining clothes, lay down on the comforter next to Greta, and closed his eyes. His mind wandered, thinking about Lou and if she was still mad at the ambush. She had a big heart, but this could be unforgivable. Still, if she could help Cud—even if it meant she dumped him as her patient—it would be worth it.

Seconds later, he imagined what kind of car he would buy on St. John. Not that there were many car purchase options on the small island. If he apologized to Robin, maybe he could borrow her car for a few weeks. This thought caused a cascade of frustration, wondering if he was ready to make peace with his sister.

Cudlow appeared in the doorway, just staring.

Johnnie whispered, trying not to wake Greta, "What do you want, buddy?"

"I want to go outside."

He got up and led Cud into the kitchen. "Why do you want to go outside?"

"Stumpy is outside."

Johnnie had completely forgotten how they dropped off the iguana plus their luggage at the house before going to Dr. Phillips' apartment.

From the view of the rear sliding glass door, Stumpy was clearly sitting on the teak dining table under the trellis, perched like a king.

"Sure, let's go see Stumpy."

They sat at the table and took turns petting the iguana, who seemed to love the attention, with an open mouth and slitted eyes.

At least Cud was calm.

Johnnie looked at the time on his phone.

Where was Jackson?

What was Lou telling him?

His stomach grumbled. They would need food within the next hour.

Was this like having a child? Not letting them out of your sight? Extreme exhaustion and simple chores became logistical nightmares?

No, he never wanted to have a kid. As awful as that sounded, he knew he couldn't take the constant worry and exertion.

When it came to having kids, he had to count himself out.

Chapter 6

Professor Elson C. Loughton wrote the word "demand" in capital letters on the whiteboard as the classroom quieted.

"Demand side economics," he boomed, "will be the focus of the next exam."

The second-year economics class at the University of Hampshire opened their notebooks and laptops with a clamor.

Elson's phone beeped with a notification.

He ignored it and started his lecture, but kept his phone on his lectern. "In chapter three, we learn from John Maynard Keynes that when demand is low, there is a higher chance of recession…" Elson glanced at his phone. An email from Felicity, the company's lawyer. He hadn't heard from her in a decade. "Who can give me an example of a low demand economic cycle?"

A few hands in the front row flew up. The usual eager suspects. *Mostly wankers.* He picked the one on the far right with the bad acne.

The student—wearing a bow tie in contrast to the hoodies of his classmates—excitedly ran on about the Great Depression. Elson resisted the urge to roll his eyes. Instead, he wrinkled his brow and pretended to be reviewing his notes while he opened Felicity's email.

Her message said she needed his signature. He hadn't signed anything related to Loughton Enterprises since his termination ten years ago.

Whatever she needed could bloody well wait.

When the student finished, he turned to the class. "Who can give me a definition of a free market and how it differs from socialist economies?"

Now he was just messing with them. No markets were *truly* free. Even the most capitalistic economies were ruled by monopolistic companies, leading to plutocratic rule, sometimes worse than communist governments. He'd disillusion them soon enough. Show them the dark underbelly of the world's economic reality.

All power came from wealth. He knew all about wealth and power. When his father disowned him, his social standing fell hard; he counted himself lucky to get this lowly lecturer position by sheer association, however tenuous, with the Loughton financial empire. His university salary was a pittance, and he wondered if his class noticed the moth-eaten holes in his tweed jacket.

A text came in from his son Jackson.. *the traitor*.

The student asked, "Professor Loughton, aren't you going to say anything?"

He placed his phone face down and continued the lecture, speaking at twice speed, and ending the class fifteen minutes early. "Tomorrow, read ahead to supply-side economics. There may be a pop quiz."

The students groaned but gathered up their belongings and stampeded out, their feet thundering down the wood risers.

One student named Sarah, sporting a blue pixie haircut, stopped by. "Professor Loughton, I saw you pick up that dead squirrel in the road earlier. What will you do with it?"

He'd hoped no one had seen. With pursed lips, he grumbled, "None of your concern."

"I'm not criticizing. I do a bit of taxidermy myself."

The enthusiasm in her voice allowed him to come clean. But he kept a wary stance. "Fine. If you *must* know, I dabble in articulating skeletons. Usually small mammals, given the space constraints of my flat."

"Really? That's bloody righteous. Do you have any photos?"

Elson lifted his glasses to scratch the bridge of his nose, wondering why this student had a sudden interest in his hobbies. Sarah was pretty, with good grades. Maybe she wasn't just sucking up for extra points. "I'll show you another time. I have some business to attend to." He waved her off.

She took the hint and gave a coy parting smile. "Have a nice day, professor." Sarah pivoted and headed out.

For a second, he admired the narrowness of her waist. *If only Henrietta would die already.* Not that his wife was sick. But he could daydream. The battle-axe never gave him a moment's peace since his father ripped away their fortune. He and Hen had the same argument every bleeding time.

He read the text from Jackson. Apparently, the old man was mentally sick. Jackson urged him to call Felicity immediately.

Chuckling to himself, he thought, *oh, yes. I'll sign the petition to the court.* Jackson asked that he agree to name Grandma Camille Loughton as Cudlow's temporary guardian, which was laughable because she was a hundred years old. Camille spent her days in the assisted-living home ranting about the mushy food and hitting people with her cane when they weren't looking.

Yes, the sooner he could put the old prick away, the sooner he could seize what was rightfully his. Jackson wouldn't like it, but he would understand with time. Cudlow never had a proper plan for the company's growth. Handing control to Jackson at eighteen was simultaneously unthinking and cruel.

His adrenaline raced as he remembered how badly Cudlow had treated his mom. Emotionally abandoning her for decades before she died of cancer. And then play acting as if her death tore him up.

Father's false claims of devotion made him boil, and he felt at the time he had no choice but to tell the damned bugger the cold, hard truth. A sweet moment of vindication. Later, he wasn't surprised when Cudlow ran away from the family and his company to sunbathe and to drink Mai Tais in St. John. *Like a genuine, fat, callous bastard.*

Elson texted Jackson. "Felicity contacted me. I'm happy to help. We've had our differences, but I still love the old sod." He hit send and smirked. Pretending to want a reconciliation would be fun and give him time to make some moves.

First things first. Hire a lawyer. Loughton Enterprises was based in Nassau. He'd need someone familiar with their corporate laws. He texted an old friend living in Grand Bahama. "Jasper, I need a lawyer. Bahamas corporate with family law as well."

Jasper called instead of texting back. "Elson, chap, what's going on? Did the old man die?"

"No. But maybe a better path. The S-O-B has gone mental. Can you recommend anyone?"

"I know just the guy. A real killer in the courtroom. But not cheap."

"Who?"

"Name of Greaves. He knows all the judges across the Caribbean, from the Keys to Barbados. A boutique firm, but very effective. His paralegals are amazing. He worked on my divorce three years ago and had the witch paying *me* alimony! I'll text you his info."

"Thanks, chum. Maybe when I have two farthings to rub together, we can play a bit of golf on your home course. Lord knows I need some sunshine."

"Good luck to you. Give 'em bloody hell."

Elson ended the call. A few minutes later, he had the website for Richard Greaves up on his laptop. The lawyer was not photogenic. But he'd worked on high-profile cases. He'd even won a multi-million-dollar lawsuit against an international oil company, which couldn't have been easy.

He dialed the number listed for Greaves' international headquarters.

A woman answered, "Richard Greaves, law and justice for all. How may I direct your call?"

"Yes, yes. I'm wondering if you can help me. I'm looking for a lawyer for…how to put this? A sensitive issue. Is Mr. Greaves available for a consult?"

"I'm sorry, sir, Mr. Greaves doesn't represent drug dealers any longer."

"What? No. A family issue. Involving a family business."

"I'm afraid he doesn't represent the Mafia anymore, either."

"No! I'm talking about Loughton Enterprises. The global real-estate investment firm."

"And your name is?"

"Elson Loughton."

After a pause, the woman said, "I'll put you through."

The conversation was brief and to the point. Greaves was a man in a hurry and eager to get started. The representation agreement arrived via email within the hour, outlining their financial arrangement. No retainer or money up front, but a hefty ten percent stake in the company for Greaves if he was successful.

Elson didn't care to barter. And the percentage, though worth millions, would be more than enough incentive to receive Greave's full attention to the matter.

Another class of students for a different lecturer began filing into the space. *Time to go home and begin gathering documents for his new lawyer.* Elson opened his briefcase to put away his laptop and noticed the clear-lidded rectangular container. In all the excitement, he'd forgotten about the dead squirrel. Through the plexi, the little guy was bloated and bleeding from its mouth. Likely hit by an automobile. He hoped the bones were still intact. Normally his articulated skeletons would garner him a good eight-hundred quid on Etsy.

It was a strange hobby, but oddly satisfying, making him feel a sense of power, even momentarily during his usually dull and put-upon existence. And he felt a kinship with the ill-fated animals, who were often left to the vultures to be picked clean.

In their new form, these rotten, tiny mammals could be transformed to something lasting and revered, for decoration or perhaps educational purposes.

From an early age, he learned that above all, Loughtons must be useful; to keep calm and carry on. To take all adversity and channel it into transformation, always striving to better oneself. He channeled this motto into his hobby, bringing usefulness to the plentiful and free rotting carcasses scattered across the city's streets.

Elson picked up his briefcase and exited the room, his posture erect, his chin up. He found a new lightness in his step, knowing his future could take a turn for the better.

People would know the name Elson Loughton again.

It was his birthright. And Loughton Enterprises would soon be his.

* * *

Ranger Merv stepped off the airplane at Miami International, his mind buzzing with too much caffeine. He wanted to be alert to accomplish his first two goals: steal back Stumpy from Johnnie and place some strategic bets at the horse track.

Miami was a big place, and he set his first priority at locating Johnnie. He found a bench outside the airline gate, rested his rolling bag on the floor in front of him and called the beach-keeper's cell.

The voice that answered was female and groggy. "Hello?"

Merv was instantly happy. Maybe Johnnie really had a girlfriend, meaning he didn't have to worry about him stealing Kemper. *Or had he dialed a wrong number?*

"Um, I'm trying to reach John Crosswell?"

"This is his phone. He's busy at the moment. Can I take a message?"

"Sure. This is his co-worker, Ranger Merv Hartley. I was wondering if John was going to be in Miami next weekend also? See, I'm going to be there next Saturday and thought we could meet up for a brewski." A bold lie, but he couldn't ask about their location outright.

"I don't know. I think we'll be back by next weekend. Depends on what happens with his friend Cudlow. We're trying to get him admitted to the hospital for some tests."

"Oh, gosh, I hope he feels better soon. Hey, since I have you on the phone, I'm trying to figure out which hotel to stay at. Got any recommendations? How do you like your place?"

"Cudlow's grandson rented us a villa. I'm not sure about hotels…"

"A villa? You don't say. Sounds fancy. In the city?"

Over the loudspeaker, a gate announcement blared at ninety decibels, piercing his eardrums. He held his hand over the receiver so Greta wouldn't hear. Clearly, it wasn't safe to talk in the terminal without giving away his location. He walked away, rolling his bag behind him, looking for a quieter nook.

"On the south end of the city, close to the hospital. I think it's called Casa Verde."

"Nice. Did he find it through one of those vacation rental apps?"

"Hmm. I don't know. But it has everything. A pool, gym, hot tub, and even a home theater."

"I've been thinking about holding a family reunion in Miami. It sounds perfect. Can you send me the details?" He ducked into a semi-quiet food court. Trays clattered and voices filled the background. But it was the best he could do. He sat at a table against the far wall, clasping the phone tightly to his ear to the point of pain to hear Greta properly.

"Sure. I don't know how much it costs, but it might be a ton."

"Well, sometimes you gotta splurge for family. Am I right?" Something sticky on his free hand caught his notice. He'd placed his arm on the table absentmindedly, not noticing the streak of ketchup on the red Formica. He grabbed a discarded napkin and tried to sop up the goo from his skin.

"Yes. By the way, I'm Greta."

"Nice to meet you, Greta. Johnnie told me he had a girlfriend. It has been a complete pleasure to talk with you. Johnnie is a lucky guy."

"Aw. That's sweet. I'll text you the address. Hey, I've got to go. Cudlow is awake. Have a nice time next week."

"No, thank *you*, Greta. Take care now."

He ended the call and shouted, "BOOYAH!"

The couple at the table next to him gave him annoyed looks.

"Sorry, folks." He got up from the table, ready to make a hasty exit, but slipped on a mustard packet. He stopped his slide before falling, but the yellow paste squirted outward, onto the shoe of the man at the next table.

And this didn't go unnoticed.

The man, in his thirties, with a muscle tee and sweat-shorts, stood, inspected his sneaker, then glared at Merv. "Mister, you owe me a new pair of Jordans."

Merv held up his hands. "Hey, I didn't put that there. These places are minefields. Let me get more napkins." He didn't wait for a reply. Grabbing the handle of his rolling bag, he high-tailed it out of the food court at a sprint, barely keeping his bag's small wheels on the floor.

He exited the terminal near the line for the rental-car shuttle bus and stopped to catch his breath. Regret overcame Merv, as he questioned his highly recognizable fashion choices: a straw fedora with a green feather tucked into the band; knock-off orange Yeezys; black acid-washed cut-off jeans embroidered with a red dragon across his hip and bum, and a Versace-style shirt sporting two golden leopards in a face-off.

If angry mustard-guy went looking for him, he'd be more than easy to spot. But he didn't have time to change.

[Bing] A notification on his phone showed a text from Johnnie's number. Greta came through with their address.

At least *one* thing went well today.

When he looked up, the man and woman from the food court approached the end of the shuttle line. The guy was short, but stocky and younger. Someone he didn't want to tangle with. Luckily, they hadn't seen him yet. Merv ducked behind a wide round column a few feet away and opted to wait for the next shuttle.

A poor start to his quest.

He looked up the address. *Maybe he should just get a cab?*

A burly hand grabbed his arm. "Mister! You gonna pay for my shoes or what?"

Merv's eyes froze wide in fear. "What?"

"That's what I thought." The man pounded him in the face, sending him to the concrete sidewalk.

Mustard-shoe guy said, "Motherfucker," and walked away.

Merv stayed on the ground and touched his nose gingerly, hoping it wasn't broken. It sure did smart.

Maybe the universe was trying to tell him something.

Like, *stop gambling.* Or, *avoid airport food courts.*

It was his own damn fault. He couldn't keep putting himself in financial and physical peril.

Just let me get through this, he thought.

I promise, I can change.

Chapter 7

Early the next morning, after only one cup of coffee and before most of Miami was awake, Dr. Louella Phillips rolled through the automatic glass doors of the hospital administrative offices and spoke to Velma, the head of the department.

"Vel, thanks for meeting me so early. Man, I hate these high-profile cases."

"I got your email. Don't worry. We'll use a pseudonym. I'll be the only one who knows."

"Thanks. All my other celebrity clients were out-patient. How do you pick the name?"

"We try to pick generic names."

"Won't this confuse our patient? He seems confused as it is. His grandson said he was calling himself Gnomey…like a garden gnome."

"Interesting. Yes, I can see how it might make matters worse. But it's more important right now to get a clear diagnosis. Depending on what we find, perhaps later he could get private care where his identity can be protected."

"Yes, of course."

"Hmm. Mr. Harold Nome, spelled like the town in Alaska. Harold is the name of my Schnauzer. Okay with you?" Velma typed something into the computer.

"Sure. Do you have a room ready? He and his family and friends are waiting in a taxi outside."

"Yes, I'll send an orderly out. Thank you for submitting the paperwork in advance. Here are the three visitor passes you asked for."

"Thank you, Velma, I appreciate your help with such short notice."

"The local court order allows seventy-two hours for evaluation. Then we have to let him go unless we can prove additional care is medically necessary."

"Exactly. Will your lab be able to expedite? I'll be ordering more tests than normal. He seems awfully malnourished. He was living on a beach; possibly without clean water. Also, scans for cancer, bloodwork for viruses. Harold just came back from a vacation in South America, plus he's been traveling recently for work. It's a long shot, but I want to be thorough.

"I'll call the lab manager now. Mr. Nome will get top priority." Velma took out a Sharpie pen and wrote 'Harold Nome' on the top label of the otherwise nondescript manila folder. "Here, I started his chart."

"Thanks. I'd better go." She took the folder, placed it on her lap; then turned her wheelchair around and pulled the handle of the office door.

"Do you want me to get that?" Velma stood as if ready to dash around her desk.

Lou was half-way thru when she laughed, "What do you think?"

"Right. Well, good luck with your patient."

Before she closed the door, she said, "Thanks, I think I'll need it."

An orderly pushing a hospital wheelchair met her in the hall. "I'm Nate. You must be Dr. Phillips? I'm ready to receive your patient."

"Good morning. Follow me."

Nate followed her to the wing entrance. They exited through the glass automatic doors. A tall overhang spanned the two-lane patient drop-off area. The sun was still low in the sky behind thick clouds and the morning air felt refreshingly cool in the shade. The minivan taxi remained parked where she had last seen it. She waved over it over.

The driver pulled around to the curb and Jackson got out first.

"Dr. Phillips, is the coast clear?"

"Yes. Jackson, meet Nate. He will take good care of *Harold*." She winked.

Jackson nodded. "Harold. I see. Great. Well, let's get cracking, I guess." He pulled open the rear sliding door. Greta got out first, wearing white Bermuda shorts and a plain gray T-shirt, followed by Cudlow, then Johnnie.

Lou noticed Cudlow's hair was silky and his clothes looked clean and crisp, unlike their first meeting at her apartment building. Knowing what a state he was in, freshening him up couldn't have been easy. Lou said, "I know you all care about him, but this is a hospital. Normal visiting hours don't start until ten and you won't *all* be able to stay with him." She handed out their visitor passes.

Johnnie closed the taxi door. "I just want to make sure he feels safe."

Cudlow looked above at the sky. "That seagull said it's going to rain."

Greta, holding Cud's hand, said in a soft voice, "Yes, it looks like it might rain. Come inside now. Look, this nice man has a special chair for you." She gestured to Nate. "See, even Doctor Lou sits in one." She walked Cudlow over.

Nate smiled and helped seat the old man. "I'm Nate. Hey, Harold, do you like Jell-O?" He lifted Cudlow's feet and flipped down the foot rests.

"Jell-O?" Cud asked.

"Sure. We have red and orange. And green." Nate turned Cud's wheelchair around and began walking at a brisk pace down the hallway to the elevator bank.

Lou showed the folder with Cudlow's new name to Jackson, Johnnie and Greta, whispering, "Got it?"

They nodded.

She stayed back and rolled behind the crew as they followed Nate.

Nate and Cud entered a large hospital-bed-sized elevator; when they were all inside, he pressed the button for five.

Lou whispered to Nate, "I thought they kept certain patients on lower floors."

He whispered back, "We didn't have space on the other floors. But, don't worry, the windows don't open."

Lou cringed inside for bringing it up. But it was her job to anticipate the worst.

On the fifth floor, the halls were empty. Cudlow's room was private, with a window, but a solid pane as promised. There was a narrow wood cabinet, like a locker for personal clothing, a television mounted from the ceiling, and a stiff-looking blue sofa that would seem at home in any strip mall doctor's waiting room.

Nate helped Cudlow from the chair to the hospital bed. "Dr. Phillips, I've got to leave you now, but a nurse will be in shortly. There's a gown on the bed."

Lou nodded. "Thanks, Nate."

Greta whispered to Cudlow. "Do you want Jackson to help you get dressed?"

Jackson said, "Johnnie, help me."

Dr. Lou said, "Greta, how about we let the boys handle this?" She rolled outside and Greta joined her, closing the door behind them.

Greta leaned against the wall. "Thanks again, Doctor Phillips. I'm sorry we ambushed you yesterday. I thought Johnnie worked it out with you before we left St. John."

Not one for small talk, and needing more coffee, she got to the point. "How long have you been dating?"

The redhead twirled a lock of hair around her index finger and her eyes went up as in thought. "Hmm. A couple of weeks?"

"And you came all the way to Miami to help one of Johnnie's friends?"

"Well, I'm also going to the Librarian Conference this week. At the convention center."

"Cud...Harold has taken a shine to you."

She smiled. "He's a sweetheart...well, at least when he isn't crying or screaming. Poor Jackson. I can't imagine what he's going through. And Johnnie feels so guilty..."

"Guilty?"

Screams came from the hospital room. Greta pulled open the door and held it for Lou.

Cudlow was in his hospital gown, revealing his knobby knees and bare feet. His eyes wild, he shouted, "STUMPY! Goodness! Where's Stumpy?" He ran towards the door. Johnnie wrapped both arms around Cud's shoulders, bracing his movements. But it was a true struggle.

Jackson sighed audibly. "I knew it."

Dr. Lou shouted into the hall. "I need an orderly, STAT!"

Greta held her hands out low. "Mr. Nome, it will all be okay. I'll get Stumpy. I promise. Remember he was sleeping? And we didn't want to wake him? Just wait. I'll get him." She approached and placed her hand on his.

Cudlow nodded and seemed to calm down.

Johnnie eased up on his hold but didn't let go. He turned and mouthed, "What?"

Greta winked. "Trust me. I'll be right back."

Lou followed her into the hall and closed the door. "Look, I know you want to help, but we *absolutely* cannot have an iguana in his room."

"I'm not *really* getting Stumpy. You'll see." Greta dashed off down the hall and turned toward the elevators.

Lou shook her head. *This case was going to be rough.*

A tall orderly with a shaved head and nametag of 'R. Armando' strode up. "What's the situation?"

"A new patient in room 504 is agitated and tried to run."

The orderly opened the door. Lou evaluated the unexpected scene in front of her. Cudlow was tucked into bed, sipping from a plastic water cup, eyes focused on Jackson. The grandson sat on the edge of the hospital bed near Cud's feet, singing the Itsy-Bitsy-Spider song, with finger movements to match the lyrics. Johnnie was on the sofa, clapping his hands in time.

"Looks okay to me," the orderly said.

"This time. Thanks for getting here so fast. I'd appreciate it if you could check on him from time to time."

The orderly grimaced. "Sure. I'll try. If you need me, dial 5911 on any hospital phone."

Lou asked Johnnie, "How did you calm him down?"

"Gertie told me that singing helps. Does the TV work? He also likes nature and cooking shows."

"The television controls are on that wired remote next to the bed. I'm going to be ordering a few tests. You can stay for ten minutes, but then you need to clear out. Understand?"

Jackson turned. "We understand." In a childlike voice, he continued singing, "London Bridge is falling down…falling down…"

The singing went on for a couple minutes, which included the nursery rhymes, Baa Baa Black Sheep, and Three Blind Mice. Lou knew there were better things to do with her time, but she wanted to see what Greta meant. She wrote a few observations in the folder while they waited.

Greta burst into the room, out of breath as if she'd been running the entire time. "I got it!" She held up a stuffed green toy. "See, Harold? Stumpy!"

Lou chuckled to herself. The plush toy animal, nearly two feet long, was clearly an alligator with googly eyes and felt teeth and not an iguana, but Cudlow opened his arms wide and shouted, "Stumpy! Come here, boy!"

Greta placed the alligator in Cud's arms; he snuggled the plush green reptile like it was a long-lost friend.

Johnnie put his arm around Greta's waist. "How did you…?"

"When we drove up to the hospital, I saw a sidewalk vendor selling toys.

Only six bucks. I thought it might work."

Lou shook her head in disbelief. "Certainly inventive."

A nurse knocked on the door. "Dr. Phillips? I'm Naomi. Nice to meet you."

"Hi, Naomi. Could you start an I-V? Did you get the list of tests I ordered?"

"Yes, I'm ready to get started on his blood draw."

Jackson interjected, "I'd like to stay."

Lou drew in a long breath to evaluate Jackson's request. Having an extra set of eyes to keep tabs on Mr. Loughton would be helpful, and she could see the desperation in the young man's face. "Okay. But Johnnie and Greta need to go." She turned to Naomi. "I have some other appointments this morning, but I'll be back to check on Mr. Nome this afternoon. I want his test results the moment they come it."

Naomi took the chart from Lou. "Yes, you should be able to see them uploaded to the portal as soon as they are complete."

Lou nodded. "Jackson, I promise we'll find out what is wrong with your grandfather. I'll be in touch soon."

Jackson got up off the bed and extended a handshake, "Thanks, doctor."

"Glad to help." She shook his hand, then rolled out of the room and toward the elevator.

In her line of work, she'd seen worse cases. But this would be one of the more difficult. Perhaps a top five.

A cup of coffee was still calling her name.

Her schedule included a ten-mile training loop after her last appointment at four. Somehow, she knew in her bones that her training schedule was going to suffer with this new case.

The race in Orlando was coming up soon, and she wanted to win this year in the push-rim division. She'd made the hotel reservation for the event months ago. But she couldn't think about that now.

She made a mental note to talk to Johnnie about his impulsive behavior. Because now it was affecting her own life. And that just wouldn't do.

* * *

Johnnie held Greta's hand, mindful to use his uninjured arm, as they exited the hospital. It was comforting to feel her soft fingers interlocked with his, yet he could tell from the way she walked a half-step ahead, she was eager to get to her destination. And he didn't want to hold her back. She'd been so nice to Cud and he would have lost his cool a few times last night if she hadn't been around to calm down both of them.

He stopped. "Oh, damn."

"What's wrong?"

"I forgot to tell Dr. Phillips something important."

Greta shook her head, "Just call her."

"Hold on. I'll text her. I need her to know that Cud is still in there."

"In where? The hospital?"

"No. Like inside. Inside his brain. Before we left St. John, Cud and I were sitting at a picnic table at Hawksnest, and he seemed normal. Almost like he knew what was happening to him. Just like the old Cud."

"How long did it last?"

"Only a minute. But it has to be important, right? I don't want her to fill him full of drugs."

"I don't know. You trust her, don't you?"

"Yes. I think so."

"Let her do her job. All we can do is stay positive." Greta looked at her phone, obviously distracted.

They continued walking to the next intersection and waited for the crosswalk signal.

She said, "I'm going to be at the convention most of the day. What are you doing?"

He hadn't thought about it. He'd assumed he could visit with Cud most of the time, but the hospital's general visiting hours were limited. Still, he had another idea of and it wasn't particularly wise. And Greta wouldn't understand. "I'll probably spend the day by the pool with Stumpy. Maybe go to a bookstore." *All complete lies.*

She kissed his cheek. "I might stay late. The opening keynote address goes until seven, followed by a happy hour reception."

"Have fun."

Greta looked at her phone again. "Text me if anything changes with Cudlow. Or if you need me. I can leave whenever."

He saw the excitement on her face. "Just go. Like you said, nothing to do but wait and see."

As soon as the light changed, she was off, speed-walking down the sidewalk.

When Greta was out of visual range, he brought up a map on his phone with directions to the J.M. Murlock Construction Company. The address seemed the same. Knowing it was Sunday, the office wasn't likely open, but he wanted to see for himself.

Johnnie hailed a taxi. A few minutes later, he paid the driver and stood outside the familiar looking single story industrial building. He stared at the facade like he had stepped back in time. No lights were on that he could tell, and only one car in the parking lot.

He'd come this far. In his mind, Robin's voice chirped at him, calling him a butthead and making a joke about his brave stupidity. He responded to this internal dialogue with the thought: *Robin. I have to.*

The front door was unlocked, to his surprise. The reception area was the same. Plywood walls and crummy Formica desks. A film of black grime covered every surface as if the office hadn't been cleaned in two decades. Muddy work boots had left a track of soiled carpet through the office to the warehouse door.

A familiar brunette came into the room from the back.

Darla.

His ex-wife's eyes went wide like she'd seen an apparition. *She wasn't wrong.*

All he could think to say was, "Hi." Instantly, he wanted to leave, but his feet wouldn't move, anxious to hear what she would say.

"Johnnie! What are you doing here?"

"I was in town. Just wanted to see how you were…but if you're busy, I can leave."

Darla's hair was longer, and she seemed thinner with very toned arms. Older by four years, but that was the nature of time. She looked good. He remembered the time she got her nose pierced in high school. The hole had filled in but still left a dent. Her brown eyes were the same, but happier than he recalled. She wore white jeans and a white T-shirt with the word 'positivity' in sequins.

She closed the distance between them and embraced him around the shoulders. "You look good."

A hug was unexpected, and he considered all his options. *Flee or be polite.* She smelled the same, with her usual wild ginger shampoo. Part of him wanted to bury his face against her neck like he used to. But that was a different him and a different her.

He pulled away and stepped backward to increase the gap between them.

She cocked her head to the side. "Do you want to get some coffee? I'm just about finished here. I needed to prepare invoices for tomorrow's mail. You remember the drill."

No, he didn't remember her working Sundays, but perhaps a part of his brain had, or he wouldn't have come. "Coffee sounds good."

They exited the building and she locked the door behind her. "What brings you to Miami? Are you still living in St. John with your sister, Robin? How is she?"

So many questions... "I'm here with a friend. Um, three friends." Immediately, he knew his mistake. *Two friends and his girlfriend. Was it a Freudian slip?* He didn't want to make a big deal about it now.

"We can go to Chuckie's Diner on Fourth Street. Remember? They still have great eclairs."

"Okay." He followed her lead down the sidewalk. Darla was taking his reappearance so well...*too well.* As they walked, he asked, "Aren't you upset I just showed up without calling first?"

She smiled and faced him. "You know, I had a dream last week. You were in it. We were at a restaurant. Do you believe in astral projection?" Darla's eyes flickered with mischief.

"Come on. You're joking, right?"

She laughed. "Yes, I'm just teasing. Don't be so serious. I don't know. Maybe you caught me in a good mood." She continued her easy stride down the sidewalk.

He recalled how they used to tease each other. And a sense of calm came over him, like he was talking with a long-lost friend. Which he was. Still, it felt both foreign and familiar at the same time.

"Whew. You had me there."

"Hey, before you get the wrong idea, I just got engaged." She held up her ring finger, sporting a respectably sized diamond on her left hand. Darla continued, "So maybe this is Karma. We didn't exactly have closure when you left."

"Do I know the lucky guy?" He exhaled, happy her head was turned, because he could feel his face turning red. *Why did he have to say the word lucky?*

It sounded so cheesy.

Without a beat, she answered, "Murlock's son, David."

"Wait…hold up. We went to high school with him…right?"

"Yep. Ugh. Remember how he dated that cheerleader, Bambi? I hated her because she always called me fat. Anyway, they got divorced last year."

He didn't remember Bambi. And the divorce was probably difficult for David. Still, he answered with the only thing he could think of. "Congratulations."

The diner was in front of them. He held open the door.

"Thanks." She walked in ahead of him.

As he entered, the diner's familiar odors hit him hard. *Stale grease and potatoes.* It felt like entering a strange portal, as if he was in a live-action Black Mirror episode. The place looked the same.

Instinctually they settled on the booth in the back. *Their booth.* He touched the wall next to him to confirm it was real. "Will Dave be upset? I mean, is this okay?" He turned the paper placemat over to the blank white side to avoid the crazy advertising that made his eyes sore.

"Dave is much more chill than he was in high school. He's gotten very spiritual."

"You don't say?" The table had the same black and white dolphin-shaped salt and pepper shakers. It felt odd, yet reassuring, to remember that detail.

They gave their order to the server. They each got coffee and a BLT club sandwich. *Like the old days.*

He checked his phone. A text from Greta with a photo of her in front of a line of people waiting for Margaret Atwood's autograph. He chuckled at the caption, *"Forgot my red robe."*

Darla rested her chin on her palm. "Who's that?" She leaned forward, as if trying to peer over his phone.

It was time to come clean. "My girlfriend. She's at the Librarian Conference downtown."

"Johnnie! That's great! I'm so glad you found someone."

"We just started going out. I wouldn't say it's serious." Again, he wanted to slap himself. *Why did he say it wasn't serious?* It felt serious. He seriously adored Greta. *Another Freudian thing? What was wrong with him?*

"Tell me all about her."

"Look, I didn't come here to talk about Greta. I wanted to see if you were okay and to say I'm sorry."

"Sorry? For what?"

"I've been thinking a lot lately. Yeah, I know. Not my strong suit." He stared at the table. "I know I made things bad and I don't blame you for leaving. I was a mess. I wasn't trying to hurt you, but I did. For that, I want to apologize."

"Wow, Johnnie. I'm sorry too."

"No. It wasn't your fault. I know that now. I was so angry. I had so much rage. But that was on me."

Darla placed her hand over his. "I appreciate you saying that."

He looked up at her face. The same face from their wedding day. And all the happy times, before the dark days. Johnnie wondered if it was possible to go back in time; completely rewind and start over. He would do so many things differently. Like not charge that Taliban vehicle. And not resist taking medication in those early months of his recovery.

It occurred to him that maybe his resistance to pills had cost him his marriage. And maybe he needed to let Dr. Phillips do her job to bring Cudlow back to reality. In any way she saw fit.

Was this the lesson the universe was trying to teach him?

He'd have to seriously consider that.

Chapter 8

Armando eyed the man in the wrinkled, pin-striped suit. The man's demeanor spelled confidence, even when his clothes did not. He'd seen ambulance chasers before. But, typically, they hung out in the emergency room waiting area. It took a really pushy lawyer to roam the halls on the upper floors.

The orderly crossed his arms, his stance wide, ready to hear the man's spiel.

The man wiped his nose with his bare hand. "My name's irrelevant. It's a hush-deal, got it? Pays handsomely."

None of this smelled right to Armando. But it could have been the man's heavy use of body spray. "Hey, I'm busy. What are you saying?"

The man with the pimple on his chin and stubby wide dress shoes pulled a phone from his jacket pocket and held up an image. "This old guy...he's here, right?"

"Maybe..." Armando needed to play his cards close. This guy might not have any money at all; if the stain on his blue tie was any clue.

"Yeah, I know that look. You think I'm full of crap. Wouldn't be the first. I'm a busy guy and don't have time for dressing snazzy. But you see this briefcase?" He held up his worn brown leather case with scratches and a bent paperclip securing one end of the handle. "Has a good amount of *paper* in it."

Armando wanted to laugh. This guy was unreal. "Show me."

Pimple-chin jerked his head to the side, and they headed down the hall to the vacant part of the wing.

The lawyer opened the case. "Twenty-K. But we need him to look...you know…cray-cray. Let me put it to you this way. Sliding scale. The worse he looks, the closer you get to the twenty. Capiche?"

"You want me to rile him up?"

"Not saying anything of the sort." The lawyer surveyed the ceiling, as if looking for security cameras, then locked eyes. "Meet me in the cafeteria in one hour to trade."

"What's your name?"

"Better not to use names."

Armando looked at his phone for the time. "Right."

The wrinkled disaster strode away with a jaunt in his stride.

Armando shook his head, wondering if this was legit. His kids' private school tuition bill was due next week, plus his car needed a new timing belt.

Sure, he could poke the poor old guy.

He ducked into Mr. Nome's room after he saw the target's grandson head down the hall.

Nome was sleeping like a baby. Kind of cute, like a Baby Yoda, with his blanket tucked under his chin and the stuffed alligator cradled under his scrawny right arm. He slid the toy out and hid it under the bed.

His plan was simple: do some annoying shit to agitate the guy. *How hard could it be?*

Naomi, the head nurse appeared. "Armando, what's going on?"

"Oh, hey. I got a call about Mr. Nome earlier. Just wanted to see how he's doing. But obviously he's sleeping."

She smiled. "Aren't you sweet? You know, word is, Mr. Nome is one of those secret V-I-P cases. Beatrice in food services thinks he might be related to the entertainer, Pitbull."

"No shit?" He studied the man's face. "Nah. I don't see it."

"He's supposed to go for an MRI soon, but his grandson insisted he sleep a little more. It was a tough morning. His blood draw went fine at first, but he knocked the vials on the ground. It was a complete biohazard scene."

"You should have called me. Hey, I can walk him down to the MRI. To give you a break."

She nodded. "Thanks. I'll take you up on that. Dr. Phillips wants all his test results this afternoon, so I can't let him sleep forever."

Armando smiled. *The perfect cover.* "I'll take him now."

Naomi woke up the old man.

The wizened guy startled; his gaze wandered around the room. "Who are you? Where am I?"

"Mr. Nome, you are in the hospital, remember? I'm Naomi. This is Armando. He's going to take you downstairs for some tests."

Nome smiled. "I had a pleasant dream about vanilla wafers. And I was talking with some birds."

"That's wonderful! Do you want to walk or take a wheelchair, Mr. Nome?" Naomi drew back the blanket.

"I like walking."

Armando stood against the wall, watching the man's slow, deliberate movements as Naomi eased him up. She helped him adjust his gown.

Armando said, "Take my arm. We'll go for a walk."

Nome squinted. "Will there be cookies?"

Armando smiled at Naomi and winked. "There might be." He directed his attention to the patient. "We can check. Hold on to me now." The man's fingers were cool and very bony. But not any different from other old people in the hospital. A magenta bruise covered the top of his hand around the needle port. And the old man's breath was awful.

A twinge of guilt pierced his conscience. The old guy was frail. Roughing him up to get a video would be truly low. But these were hard economic times. A couple minutes of torment would pay his kids' education for an entire year. On balance, he could live with that.

All during the MRI, Mr. Nome was cheerful and smiling. He even laid still during the procedure, which he hadn't expected.

On the walk back, he guided the old man on a detour to the empty part of the fifth floor, furthest from the nurses' station, and separated from the rest of the wing by double doors.

Mr. Nome waved his arm above him. "Do you see the cookie people?"

"What?" The room he had in mind was just another twenty paces.

"They are pink and smile; look above you! See? Oh, I'm so hungry. Come here, you naughty cookies! I will munch you!" He swatted the air in a scooping motion, hammering imaginary food into his mouth, saying, "Nom, nom, nom."

Armando nudged the guy into the room and shut the door behind him, turning the latch to lock it from the inside. He took off his nametag and put it in his pocket. "Mr. Nome, who are you?"

With a blank stare, the man in the hospital gown and white hospital socks replied, "I don't know. Who are you?"

Armando smirked. "No one." He took his phone from his pocket and hit record. With his free hand, he slapped the old man across his stubbled face. [Whack] *Not too hard. Just enough…*

Nome's hand flew to his jaw. "Ow! No! You are bad!"

He tried again, with more authority in his tone, "WHO ARE YOU?"

Nome's face turned red. "I want to go!" He broke for the door.

Armando grabbed him one-handedly and shoved him backward. His two-hundred-and-thirty-pound frame was no match for the old guy. Instantly, he sensed he'd used too much force, but what was done was done.

Nome stumbled and face-planted onto the hospital bed to his left, but quickly righted himself.

"Let's try this again. WHO ARE YOU?"

"I am GNOMEY! I hate you! Where is Stumpy? I want to go home!" Nome threw fists against Armando's chest, but they barely made an impact.

Armando chuckled. It was working. All he had to do now was get clear video. He kept the guy's seething face centered in the video frame.

"Where am I?! Take me to Stumpy! We are USEFUL!" The old man grabbed the empty plastic water pitcher on the tray table and threw it at the lens…*awesome stuff.* Armando let the guy rave.

"You are bad! I am useful. She still loves me! You will see!" The veins in the old guy's neck bulged, his teeth bared like a trapped animal.

Only thirty seconds of video, but it was enough. Armando put away the camera. "Sir! Mr. Nome! Relax. I'll bring you back to your room. I'll get you some ice cream. Do you like ice cream?"

His victim looked around, as if seeing the room for the first time. "The cookie people like vanilla."

"Right. Vanilla ice cream. Come with me. Back to your grandson." Armando opened the door and took Mr. Nome by the arm again, as if nothing happened.

He escorted Nome back to his room. The grandson was there, but preoccupied by his phone.

Armando put on an authoritative tone, "We just got back from his MRI." Noticing the patient's face was still red, he added, "The machine noise upset him, but he settled down after."

The young man with the preppy blue Izod shirt nodded. "Thank you. I'll help him back into bed. Do you know when Dr. Phillips will be back?"

"Naomi will know." He handed the patient over to the grandson and high-tailed it out of there.

Out in the hallway, Nurse Naomi approached. "That was fast."

"Yeah. Hey, he was asking about vanilla ice cream."

She grinned, "Oh, he was, eh? I might be able to scare some up."

He regarded the head nurse. She was a good person and, in that moment, he felt he had no right to even speak to her. "Thanks." With his head down, he strode away and found the door to the stairs, not feeling safe until the metal door had shut behind him.

At the cafeteria, he reviewed his work. The video needed some editing, but not too much. He bought a stale pre-wrapped sandwich from the prepared foods case and ate it half-heartedly while he edited and waited for the greasy lawyer.

Five minutes after their agreed upon meeting time, the lawyer showed up and sat at the table next to his. "You got it?" he asked with a whisper that sounded like a hiss.

"Yep." He passed a hand-written note on the back of his food receipt that had the online drop box address and passcode.

The lawyer took off his jacket and rolled up his shirt sleeves, his forehead beaded with perspiration. He squinted at the note. "Is that a one or the letter L?"

"Letter." Armando stared straight ahead. This was taking too long. He wasn't the nervous type, but there was something about this guy that was sorely off—and it wasn't just the dark pit stains on his dress shirt.

"Got it." The lawyer studied his screen. "Oh yes, Wonderful!"

Armando tidied up his lunch, placing his crumpled napkin and empty paper cup on his tray. "Well? I got things to do."

The lawyer shoved the brief case on the floor across the distance between their tables with his foot. After tucking his phone into his pants pocket, the sweaty twerp got up and left without another look or sound.

Armando waited a full minute before pushing back his own chair to leave. His heart raced. He'd bought drugs from a street dealer once in high school. In contrast, this transaction seemed worse. Probably because of the dozens of coworkers within the cafeteria at this hour who could have easily noticed the exchange. Including the hospital administrator, who seemed to head directly towards him.

Time to go.

He left his tray, picked up the briefcase, and headed to the closest exit.

The case felt heavy, but he couldn't be sure the money was in it without looking. He kept a deliberate pace until he exited the hospital and found a park bench two blocks away.

Armando scanned the surroundings and waited until the coast was clear before unlocking the top clasps.

Stacks of hundreds. He didn't have time to count it, but it sure looked right.

He closed the briefcase and wondered who Mr. Nome was and why someone wanted evidence of his insanity.

Racking his brain, he remembered his daughter showed him an app once that could perform a reverse photo lookup. He gave it a go and uploaded a still image of the angry patient.

There were three hits. The first was the actor Ben Kingsley. *Definitely not him.* The second was Sir Patrick Stewart. Again, not likely. The third was a man named Cudlow Loughton, a once noteworthy entrepreneur. He'd never heard of that guy.

The sun was scorching, and he needed to finish his shift. The old guy's true identity didn't matter. After his shameful behavior, he planned to lie low for the next few days. He'd avoid the fifth floor when possible.

But he certainly couldn't bring the briefcase back into the hospital and he didn't have time to go home to store it.

The fancy hotel across the street was the answer. He strolled inside, feeling out of place in his green scrubs, holding the worn-looking brown case. The bell captain greeted him. "Hello, sir, are you checking in?"

Armando wanted to laugh. Instead, he got down to brass tacks. "Can I store my case here until I check in later?"

The bell captain ushered him to a side vestibule and exchanged the case for an bright yellow cardboard stub with a pre-printed black serial number.

Armando placed the stub in his rear pocket, thinking this was the most valuable piece of paper he'd ever held.

Only three more hours to the end of his shift.

He'd stop in the Haagen Daz next door for some vanilla ice cream. He'd get a pint and have a coworker send it up to room 504.

It was only right.

Chapter 9

Locating the house based on Greta's information was easy. A tall hedge with a wood access door surrounded the backyard. No car in the driveway or along the road. The place appeared deserted.

Merv drove up and down the street a few times, just to be sure there weren't any looky-lous to witness his endeavor. His rented ten-year-old metallic lime Kia seemed out of place with the surroundings of multi-million-dollar homes with manicured lawns. But he couldn't dwell on this detail. He parked on the street, straddling the property line. The house looked like the picture; it had to be right.

In the rear-view mirror, he inspected his nose. It still throbbed, and there could be noticeable bruising in the morning. But he looked okay for now. Again, his flamboyant clothing choice might be a problem. As he contemplated a quick change of clothes, a rail-thin, middle-aged man roller-bladed down the street towards him in a very similar, brightly colored outfit, except with tight white shorts instead of black jean shorts. Merv chuckled. Maybe he would 'blend in' after all.

He grabbed the snack-size bag of cheese puffs and approached the rear gate. It was unlocked. After he entered the backyard, he closed the gate quietly, but a metallic creak rang out, seeming to echo off the stucco sided house. *Dang!*

Merv pressed his back into the hedge while he scanned the area for better cover. There was a cabana opposite the pool. A beamed portico covered a beautiful patio with teak furniture sporting crisp white cushions and a built-in outdoor kitchen that included a grill that could cook an entire pig.

The dining table was adorned with a vase of dried flowers and an artful arrangement of rectangular black iron lanterns; but he found his target. Stumpy was asleep on the wood-slatted table, sprawled out with his rear legs akimbo.

Pink and red bougainvillea flowers scented the air and the ripple of water from the pool added to the overall drowsy mood of the scene. A sumptuous hammock with inviting-looking pillows seemed to call his name, making him ache for a mid-day siesta under the shade beside his pal. Contemplating all the stress of the last few days—dodging his creditors and the punch in the face—made him wince. He would give his eyeteeth for a peaceful afternoon in this beautiful oasis. Although it occurred to him, if he didn't pay Bisbee soon, he would lose his teeth regardless.

Merv shook his head, wondering what Johnnie did to deserve this kind of luxury. *It wasn't fair.*

"Hey, Stumpy," Merv whispered, hiding behind the column supporting the roof. He pulled out a cheese puff and dropped it on the ground next to his feet, out of visual range of the home's rear-facing glass doors.

Stumpy lifted his head, blinked twice, and went back to sleep without moving a muscle.

Was Stumpy drugged? Normally, the iguana would become frenzied at the sight of a cheese puff.

The sound of a vehicle pulling up and voices startled him. Panic seized his chest. If Johnnie came home and discovered him, how would he ever explain his presence? He needed a place to hide.

Think! Think, damnit!

He heard the front door open and close, and the voices inside the house seemed to come his way. He could grab Stumpy and run for the gate if timed correctly.

Mid-way through his lunge to grab Stumpy, the glass patio door opened.

A dark-haired man in coveralls and a tool belt stared at him.

Merv put Stumpy down. "Um. Hi."

The man waved with his screwdriver. "You call in the door?"

"What?"

"The door…she's broken. Management company sent me to fix the lock. Okay by you?"

Merv took off his straw hat and wiped his tall forehead. "Yes, great, thank you. I… I mean, we'll get out of your way."

The man flicked the door's locking mechanism up and down and knelt to inspect the latch. "Sure. Ho-kay."

Merv picked up Stumpy and sauntered around to the side gate, his heart beating out of his chest. *That was a close one!*

As he passed the driveway, he read the sign on the van parked there. It read "Miami-Dade Handyman Services".

He grinned as he strolled to his economy car and clicked the key fob to unlock it.

Placing Stumpy on the passenger seat, he dumped three cheese puffs on the seat cushion for his old friend. "Stumpy, what do you say? Want to watch the ponies first?"

The iguana chomped down on the puffs with little regard for Merv's attempt at conversation.

"Right." Merv pressed the ignition and the engine shuddered. His bargain-basement rental car had obviously lived a hard life based on the whirring noise under the hood.

"I bet we can make the two o'clock race at Dade Winds Downs." He had a strong hunch about that race. With only two hundred dollars in his pocket, a winning longshot could make all the difference. He continued driving, winding through the posh neighborhood and finding the highway. Soon, brightly lit electronic billboards signaled proximity to the racetrack. He held his breath as he neared the parking entrance. Glancing at Stumpy, he asked, "What do you think? Mister Ed Harris for the win? Or should I go for place?"

Stumpy just blinked at him.

He found an empty spot near the entrance—a lucky omen—and turned off the engine. "Come on, I need your input. Blink once for place and twice for *win*."

Stumpy blinked twice.

"I knew it!" Merv yelled. "You'll be my lucky charm, you'll see." He pulled a backpack from the rear seat and placed Stumpy inside with more puffs. "Sorry, guy. But the park has a 'no pets' rule. You'll have to stay hidden."

It was five minutes until two o'clock. He paid the admission fee and dashed to an open betting counter. "A hundred and fifty on Mister Ed to win." The worn bills represented most of his remaining cash. His credit card's available balance had enough left to buy a plane ticket home, but not much else.

The cashier behind the plexiglass took this sacred currency swiftly and without care, counting it with a speed that caused a distinct slapping sound.

Seconds later, he clutched his orange receipt and headed to the viewing stand. The sun was oppressive and the plastic seats were like lava, but his excitement masked any discomfort. The familiar smell of manure, old cigars and spilled beer wafted through the steamy air; he felt the subtle stir in his loins, punctuated by an endorphin rush. His ears stiffened with alertness. He whispered to Stumpy with shallow breath, "Buddy, keep your fingers…I mean, your talons crossed."

Horses and jockeys were poised at their gates. A pistol rang out. Horses rumbled out of their gates. People in the stands jumped to their feet. His horse, number ten, held with the leaders around the first bend. With his heart beating fast against his breastbone, Merv yelled, "Go! Go, Ed! Go!" He swayed, shifting his weight from foot to foot, trying not to jump, wiggling like a toddler that has to pee but won't admit it.

"Please! Lord! Help a bro out!" he yelled to the heavens. As they came to the last straight-away, his pick and another horse, number two, ran neck and neck. Side by side, numbers two and ten galloped with identical strides, kicking up dirt as their jockeys held on. Merv took off his backpack and left it on the seat, unable to contain himself, jumping in place, screaming, "Go! Go! Please! Yes! YES!" The race was incredibly close. He crossed his fingers and held his breath, hoping for a win like his life depended on it. Because, in a way, it did.

Both horses crossed the line simultaneously among the roar of the spectators. Over the loudspeakers, the announcer belted out, "Gracious James Monroe, number two, is the winner!"

Merv threw his hat on the ground. "Fuck."

A trio of middle-aged women to his left yelled, "What?" "Is that guy blind?"

He asked the women, "Did you have money on Ed also?"

The woman in the tight silver jeans and big hair sighed. "Yes, we got an inside tip. This wasn't supposed to happen!" She shook her head, "Motherfucker!"

"Damn. I lost too."

Another woman in the group, somewhat older, snarled, "Come on, let's go to the bar."

Big hair dropped her ticket on the ground and they stomped off, still muttering obscenities.

Merv dropped his backpack, sat back in his super-heated chair and rubbed the perspiration from his face. "Stumpy, I can't believe it. I am sooo screwed."

The top zipper of the pack squeaked open a centimeter, then five centimeters, until the iguana's face poked out. [Tough break, Merv].

"Don't I know it." He didn't bother zipping up the pack to conceal Stumpy. After this loss, the horse track management could go bite his ass with their dumb rules about pets. He only had a few dollars. Not even enough to get a hotel room. *What was he going to do? Another payday loan?*

The loudspeakers squawked above him. "Correction. Correction. Video replay shows Mister Ed Harris is the winner. I repeat, number 10, Mister Ed Harris is the winner."

Merv's eyes bulged. "Stumpy! Did you hear that? WE WON! Wheee! Yes! BOO-YAH!"

Stumpy extricated himself from the backpack and wandered down the concrete riser a distance of two seat lengths. He picked up something orange with his mouth and began chewing on it.

Merv followed him, wanting to see what he found. As he bent to investigate, he couldn't believe it. It was the bet receipt from the folks that just left. Merv reached for it and rubbed the iguana saliva off. *Finder's keepers.*

"Come on, let's cash in!" He stuffed Stumpy back into the bag and slung it over his left shoulder.

As he jogged up the steps, the female trio walked towards him in the direction of their former seats.

He waved to them. "I guess we won after all!"

The older woman hi-fived him. "Yes, we need to get that blasted ticket. Did you see it?"

"Nope. Sorry. I *bet* you'll find it." He chuckled, "Get it? Because it's a bet?"

Silver pants smiled and wiggled her hips. "Aren't you cute?"

Merv shoved his hand into his front pocket, feeling a pang of guilt as he ran his index finger over both stubs. "Hey, you're pretty cute, too. Save my seat. I need to use the little boy's room. I'll be right back."

She smiled, revealing a thin line of pink lip-gloss on her teeth.

He continued past them and skedaddled inside; he race-walked to the furthest and most secluded cashier station. Tucking the two slips under the plexi-glass, he tried to look natural.

"Congratulations," said the cashier robotically as she counted out a series of hundreds, until reaching three-thousand dollars.

He kept his gaze on the floor, away from the security cameras. "Thanks." He placed the cash in the smaller front pocket of his pack and exited the racetrack. He didn't stop until he was safely inside the Kia with all the doors locked.

"Damn. Stumpy, I owe you one. You really are my good luck charm."

Stumpy wiggled in the bag.

"Sorry, dude." Merv unzipped him and gave him the rest of the cheese puffs. "We should go get a steak dinner tonight."

Stumpy blinked at him twice. [You know I don't eat steak.]

"Hmm, you know," Merv's eyes danced with thought, "there's a five o'clock race at Merryknoll Downs. What do you say? Are you thinking what I'm thinking?"

The iguana continued munching on puffs, breaking them into pieces. Orange dust spewed onto the seat and onto the floor.

"I thought so." Merv revved the weak engine and headed toward the next horse track. He could place a few epic bets with three grand and win back all the money he owed his bookie, plus keep a little extra for his trouble. And maybe he didn't need Stumpy to steal jewelry and wallets on Miami beach after all. Not with *this kind* of winning streak.

Stealing back Stumpy from Johnnie was the best decision he'd made in months.

The universe was on his side for once.

It was inconceivable that he could lose.

* * *

Cud ate his ice cream, licking the spoon. His head still pounded, but the sweetness on his tongue diverted his attention to happier thoughts. The nice young man in the blue shirt was asleep on the sofa, lightly snoring, his head drooping across the armrest.

"Do you want some ice cream, Stumpy?" he asked the furry creature on his lap.

Cud mimed a squeaky voice. "Yes, I like ice cream."

"I do too. Let's sing a song. *Where is the muffin man? The muffin man…the muffin man."*

A woman in light green scrubs, almond complexion and short brown hair walked in. "Mr. Nome, you are in a good mood. I need to check your temperature." She pulled a plastic tube from a cardboard box on the shelf behind him and affixed it to a metal probe. "Can you say 'ah'?"

He opened his mouth and stuck out his tongue. "Aaaah!"

"Great!" She held the thermometer steady until it beeped. "Hmm. A hundred point three."

As he studied the woman's face, he perceived her green aura that matched her outfit. "Nurse Green? My head hurts."

She checked his chart. "I can give you some aspirin."

The nurse left the room and came back a few seconds later with a tiny paper cup with two pills.

He swallowed the aspirin with a sip of water and the nurse left again.

Cudlow turned his attention to a cooking show on the television mounted to the ceiling. Not long after, a sports fishing show came on and he lost interest. Sleep overtook him.

He woke sometime later to an empty room. The pounding in his head was gone. Yet, an uneasy feeling came over him.

Scanning his environment, he had a vague recollection of his admittance to the hospital and the flight the day before. But he understood little else. At the moment, he felt fine and his conscience told him he shouldn't take up a hospital bed that could be useful for healing those more ill than himself.

He threw off the covers and swung his legs around, his socked feet hitting the cool linoleum floor. A stuffed alligator doll by his pillow looked adorable, and he tucked it under his sheet to keep it warm.

In the cabinet locker next to the bathroom, he found clothes and quickly got dressed. The slip-on loafers at the bottom didn't look familiar, but they fit. For good measure, he used the toilet, splashed some water on his face, and brushed his teeth with the toothbrush he found in a toiletry bag sporting his initials. He didn't remember owning such a bag.

The fog in his brain was still present, but his head felt much clearer than before. He knew one thing: he must find Johnnie or Jackson to tell them he felt better and wanted to go home. Cudlow peered into the hall. The aid station and hall were empty. No sign of any staff to discuss his situation with.

A red exit sign on the ceiling beckoned him. If he could go outside, into the sunshine, it might clear his head and he could figure out how he arrived at the hospital in the first place.

The exit sign pointed to a stairwell. He went down a flight and his legs wobbled. He gripped the handrail, hand over hand, making his way down the rest of the steps, slowly but surely.

Once on the first floor, where the stairs ended, he pushed the exit bar onto the metal door and found himself in a parking garage. The door slammed behind him. *Locked.*

Contemplating his next move, Jackson's phone number popped into his head. Clear as day. But then evaporated, like his brain was an Etch-a-Sketch and someone shook it up and down. He rubbed his skull. *Think! What the devil is wrong with me?*

He sat on the concrete curb—his scrawny bottom sore where his ischium bones met the hard surface—concentrating on any snippet of recollection that could help his predicament. A vision of Gertie singing in her garden crossed his mind. Beautiful Gertie. *A happy time.* He didn't know much, but he knew he still loved her. In a whisper, he said, "Gertrude, I'll come back to you. I must see you again. I promise." A vision of her in her white flowy gown appeared before him; her hair in soft waves. Vows of everlasting love. The small flower ring in his hand…his life beginning all over again. Before he fucked it all up.

A red sedan whipped around a corner, its engine roaring and tires screeching, echoing off the concrete surfaces. The vehicle sped past him, spewing thick black exhaust.

He gagged on the fumes and swatted at the air in front of him.

Coughing to clear his lungs, the pounding in his head resumed, like the horns and cannons of the 1812 Overture. He held his ears, trying to hold back the ache. A wave of nausea seized him and he collapsed face down on the concrete, throwing up only liquid into the gutter. A white frothy substance dribbled from his mouth.

His face felt hot and he righted himself. After some deep breaths, another vision came: the cookie people were back, dancing and giggling in the surrounding air.

A grin spread across his face. "I see you! You naughty cookies!" He swatted the air. "Yes, I'll follow you. Come back. No! Don't go!"

He got to his feet and chased the largest cookie face down the garage ramp until he met the sidewalk outside.

The sun's rays blinded him and he lost his target. A disembodied voice ordered, "Go that way," meaning to his left. Cud obeyed. After walking several blocks, the beach appeared. The ocean looked so inviting, like an old friend.

A seagull landed on the metal fence post next to the beach entrance. Its eyes fixated on his and it spoke to him. "Cudlow, do you want to fly with me?"

"Yes, Gully. Teach me to fly!"

The bird took off and fluttered further down the sidewalk. He gave chase. As he neared the bird, it continued on and landed again. His chase continued several minutes until he was out of breath and his feet hurt. He leaned against a wall.

A different seagull swooped in and pecked at the ground a few feet away. "Cudlow, we need to get some snacks first!"

He nodded. "Yes, snacks are always fun."

As if on cue, a commercial delivery truck—advertising ice cream on its side—drove by.

He chased the truck. "Stop! I want vanilla! And Gully too!"

For blocks he chased the truck, catching up to it when it stopped briefly for a red light and losing sight of it between traffic stops. His feet ached.

After unsuccessfully chasing the truck, he had no concept of how much time had passed since he left the hospital. His legs felt weak and he needed to rest somewhere. Cudlow took stock of his new surroundings.

An underpass in front of him, where the chain-link fence had a gaping hole, had a linear community littered with several tents and tarps; men of different shapes and ages, with scruffy beards and wild hair, all stared in his direction.

He called to them, "Did you see the cookie people?" He walked toward them, hoping they could help. If they were nice people, they could share the cookies. And maybe they had something for his thirst. "Do you have any milk?"

A skinny man, wearing a shirt made of plastic shopping bags, with a dark tan and yellow teeth, sat next to a pile of rocks and a rusted fifty-five-gallon drum. He responded, "Nah, man. What you want? I got some powdered milk, you dig?"

Cudlow nodded and ambled towards his new friend.

A woman, pushing a dented shopping cart, rushed up. "Mister, are you okay?"

"Do YOU see the cookie people?"

The woman, with shoulder-length reddish-gray hair and a black baseball cap, shook her head. "Mister, you gonna get yourself kilt, you hear?"

He squinted at the woman. Her aura was white, just like his friend Johnnie's. *A rare one.* "Who are you?"

"Look, my name is Rosalie. Come with me, okay?"

The skinny guy, still sitting on the dirt a few feet away, yelled, "He's mine. You GOT THAT? Sheeeet." He picked up a fist-sized rock from ground and hurled it in their direction.

Rosalie grabbed Cud, "Duck!"

The rock sailed past them.

She shouted, "Terry, you throw ONE MORE ROCK, and I'll beat you with your own goddamned femur!" She whispered to Cudlow, "Come. We need to get away from here."

He didn't like rocks. His new female friend seemed nice, just like Gully. He scanned the sky, seeking his feathered friend. "Are we going to learn to fly?"

"No! You don't want Terry's shit." She pulled his arm. "Come on. I have a Snickers bar. Follow me and I'll give it to you."

Cudlow blinked a few times, unsure of what to do. "Okay." The arthritic pain in his left shoulder intensified and he looked above. Dark storm clouds moved swiftly, coming in-land from the water.

"Here, you hold on to my cart, got it? Stay with me." She put her arm around his shoulder and hustled him away from the underpass.

Cud smiled. "You are nice."

They rolled along the bumpy sidewalk, next to a busy street, and turned into a rear parking lot. The smell of food was pungent. Like fried fish. Not at all like fresh cookies.

Rosalie said, "We're almost home."

He nodded. "I'm sleepy now."

A few drops of rain fell and a powerful gust of wind created a tunnel-effect along the back of the strip mall. Bits of litter and paper swirled around them. A plastic garbage can fell over and came at them like a projectile; Rosalie threw her arms around him, shielding him from the impact. She grabbed his arm, lengthening her stride. He tried to keep up.

Drops of rain came down like a burst water balloon. He shivered from the cold; the rain soaked his shirt.

Above the deluge's roar, Rosalie shouted, "Just a few more steps. See over there?" She pointed to a small single-axle camper with a rounded metal exterior next to a wood fence. Flowering vines creeping over the fence had nearly covered the entire camper. "You'll be safe inside. And you can sleep as long as you'd like."

Chapter 10

Rosalie knew right away that she'd found an interesting case. The old man was clearly not local. Sure, he was insane, but there was a sweetness about him and he wore new-looking shoes. Which meant he probably hadn't been living on the streets for very long.

The rain blew sideways just as she pulled on the door of her mini-camper parked illegally on the vacant lot. The oval-roofed aluminum trailer was only nine-feet long, but it was secure from the weather and other foes.

"Get in."

The white-haired man with the deep tan stepped up into the camper and she climbed in after, locking the door and inserting an iron rod mounted on the floor at a 45-degree angle. The rain on the aluminum roof was deafening, as if they were standing inside a kettledrum.

She guided her guest to sit on the small bench over the wheel-well, the bench she'd fashioned from a discarded wood pallet a year ago.

He looked around. "What is this?"

"This is my home. Can I see your bracelet?" She kneeled and placed her hand on his wrist, turning the pink plastic band to read the writing. "Harold?"

"Who's Harold?"

"You. Harold Nome. Princewood Hospital."

He just blinked at her.

She had to try a different approach. Maintaining eye contact, she asked in a measured tone, "Why were you in the hospital? Are you sick?" She took a blue towel from under her bed and began rubbing Harold's hair and face to dry him off.

"I don't know. My head hurts."

She dried his arms next. "Do you have any family nearby?"

"I don't know."

Rosie tossed the damp towel over a hook; her eyes darted in thought. *What to do?* She reached into her tiny kitchen cupboard, only a foot in width, mounted from the ceiling, and handed him her prized Snickers bar. The one she'd been saving for her birthday two days from now. "Here, enjoy."

Harold pulled on the wrapper, but couldn't open it. He brought it to his mouth, as if he would eat through the plastic; she grabbed it from his hands. "Please, let me." She unwrapped it and handed it back.

"Yum time!" he smiled as he licked the end of the bar and began gnawing on it.

"Harold, I need to get you back to the hospital."

He continued to chew, but without fully closing his mouth properly. "That was a bad place. He hit me."

"Who hit you?"

With a mumble, "Bad man. No hair. I am useful." He finished the candy bar, wiped his chocolate-covered fingers on his shirt, and let out a long yawn, exposing surprisingly straight teeth. "Can I take a nap?" He pointed to her twin mattress with the white sheet and eyelet pillow case. His lids drooped and he swayed like he could pass out.

"Yes, sleep. I need to run some errands. Don't leave. If you need to pee, use the bucket." She pointed to the orange contractor five-gallon pail opposite the door, which she only used for nighttime emergencies. But this current situation was certainly an emergency. Harold didn't belong on the streets with his clean fingernails and designer shoes. Someone would come looking for him.

The boys under the bridge would have done terrible things to the old man. Rosalie didn't even want to imagine what could have happened.

Normally, she wouldn't get personally involved in a homeless case like this and bring a stranger into her sanctuary, no less allow someone to sleep on her clean bedding. But this one called for drastic action.

Harold crawled up onto the bed and curled into a ball on his side. Somehow, his breathing changed, as if a light switch was thrown, and he seemed to be asleep.

She waited a few seconds, then whispered, "Harold? Harry?"

No response.

Rosie exited the trailer, locked it with her key while getting soaked again, then ran across the alley for the shelter of a nearby awning of the convenience store's rear door. Huddling from the rain, which fell vertically now, she dialed her friend Sondra using her flip phone.

Sondra answered, "Hey you."

Rosie smiled. Sondra had finally broken the habit of using her name on calls.

"Hey, I got a new one. I need a favor. He doesn't belong out here. He has a wrist band from Princewood. Can you pick him up and drive him back?"

"I'm busy right now delivering meals. Can it wait until six?"

"I guess."

"You know, you could just call the police."

"Ha. You know I can't."

"Why not?"

"They'd ask questions."

"It's been five years. They aren't looking for you anymore. You are a dead woman, remember? With the scarring from the explosion, they won't recognize you."

She ran her finger over the numb skin on her right cheek, where the burns had left scar tissue. "I can't risk it."

"Fine. Put him in an Uber."

"I don't have any money or a credit card."

"Look, if he escaped from the hospital, order a cab and I'm sure they would pay the driver."

"I don't know." She rocked back and forth on the heels of her wet yellow canvas sneakers.

"Or just call the hospital, anonymously."

"What if they record the call?"

"Rosie, you can't be paranoid your entire dead life."

"Yes, I can. Remember, I hit a guard during the prison riot."

"You said that was an accident."

"It was. But I'd get another ten years. Maybe more."

"Then wait until I'm free later. Okay?"

"Fine." She ended the call.

The rear door to the convenience store flew open. A young man with a hispanic complexion, holding a clear trash bag, appeared startled.

"Sorry." Rosie held the door for him. "I was...never mind."

He shot her a suspicious sneer that said, "You don't belong here." He put his free hand out in the rain and muttered, "Motherfucker."

Rosie smiled. "I'll toss your trash for you." She pointed to the green dumpster across the alley; the alley that was now turned a river.

He shook his head, dropped the trash bag, and went back inside. The clank of the lock snapping into place reminded her of her unwelcome social status.

She lifted the bag to inspect the contents. *Jackpot!* Clearly, most of the bag was full of expired bread, but a pocket of pink frosted doughnuts looked promising. Plus, some coffee grounds. A feast for tomorrow's breakfast.

Her watch, with Wile E. Coyote on the dial, showed it was close to two o'clock. Babysitting a sleeping crazy man seemed unproductive compared to other things she could be doing. With this rainstorm, the five homeless ladies on Fourth Street could really use those tarps she'd collected last week.

Rosie dashed through the rain back to her camper. Harold's snores radiated through the small space, but she found his intermittent gurgles and snorts endearing.

Silent as a mouse, she left the bag of discarded food near the door and locked the door again. Under her trailer, she grabbed her stash of neatly folded green construction tarps and placed them in her shopping cart.

Rain streamed down the brim of her baseball cap and soaked her hair, causing it to resemble wet string, but a little poor weather never discouraged her from an opportunity to ease suffering for the indigent.

Her plan was simple. Deliver the tarps and be back within two hours...tops.

Mr. Nome would be safe as a bug in a rug until her return.

* * *

Johnnie ate his sandwich in small bites, dragging out his meal, letting Darla talk about her wedding plans and other superficial things, happy to not have to make further conversation. Because he could see they had little in common to talk about. Eventually, Darla stopped to sip her soda and Johnnie seized the lull in her speech to say he should be going.

"Oh, of course. I've been babbling. Well, it was great to see you. You seem better." She waved in the air to the server to ask for the check.

"Yeah. Same. I feel better. Like… hopeful." He paused to evaluate. *Yes, that seemed a correct term. Was it because of Greta?* With his luck, he assumed this state of bliss was a mirage and some kind of disaster had to be waiting around the corner.

"That's wonderful. See? Maybe things work out for the best after all." She grinned and grabbed the check the instant the server slipped it on the table between them.

"No, let me."

She shook her head. "Tell you what, you get it next time."

They both knew there wouldn't be a next time, but he admitted defeat. "Thanks. I'll walk you back to your car."

A short time later, they entered the parking lot to the construction company office. Darla's blue Hyundai was the only car left. "Still got old…hmm, what was it again? Blue Bunny?"

She giggled. "Ha, I haven't heard that name in a long time. Why did we ever start calling her that?"

Now it was his time to laugh. "You expect *me* to remember?"

"No, I guess not."

Her eyes widened and her mouth gaped. "Oh, you won't believe this. I know you'll think I'm nuts, but I swear I think I saw your mom last month."

"What? No way." Instantly, he knew she was mistaken or crazy, because his mom died in a prison riot. The explosion in the sewer—where some women had tried to escape—was supposedly caused by a lighter and a natural gas leak. It took weeks to sort out the bodies, many not recognizable. But some dental work confirmed her passing.

"I know there is no way it could have been Rose, but this lady was a dead ringer. Pushing a beat-up shopping cart near the freeway."

"Huh. That's weird." He stared at the ground. At the time of mom's death, he'd been in the hospital, still trying to re-learn how to form words. He'd only found out months later from Robin what had happened. And he didn't remember why mom was in prison to begin with. It took several explanations for him to comprehend the story.

"Maybe I shouldn't have mentioned it." Darla hit a button on her key-fob and the rear lights flashed.

"No, it's fine. I haven't really thought about her in years. Sometimes I have memories of her from when I was little, but they are flashes, like dreams; then they disappear the next instant. I know I should miss her more, despite the rotten thing she did. But I can't miss someone I don't remember much."

Darla nodded. "I understand."

"Embezzlement is stupid. I'm not saying she didn't deserve prison, especially stealing from a homeless charity for God's sake, but she didn't deserve to die, burned alive in a fire. No one deserves that."

She pursed her lips and tsked. "In my religion, everyone gets a second chance. In her next life, I'm sure she'll do better."

He squinted at Darla, trying to detect if she was serious. "What?"

Darla opened her car door and grabbed a pamphlet off the seat. "What do you know about Scientology?" She handed him a booklet titled, "Many Lives to Reach Your Clear Self."

He scoffed, snorting disbelief through his nostrils. "You're kidding again, right? Okay, you got me." He leafed through the book. It had pictures of families wearing forced smiles, like a children's book. He handed it back.

"No, you should come with me to a meeting tonight. It's brought me so much peace. It would help you with your anger." She placed her hand on his shoulder; her eyes searched his as if yearning for connection.

He turned away. "I don't think…"

"Look, I get it. I was skeptical at first. But is such a great community. Everyone really cares about each other. Truly uplifting. It will change your life."

He took a couple of steps back. "You really *aren't* kidding…wow."

Her face seemed red. "Johnnie, I'm not bitter anymore. I learned to accept you and your choices." She scowled. "You *need* to accept mine."

Scratching his head, he blinked. "You know it's just a total scam, right? Come on. You can't be that dumb. I mean, I'm missing a few centimeters of brain matter and even *I* wouldn't fall for that crap."

Darla tossed the brochure back in her car and put her hands on her hips. "Johnnie, you were always a raging asshole! Even before Afghanistan. Always judgmental…acting like your shit doesn't stink. A macho dick-head, putting folks down. Maybe you don't remember. But that doesn't change the truth. You were a fucking lousy husband and a lousy human being. Go fuck yourself." She walked around to the driver's side of her car and sat behind the wheel. The slam of the door coincided with the start of the engine. Through the glass, Johnnie saw her slam both fists on the steering wheel.

"Yeah, well...." He couldn't think of a comeback.

She drove away, spraying loose sand from her rear tires.

He took a deep breath, processing this new information.

Had he always been an asshole? He honestly didn't know. Which shook him to his core and made his stomach churn. Because this meant that he was *never* good at relationships and this didn't bode well for his new romance with Greta.

Was he doomed to fuck it up? To drive her away? To be cruel?

"FUUCCCKK!" he shouted to the sky above.

When he stopped screaming, he stared at the dark clouds racing in from the ocean. The wind gusted, followed by chubby drops of freezing rain that pelted his head and forearms.

He should have run for cover.

But what did it matter if he got soaked when his whole life had been a shitty series of lies to himself?

No, maybe the rain was a small, but deserved punishment for his crimes against Darla. He hoped it would wipe some of the stink off his pathetic existence.

Along the street, a city bus came to a halt at a bus stop and let off two short men.

He contemplated walking in front of the next bus or tractor trailer that came along...*to just end his worthless life.*

But then he thought about Cud. There was still a chance he could help his friend.

He walked over to the bus shelter, now empty, and looked up mass transit options to get to the hospital.

It was the least messy choice. At least for now.

Chapter 11

Elson soaked the tiny bones in a solution with lye. With a tweezer, he picked out a slender rib, now white and smooth, with no trace of flesh, and held it under his illuminated magnifying glass. Although nearly perfect, the skull on the table to his right revealed a chipped front tooth, which could diminish the value of the piece. But he knew some tricks of the trade to repair it with epoxy filler.

He named his new furry friend Preston and thought himself brilliant, as the car, weighing tons, had pressed the squirrel beneath its tires. When he tried to explain his joke to his wife, Henrietta, she put on her usual cross face, sucking away all his joy.

Elson picked up the skull and ran his finger over the tooth. "Preston, you will be good as new. Better even."

Heavy footsteps rhythmically battered the wooden treads of the basement stairs. He steeled his nerves and eardrums to brace for impact.

"Well?" Hen's sneering tone—like a high-pitched weasel with a deviated septum—broke his reverie. "Are you coming up for supper? I made lamb and potatoes."

"No. I'm busy." He didn't look up, but felt her presence looming over him, knowing she likely stood there in her flowered pajamas and bunny slippers, with her brown bowl-cut hair and ruddy cheeks, arms crossed.

"You spend more time with those disgusting rodents than you do with me."

A valid point. He wanted to say he thought *she* was a disgusting rodent, but didn't want another one of her crying fits. "Sorry, just put a plate in the fridge for me…thanks, honeypot."

"I don't know why I bother." She stormed back up the stairs, so loudly he worried the brittle wood treads would break. Her hand turned the knob at the top, but instead of departing, she called out, "Honestly, first you destroy our lives because you can't keep your yap shut. Now you spend every waking hour playing with bloody mangy vermin. We could have gone to the Society Ball last month. Lived without a single care! You bleeding wanker!" She exited and slammed the door shut.

The Annual Royal Society Ball. They had attended twelve years ago. Him in a white tie and tails. Hen—forty-pounds slimmer—in a low-cut silver sequin dress that made all the men's heads turn. How they had been the envy of all. At the height of prestige, mixing with the upper echelon of British society. Drinking brandy and discussing the stock market with titans. Where the bankers called him affectionately by his first name, all vying to gain his favor with offers of a golf outings at an exclusive Scottish course, or a paid two-week safari in Africa. Literally having the world in the palm of his hand.

All of this power was once again within his grasp. Loughton Enterprises would soon be his.

A smile crept along his face and he closed his eyes, envisioning the estate he would buy with his new wealth. Of course, he'd bulldoze Cudlow's estate on Grand Bahama into the ground first, leaving no trace of the home his beloved mother had found so much unhappiness in.

The video his lawyer sent a few minutes ago was pure legal gold. At the rate Greaves was proceeding, he had his own happiness to think of. If he received the company right away, he may never be rid of Henrietta. *What good was money if he was tied to her forever?*

Sure, divorce was an option. But she would get half, and that would *not* do.

Panic coursed through his body. *No, if he were to cut her loose, he needed to do it now.* He'd have to pick a fight with her...give her no choice but to leave. Or he could kill her now and make it appear like an accident. Surely, the second option was the swiftest.

He went up the stairs and located Hen in the kitchen. She appeared preoccupied ladling potatoes into a Tupperware container.

"Dear heart, don't be cross. You don't have to tell me again how I bollocked up our lives. Besides, who needs fancy parties and titles when we have each other?" He crossed to her and rubbed her shoulders from behind.

"What's wrong with you? Why are you talking so oddly? Are the chemicals going to your head again?" She pulled away and aimed the end of the wooden spoon in his face, as if she would strike him.

"No, it's just that our situation has brought us closer, don't you think? Living in this small flat. Remember how it used to be? You with your garden club lunches and me jetting about to financial conferences? We never spent time together then. I like our new life. I've grown content, like a baby bird in a nest. How about you?"

She shook her head and squinted at him. "Ha! I would leave you if I could afford a barrister! I'd be better off with that skeevy toothless grocery bagger who keeps giving me the once over." She whacked him sharply in the chest with the spoon.

"Dearest, you don't mean that. Can I draw you a nice bath? Maybe a back rub? You look tired."

She turned back to face the kitchen counter and affixed the Tupperware lid, pressing it with her palms until it clicked. "I think you must have a fever."

"Honeybun, I've got to finish this little project with Preston tonight, but would you like to take a walk tomorrow? Along the canal like we used to? My lecture will be over by noon. We can go straight away and then pop into that gelato place you like." In his mind, he wondered if the canal was truly deep enough to submerge a body. *Perhaps he'd need some weights?* He could easily hide the syringe in his fanny pack.

"You know I've got bunions. Honestly, I think you've gone daft!"

He took her shoulders and turned her around, cupping her chin. "Let me make it up to you. We could be close again. You'll see." He kissed her cheek.

She recoiled and scowled. "You wanker. You destroyed our family. Gelato doesn't change that. Our precious boy won't speak to me because of you." She hissed, "There's no bleeding way to make it right."

Elson's eyes widened. Here was his opportunity. Maybe he didn't need to push her into the river and kill her. "If you feel that way, then perhaps it would be best if we separated. Amicably. Of course, I would agree to half my salary as alimony. Not that it is much to live on. I suppose I could make ends meet living with roommates. That chap in the English department has an advert for a spare room. I know I've made things impossible for you. I just want you to be happy, Hen."

"See? This is my point. You don't fight for me. You give up too easy in life. Instead of challenging your dismissal those years ago, you could have fought! Gotten a better severance package. Ha! You claim to be a financial genius, but you couldn't negotiate a ten quid raise if your life depended on it." She took a seat at the dinette table, a heaping plate in front of her. Shoveling lamb into her face, she mumbled, "My sister was right about you. Always said you were too passive. A real puss."

Gleefully, his inner monologue whispered, *yes, hate me!* Outwardly, he hung his head and softly said, "You don't have to be cruel."

With a wave of her hand, keeping her face downward, she announced, "Fine. Leave tonight. I don't want to see you—or your sorry maggot-ridden rodents—one more second. I want those blasted dead things out of my home. Don't you leave one bleeding corpse behind."

"As you wish. I'll leave straight away, but know this. If I go, I plan to pursue a divorce post-haste. I hope, for both our sakes, that we can part as friends. For Jackson's sake."

Hen clasped her hands to her face, covering her eyes. Her shoulders shuddered, and she sobbed. "I knew it."

"Knew what?"

"You may be a wanker, but I see through your little scheme."

"Scheme?" He leaned against the wall, terrified that she knew about the new legal proceedings to assume control of Loughton Enterprises.

Her crying stopped. Her earlier bitter tone resumed. "Joan at the supermarket told me, but I didn't believe it. Said you were having an affair with a student. What? Did you get dumped? Is this why you wanted to reconcile? Or are you shacking up with that tart?"

"Tart? No! What? I am certainly not having an affair. God damn it. I spend all my waking hours at university or in the damn basement on my hobby. Ha! And what young thing would want the likes of me? Honestly, do you even hear yourself?"

"What about your long walks? How you disappear in the middle of the night when you say you can't sleep?"

Elson couldn't take it anymore. Playing nice wasn't getting him anywhere. The gloves were coming off. "I go for *walks*. You should try it. Ha! Bunions my arse. God knows you could use the exercise, ya lazy, flabby hag."

Henrietta flung her half-eaten pork chop at his face. She rose to her feet.

"Oh, you are a fine one, aren't ya! Well, I don't care what you do or who you are with. Just GET OUT! Fuck off!"

He wiped the grease from his forehead and grinned. "Great. Have a wonderful life." He strode to their bedroom and packed a suitcase, throwing clothes in without care. After stuffing his laptop into his briefcase, plus his charging cords, he stormed to the front door. There was no sight or sound of Hen.

Elson opened the door with a flourish, hoping the sound would irk her. The sun was setting and the building across the street created long, cool shadows. He should have taken his car, or hailed a taxi or summoned an Uber, but he walked, dragging his rolling bag over the uneven sidewalk. Not sure where he was going, he just walked, as if he had a purpose, when in fact he had none.

Instinctively, he headed toward the university, three miles west. His home away from home. The wheels of his bag snagged at every crack in the sidewalk, the sound echoing off the torey old townhouses—with their Victorian brickwork and pristine landscaping—lining the street. He walked and walked, muttering to himself phrases like, "I'll show you," and "Just you wait." As he neared the campus, with its stone-arched sidewalk entrance, the sweat along his back grew cold. The courtyards were alive with students scattered on the grass or walking in intimate groups. He hoped they wouldn't notice him.

At last, he reached his office. He usually shared the space with another professor, but at the late hour, he had the room to himself.

Sitting in his high-back rolling chair, he stared at the leather-bound books on the shelves that seemed to mock him. Because now he was both homeless and nearly destitute.

Not for long, he told the brown tomes. *You'll see.*

He put up his feet on the desk and leaned back, arms crossed above his head. *Soon,* he thought, *everything will fall into place and his former friends would come crawling back, like slimy earthworms.*

The articulated bat skeleton hanging in the corner of his room spoke to him in a mocking tone, his hollow eye sockets staring at him. "Elson, don't you know WE are your real friends? You don't need those bleeding windbags."

He shook his head. Maybe the chemicals had gotten to his brain. "You aren't real."

"Oh, I am real. Just like Preston, who you left dismembered in dozens of pieces on your workbench. You must go back and finish him. It's only right."

In the shadows of his dark office, Elson thought he saw the bat's wings point east, towards home.

"No! I'm never going back. NEVER!"

He stared at the bat skeleton, which now appeared to be as lifeless and inanimate as it ever was.

Perhaps he was cracking up. Losing his marbles.

But there was a single truth. He was never going back. Not to the flat. Not back to Hen.

His new life was just beginning. And he didn't need his little vermin friends any more.

* * *

Jackson sat on a bench outside the hospital, pressing his phone against his ear, straining to hear.

"Felicity, say that again?"

"A VIDEO. Your father's lawyer filed a motion in the Bahamas."

"No. He wouldn't do that."

"I'm sorry. But he did. I'm sending you a copy of the affidavit. The footage is shocking. Is Mr. Loughton really that far gone?"

"Yes. I mean, no. Oh, I don't know. He's been under such strain. Perhaps he's simply malnourished. Or something equally temporary. But father has no right. Bastard!"

"Unfortunately, your father has every right. He's asking for medical proxy and on the last page he petitions the judge for full control of Cudlow's shares in Loughton Enterprises."

"Which means he would have a controlling stake."

"Precisely."

"What can I do to stop this?"

"The hearing is scheduled for tomorrow morning in Nassau. You need to tell your side of things."

"But…I can't leave him."

"You have to. If you don't want your father in full control of his medical treatment."

Jackson sighed. "What if…what if this is just a misunderstanding? I'll call father right away and sort this out. Let me call you back."

"I hope you are right."

"Me too. Bye."

Jackson tugged at his shirt to break the cling of sweat. He knew his father was prone to small-minded, petty grievances, but would he really put Pawpaw away forever? Just for money? He knew the answer, deep down.

With the time difference, it was ten o'clock at night in London. But he called anyway.

On the third ring, he heard, "Hello, son."

"Dad, what in blazes are you doing?"

"What do you mean?"

"Don't play stupid. If it's money you want, take my blasted shares of the company and leave Pawpaw alone."

In a calm tone, Elson said, "It's for his own good. He's gone stark raving, he has. He needs medical attention. For the sake of the Loughton legacy, he needs someone to take the burden of the company off his shoulders."

"Ha! You only care about your own legacy."

"You know, when he leveraged the company last month, it made headlines in all the financial magazines. He nearly put the whole thing in the toilet. Think of the employees. And what about you? After all your hard work, you can't leave decisions to that looney."

"Father, the company is in good shape. You should have seen him last month, working around the clock. He made deals in thirty days that you couldn't make in thirty years. He's just suffering from exhaustion. Please, if you ever loved me, stop this nonsense!"

"I'm sorry, son. I really can't do that."

"You mean you won't do it. Why do you want to hurt him so badly?"

Jackson waited for his father's reply, but only heard silence. "Are you still there?"

"He's not the hero you think he is. Look, he fucking owes me. And I'm rightfully going to take what is mine."

Jackson had heard enough. "Just as I thought. Fine. See you in court."

"Looking forward t—."

He ended the call before his father could spew more venom. With a deep breath, he shook off his frustration and called his newest employee, Mo.

Mo answered on the second ring. "Hey, boss man! How is Miami? Did you go salsa dancing at that place I recommended?"

"No, Mo, I need you to listen. Cudlow is in real trouble and I need your help."

"Sure, anything. What can I do?"

"I need the company jet to pick me up. I must fly back to Nassau, straight away. Get my blue suit pressed and ready. Work with Felicity on getting all the latest financials together. We need an expert in warding off financial takeovers…"

"Got it. What else?"

"Mo, do you think Pawpaw will be safe if I leave Miami? What I mean is, I know Dr. Phillips and the hospital will do right by him, but what about Johnnie? Will he take good care of Paw while I'm gone?"

"I've only known John a short time, but he really cares about your grandpa. It's only one day. Johnnie will do a great job."

"I hope you are right. I know he loves Paw, but he's not the most reliable person."

"Well, it seems you don't have much choice. Hey, isn't his girlfriend, Greta, with him?"

"Yes. Right. She seems a bright woman. Yes, I think Paw will be in good hands with her around."

"See, problem solved. Let me work on your flight. Don't worry. Everything will be fine."

"Mo, you don't know my father. This is deplorable, even for him."

"The judge will see the truth. Just speak from your heart."

"Thank you, Mo. See you soon."

Jackson ended the call and rubbed his hands over his face. Something his father said bothered him. *What did he mean by "he's not the hero you think he is"?* He knew their falling out had something to do with Grandmaw Winnifred's death. But he was only eighteen at the time and the grownups had shut him out of the shouting matches. He had heard snippets of their fights, but he assumed it was just grief and nonsense anger. Poor Pawpaw was so upset at her death that he left the company and disappeared to St. John.

Why did his father feel the need to keep kicking Pawpaw after all these years? What could Cudlow have done that was so terrible to make father hate him so much?

Whatever the reason, Jackson had to stop this madness.

The company didn't matter. He had truly meant it when he offered his own shares up.

But he couldn't let Cudlow's life fall into the hands of his greedy, rotten father.

Not now.

Not ever.

Chapter 12

After exiting the air-conditioned convention center, Greta basked in the warm sunshine breaking through the clouds. She tied her long hair in a ponytail with a scrunchy she'd worn around her wrist.

Her canvas satchel, silkscreened with the phrase, 'Libraries = Love', was heavy, laden with bookmarks, brochures, pens and other swag. The long fabric handles dug into her shoulder; her sore feet added to her overall state of weariness. Yet, it was a fantastic day, and she met so many interesting people.

Her best purchases of the day were a bobble-head figure of Jane Austen—a gift to herself—and a signed paperback edition of The Martian as a surprise present for Johnnie.

Forgoing the keynote speech and reception, she decided to head home early, take a nap, and hopefully convince Johnnie to go with her and her new friends to an awesome neon-themed drag show later tonight.

She texted Johnnie while she waited for a taxi.

"I'm heading back to the house. See you soon."

Excitement bubbled and she bopped her head sideways to a silent beat as she scrolled through social media sites. Twenty minutes later, her taxi pulled up to the house.

After paying the driver, she lugged her bag up the driveway. The house was eerily quiet, with the shades drawn. Johnnie hadn't texted her back, and she wondered if he was napping.

She entered the key code at the door and entered like a mouse, taking off her sandals and leaving her bag on the floor in the hall. She padded to the kitchen first and got a glass of water from the tap. The view out the back windows showed no sign of Johnnie, Jackson, or Stumpy.

Maybe the bedroom? She checked.

Did he take Stumpy for a walk? Is that a thing...walking your iguana? Admittedly, Johnnie had done stranger things.

She consulted her phone. Still no response. Greta typed again, "Where are you?" But before she hit send, she shook her head, resolving not to be the kind of girlfriend who was always checking up on her man. She deleted the words and settled into the bed—still unmade from the morning—to read. As she placed an extra pillow under her head, she felt something odd.

A bar of Irish Spring soap? Why would Johnnie put that there? It smelled awful. Maybe it fell out of his bag when he was unpacking yesterday and it landed there? Nothing else made sense.

Alone in the house, she considered taking a nap but felt too spun up. Instead, she looked for the television remote. She had seen it last night. She checked the top of both nightstands, on the floor, and even under the bed.

"Hmmm…" she wiggled her nose in contemplation. *Would it be okay to check inside Johnnie's bedside drawer? A quick peek wouldn't be an invasion of privacy, right?*

Easing the drawer open, she didn't find the remote, but Johnnie's soft-bound journal was where he had stowed it. The journal he had felt so protective about.

Should she?

No. She shut the drawer and returned to the center of the bed, resting her head and staring at the unmoving ceiling fan.

Did he write short stories in there? Notes from his pirate adventure a couple of weeks prior? Or did it contain more personal thoughts?

Curiosity inflamed her mind. Johnnie didn't like to talk about his accident in Afghanistan or his recovery. Was this journal a record of his feelings to help with PTSD? Perhaps if she had insights into his inner workings, she could help him. Or at least not tread on painful subjects. Yes, reading his journal could be a real benefit to their relationship. Convinced this altruistic goal would make it all right, she rolled over and opened the drawer, lifting the precious book. Before opening the cover, she froze like a statue to listen for stray noises; but hearing none, the coast was clear.

The first page was dated January 5th, three years prior. The handwriting was loose, with letters of different sizes shifting outside the ruled lines. Plus, some squiggles in the margins.

Dear Diary, Dr. Lou says this will help. But writing won't put my brain back together or bring back Darla. I'm done with physical therapy, but I still want to hit things. And people. Gertie says I need a girlfriend. I just laughed.

I saw the Goddess today out in the bay. Perfect and dazzling. That made me happy for a few minutes. But my good mood never lasts. Mostly, I want to drown myself every day. What do you have to say about that, dumb diary? Yeah, nothing. Just like I thought.

You stink, Diary.

Love, Johnnie

Greta closed the journal. *He wanted to kill himself EVERY day?* Surely, he didn't feel that way now...did he? Now she simply had to know what was in there. *And what was the Goddess? Some kind of boat?* Questions circled her head.

She left the journal on the bed and bounded out of the room, hastily racing to the front door to lock it and she latched the back door for good measure. It would take time to read or skim through the entire diary. And she didn't want to be caught in the act.

Back in the bedroom, she secured the interior lock, then checked her phone.

Johnnie had texted back two minutes ago:

"I'm going to check on Cud at the hospital. See you at dinner time."

She exhaled. Johnnie wouldn't be back for a couple of hours.

Skipping to a page near the end, there was a passage about how he had run into the Goddess at the grocery store and how she smelled like Irish Spring soap.

The hairs on Greta's neck stood on end.

Flipping a few pages, she scanned the new page and noticed her name. Yet she couldn't believe the words in front of her and they stopped her cold.

"Is it fair to be with Greta if I'm still in love with the Goddess?"

Fucking asshole! Who the hell was this goddess chick?

Her face felt hot, and she blinked in disbelief. No wonder he wanted to hide the journal. *What other terrible things was he hiding?*

Thankfully, speed-reading was her superpower. For good or for bad, she would get to the bottom of this and find out who the real Johnnie Crosswell was.

Because in the words of Ralph Waldo Emerson, "truth is handsomer than the affection of love."

* * *

Johnnie finished his text to Greta as his bus pulled up in front of the hospital. He immediately noticed Jackson, who was sitting on a bench under some palm trees, obviously in some distress because he was slowly but steadily pounding his forehead.

He walked up and sat next to Jackson. "Hey, are you okay? Any word on Cud's prognosis?"

"Thank God you are back. No. It's…bollocks. My wanker of a father." Jackson continued, staring at the ground between his knees. "It's a long story. I need to be in court tomorrow in Nassau. If father gets his wishes, Paw will be sent away forever. Probably to some dank, miserable mental ward in London."

A mental image of Cud in restraints in a dark room flashed through Johnnie's thoughts. "What? Why?"

"Father hates grandfather. They had a vicious falling out right before Paw left for St. John. After that, Paw took away father's stake in the company. My old man still holds a grudge. He is asking the court to grant him medical power of attorney and full control of Loughton Enterprises. I tried talking to him just now, but he won't listen to reason."

Johnnie shook his head. "No! He can't do that!"

"I know you don't want to hear this, but *he can*." Jackson raised his head and met Johnnie's eyes. In a soft but serious voice, he said, "While I'm away, I need to know I can rely on you. That Pawpaw can rely on you. Do you understand?"

The gravity of the situation sank in. Johnnie recalled the times he'd been intubated him after surgery. How the inability to speak and restraints on his arms made him feel a level of despair and anxiety no one should ever live through. How he had wished to die instead. Now, imagining Cud locked up, his throat tightened and his emotions spiraled into turmoil, causing his ears to feel on fire. "Sure, whatever you need."

"I'm trusting his care to you while I'm gone. Stay with him…ensure he gets all he needs. I'll be away twenty-four hours at most. Can you do this? I can't…I won't leave unless I know you are up to this."

"Yes, don't worry. Greta and I will make sure he is safe and sound."

Jackson nodded, as one does when they are convincing themselves of new information. "Thank you. By the way, I've been meaning to say…Greta is really top-notch. You outdid yourself finding her."

Johnnie scoffed, "I'm still pinching myself. I just hope I don't screw it up."

Jackson steered his attention toward his phone. "I need to head to the executive airport." He stood and clapped Johnnie on the shoulder. "I suppose you have *the Con*, chap."

"I promise, I won't let you down."

Jackson nodded and walked toward the taxi that had just pulled up.

After the taxi pulled away, Johnnie was relieved he chose not to turn himself into a road pizza earlier, because maybe, just maybe, he could do some good in the world by taking care of Cud.

It was close to three o'clock now. Dr. Phillips said she hoped to have lab results back by five. Maybe there was some kind of quick medical intervention, like a pill, or antibiotics, that would snap Cud out of his mania. It was a long-shot, but he needed to believe Cud would be back to his old self.

The idea of Cud sitting alone in a padded room sent a shiver down his spine.

No one deserved to live like that.

Especially Cud, a free spirit who loved nature to his core.

Before entering the hospital, he looked up at the building and made a vow to himself.

Nobody would put Cud in a cage on his watch.

* * *

Johnnie entered the hospital and headed to the front reception desk to get a new daily visitor pass. Somehow, his earlier one had gone missing, which didn't faze him, since he lost items often and the morning had been unsettling and strange because of his visit with Darla. Any hiccup in his routine usually resulted in lost items. It was just a fact of his current existence.

At the counter, he smiled at the receptionist, a tiny Asian woman with black cropped hair with blunt bangs and a gold sea-turtle charm necklace. "I need a pass to visit my friend Cudlow Loughton."

She typed into the terminal, "How do you spell the last name?"

"L-O…wait…is there a U?" He scratched the scar above his left ear.

"What was the first name again?

"Cud…" He realized his mistake. *The alias!* He wanted to pound his stupid skull for making such a bone-headed mistake, but took a step back, wondering what to do next.

She peered up from her screen. "Cudlow…the billionaire? Huh. I thought he died years ago." Her eyes squinted at him questioningly, but her tone showed a hint of excitement.

"Oh, no. Sorry. My mistake. I get confused when I get dehydrated. Whew, sure is hot outside today, isn't it? I thought the rain earlier would cool things off." He flashed a gummy smile, but realized it probably didn't help his case. He rubbed the sweat on the back of his neck for good measure.

"So, he isn't alive?"

"Um. No, I don't…I must have overheard someone talking about him. Could you look up Mr. Nome?" *Why couldn't he remember the room number? Something with a five?* "Fifth floor?"

"Spelling?"

Why was everything a spelling contest today? "G-N-O…wait…no G. Like the town in Alaska. Yes, that's right."

She looked up from her screen and arched a brow. "Sir, are you on the visitor list? Do you have ID?" She gave a small wave toward a bald-headed man in green scrubs, who looked more like a night club bouncer than a hospital employee. The tattoo on the man's forearm of a motorcycle included thorny roses and a skeleton rider. Not a wholesome looking fellow.

Johnnie handed over his St. John driver's license as he felt the orderly's eyes drill into the side of his head.

"Hey," the man said, "I recognize him. He came in this morning with the new patient, Mr. Nome. He checks out."

The receptionist chuckled. "You mean Mr. Loughton. Cudlow Loughton. Golly, I haven't heard that name in ages." She examined Johnnie's license. "Mr. Crosswell here seemed a little confused. He thought his friend was a dead billionaire."

The orderly stroked his chin. "Huh, you don't say?"

Johnnie couldn't take it anymore. His hands coiled into fists and he exploded. Dripping with sarcasm and fury, he yelled, "Yeah, ha, ha! Listen, you don't fucking know me. For fuck's sake, I had my brains blown out five years ago by the fucking Taliban!" He kicked the front of the desk. "But sure, let's all make fun of a brain-injured veteran! And ask him to SPELL every...fucking...WORD!" He wanted to spit, but didn't. "Fuck!"

The orderly grabbed his arm. His arm had unknowingly had been waving threateningly at the receptionist.

"Dude, calm down! Don't make me throw you out."

The sudden tug on his right arm sent a shock up to his shoulder, the one he dislocated the day prior. "Ow! Stop. I'm fine." He took several deep breaths, counting to himself, shutting his eyes to relax. All the techniques Dr. Lou had taught him.

The orderly released his arm, but guided him to the center of the lobby. "Sir, calm down. First, let me say thank you for your service. Are you okay? Can I get you some water? Do you want to sit?"

Johnnie recognized the de-escalation techniques the man was using and instantly felt like a schmuck. *Why couldn't he be normal? Would he 'go off' like this on Greta one day? Make her cry?* It all felt like too much.

"No. I'm sorry. I've just had some bad news. I'll be okay. I didn't mean to lose my cool." He looked over at the receptionist, now several feet away. He called out, "Sorry, Ma'am!"

She called back, "No problem, sir! Come get your license and your pass when you are ready."

The orderly looked him in the eye. "Hey, I'm heading up to the fifth floor myself. I'll go with you." He crossed over to the receptionist and picked up the pass and license. "Here ya go."

Johnnie felt uneasy around this guy, but to say no would only bring more awkwardness. "Um, sure." He took a turn to the right.

"Mr. Crosswell? The elevators are to the left."

"Right. I mean, sure. Thanks."

Once inside the elevator, they stood side by side, not making eye contact. The upward progression of the elevator seemed to take forever; Johnnie debated whether to make small talk, but after the whole kerfuffle, he worried about saying something even more disturbing. After a stop at the third floor, he took a chance and discussed the weather. "That was an intense storm."

"Looks like you got caught in it."

"I didn't have an umbrella."

The orderly kept his eyes front toward the door. "That sucks."

Another painful silence passed, lasting for ten seconds, but seemed more like ten minutes.

Johnnie let out a small exhale of relief when the doors finally opened at level five.

A nurse jogged up to the orderly.

"Thank goodness! I was about to call you. Have you seen Mr. Nome?"

"No. I took him to get his MRI earlier. Maybe two hours ago."

"He's missing. I gave him some aspirin an hour ago. I checked on him afterward and he was sleeping. He must have eloped. God, not another code 'green'."

Johnnie shook his head. "What? Cud is gone? Fuck, I mean... Harold?" *Why couldn't he get the name straight and remember one fucking thing today?*

The orderly grumbled, "Send out the alert. I'll coordinate with the exit monitors and security." He pulled out his phone and began scrolling.

Johnnie strode past both of them to Cud's room. It was empty except for the stuffed alligator, tucked under the sheet with just its head visible. He opened the locker to find Cud's clothes and shoes were missing. *A fucking disaster!*

He jogged back to the nurse, who was on the phone at the station. No sign of the orderly. "Does Dr. Phillips know?"

She pressed her hand over the phone receiver. "No. I wanted to be sure first. I called the X-ray and MRI labs, no sign of him. And I checked the restrooms and all the empty rooms on the entire floor. Don't worry, he probably hasn't gone far."

"Are you kidding? He's confused and frail. He might be OUT THERE! ALONE! What if he collapsed in the road or got hit by a car? Fuck you! FUCK ALL OF YOU!" His anger was back, and he needed to smash something or someone this time. He sent his fist into the sheetrock wall behind him, leaving a small dent. "AAAAGG. Fuck!" Pain radiated through the bones in his hand, and he wondered if he broke something.

The bald-headed orderly strode down the hallway, arms gorilla style. Without warning, he grabbed Johnnie and put him in a head lock. "STOP! I warned you!"

The guy's arms were like steel. He wiggled to get free, but the man's vise grip was unwavering. "Fuck, I'm sorry. Let go, ya fathead."

The large man let him go, but poked him square in the chest. "Get out of here. Now!" He pulled Johnnie's nametag off and crumpled it in his hammy fist. "I don't want to see you back here again, UNDERSTAND?"

Johnnie straightened his T-shirt, still moist from the rainstorm, and rearranged his glasses. "Yes, sir." He stepped onto the elevator and pushed the button for the first floor.

The orderly glared at him until the doors closed.

He promised Jackson he'd watch out for Cud. *How would he ever explain this to him?*

And where could Cud have gone to?

This was all his fault. It was his bird-brained idea to come to Miami. It was dumb to think he could help anyone with his half-baked plans.

And now he was banned from the hospital.

Once outside, he sat on the same bench as earlier and called Greta. On the seventh ring, he heard a quiet, "Hello."

"Hey, it's me."

"Hey."

Her tone was odd. As a normally upbeat and chatty person, he never heard her voice so distant and quiet.

"Did I wake you?"

"No. I've been reading."

"Cud's missing."

"Missing what?"

"The hospital staff can't find him."

"Hold on. Like, he left the hospital?"

"Seems that way. His clothes were gone. I need to find him."

"Okay."

"Do you want to meet me here? We could look together."

"Um…no. I don't think so."

This wasn't the answer he was expecting. "Oh." The silence on the other end was thick. "Are you okay? You seem different."

"I'm packing. I'm going to stay at the hotel tonight."

"What? Why?"

"I don't want to talk about it. Shouldn't you go find Cud?"

"Yes, right. Um, I may be out for a few hours. Could you feed Stumpy before you leave? There are some grapes in the fridge. You know how he loves grapes."

"I haven't seen him. I thought maybe he was with you."

"Wait, Stumpy is missing too?"

"I guess so."

"Huh." None of this made sense. *Was there some kind of cosmic black hole that was sucking up old men and iguanas?* Or had Stumpy simply wandered under the fence into the neighbor's yard?

"I've got to go. You should look for Cud."

She was right. Nothing mattered now except for finding Cud. "Yes, of course. I'm on it. Um…can I call you later?"

Greta hung up without a word.

What was going on? Had he fucked up his romance with Greta already? But how? Everything was fine this morning.

Air left his lungs as he contemplated losing Cud, Greta and Stumpy all in the space of an afternoon. *Why was the universe persecuting him? Was it some evil hex brought on by Darla and the realm of Scientologists?* If so, it was some powerful shit.

Maybe his sister Robin would know what he should do. He stared at her contact icon on his phone and instantly ran through all the things she would say. Like 'I told you so', and 'Butt-head'… or worse, she would offer to fix his mess, as she did all his other messes. And he refused to let that happen. Especially after the fight they had two weeks ago. She hadn't talked to him since, and even though she was probably right—as always—he wasn't prepared to apologize.

He needed a plan. A simple plan. To find Cud, he needed to cover lots of ground. Which meant he needed transportation.

Where would he begin to look?

Cud liked sweets and ice cream. Plus dancing. And swimming in the ocean naked. But lately, being so weak, he was sleeping more than usual.

Johnnie consulted a map on his phone to check for nearby parks in the chance Cud was simply napping contentedly under a shady tree. As his mind raced, dark thoughts took root, imagining his friend collapsed in an alley or drowned in the ocean.

A large woman on a pink Vespa sped by on the street; she wore combat-style boots and a spiked black helmet with a zombie face decal on the front. As she passed, he noticed a tiny dog peering out of her clear bubble backpack. The dog's eyes were wide with fear, somehow pleading for help, but that isn't what caught his attention.

A scooter! It would be the *perfect* way to get around Miami.

Using his phone's browser, he quickly located a rental shop four blocks away. With a quick call, he learned they had only one scooter available: a baby blue Vespa. It wouldn't be his trusty, yet recently demised, red Piaggio, but it would have to do.

Chapter 13

The first thing Cud noticed was the curved metal ceiling, followed by the tin-foil lining the windows. It was as if he were sleeping on soft cloud inside an old toaster. He sat up and rubbed his eyes, trying to recall how he had gotten there.

A photograph on the tiny kitchen countertop showed a smiling woman with red hair, likely in her thirties, standing on a beach with her arms around a pre-teen girl and boy.

He recalled a woman helping him earlier, but older looking than the picture, with discolored skin on her face that appeared to have been melted at some point in the past. *This must be her place.*

Unsure of his larger surroundings, he opened the door and looked around. A long alley behind some retail buildings, dotted with green dumpsters and piles of bulky trash. He recalled the earlier rain storm. But no rain currently.

He needed to call someone. *Anyone.* Back inside the trailer, he wondered if he should leave a thank you note. Not that he knew exactly *what* to thank the red-haired woman for, but he must have been in quite an awful state for her to share her home and let him nap there. He found a pencil in a drawer and wrote on a napkin, "Thank you, miss. I'm going to find my family. All the best."

But how to sign it? What was his name?

Out loud, he stumbled along as his name came into focus, "I am Cudlow…Eldrid…Loughton!"

Somehow, just recalling his own name gave a feeling of elation, as if he could do anything; feeling that whatever had set him back in the last few days was over. As he continued concentrating, he came up with only two phone numbers, Jackson's and Gertie's.

He jotted down Gertie's number on a separate napkin, afraid the information would leave him again. As he stared at the area code, doubts lingered. *Was it '304' or '340'? Or did it begin with a four?* He wasn't sure. But he longed to hear her voice.

After exiting the camper, Cud walked down the alley to a main road and dodged a few puddles. On a bench outside a barber shop, a woman with white hair, wearing a sparkly jacket, a cane leaning on her knee, was playing some kind of game on her phone.

"Pardon me, miss," Cud clasped his hands together in a pleading manner. "I don't have my phone with me and I need to call a friend. Would you be willing to let me borrow yours?"

The woman looked up. "What, are you British or sumthin? What you doing in Miami? And how do I know you won't run off with it?"

"Madam, I assure you. If I had anything for you to keep as collateral, I would offer it to you. But I'm lost and don't even have a wallet. But I understand. Do you know if there is a pay phone close by?"

"Ha! A pay phone! Ha, ha. Old timer, I thought I was out of touch with technology. Here. Sit down and take a load off." She patted the space next to her on stone bench. "I'll let you call your friend. Just let me finish this level…I love this Candy Crush!"

He sat. "Thank you. Actually, she's my girlfriend. Although we had a bit of a falling out."

"Oooh, love on the rocks. I hear that. At our age, it can be worse than middle school. My last man-friend wanted to see other people. Ha! Like he was 'all that'. I'm ready to tell *all* men to fuck off, excuse my French. Too much drama and you know I ain't gonna chase anyone with these bad legs."

"I'm sorry to hear that."

"Well, *someone* should be happy, even if it *ain't* me. You call your woman. Tell her you're sorry. But only if you mean it." She handed him the phone. It had a sparkly case covered in rhinestone hearts.

"Yes, thank you…"

"Monique."

"Monique, I'm…" *Should he tell her his real name?* "Just call me Cud."

"What, like the stuff cows chew on? Or like the Kudzu vine? How d'you get a name like that? I hope your momma didn't name you that."

"Yes, it's an odd name." He wasn't sure how much to explain to her. "I'm going to call my girlfriend now."

"Look, I'll just scoot over a little and you go pretend I'm not here while you sweet talk your lady."

He smiled, "Thank you, Monique."

He dialed the number he'd written on the napkin.

On the second ring, he heard Gertie's silken voice. "Hello?"

"Gertie, it's me."

"Oh, thank goodness! Are you okay? Are you in Miami? How are you feeling? I was so worried."

"I'm sorry. I haven't been myself. But I feel fine now. I just wanted to hear your voice."

"Are you with Johnnie?"

"No, I…I don't know where I am. A lovely woman let me borrow her phone." He glanced over at his new friend, and she nodded along, obviously listening to every word.

"Aren't you supposed to be in the hospital?"

"I don't know."

"What about Jackson? Does he know where you are?"

The throbbing in his head began again. Like a slow drum beat. Shutting his eyes tight, he needed to get out his words before his brain shut down again. "I don't know what is happening. But I want to say I'm sorry for any pain I've caused you. I can't remember much of the last few days. All I know is that I love you, Freddy."

"You can't keep calling me that. Don't you see? You're confused. Where are you? Give me a street name. Something."

His thoughts turned blank. The pounding in his skull made his eyes ache and his muscles weak. Cud handed the phone back to Monique.

"I'm sorry, miss. I need to go."

"You don't look so good. Your face is green."

"Is there a pharmacy nearby?"

"Yes, go to the end of this block, turn right, and then two more blocks. You can't miss it."

"Thank you." He stood up, holding the top of his head with one hand and steadying himself with his other.

As he headed down the block, he kept one palm against the rough brick wall, trying not to faint. His steps grew closer together, slowing to a shuffle.

Gazing at the sky, now getting darker, he chided himself for not calling Jackson instead. If he could only get some aspirin, perhaps he would feel better.

He straggled along, taking rests every few feet, taking deep breaths, hoping the pain would stop. The pharmacy sign came into view.

The automatic door opened and a blast of air conditioning hit him, causing a shiver and gooseflesh on his arms. He asked the man at the register, "Aspirin?"

The man pointed, "Head back and then over one row."

Cud nodded and kept going. The music playing over the speakers was some soft rock, but it may have been a quartet of tubas for all he knew, because the sound amplified the pressure in his head.

He found some generic aspirin. A plastic anti-tampering ring protected the lid, thwarting his attempt to open it. Instead, he gnawed on it with his front teeth to work it free. Accomplishing his goal, he poured a few pills out into his palm and tossed them in his mouth, chewing and swallowing with gusto. He closed the lid and carried the bottle out the front door. With this task finished, his next step was to find a payphone and call Jackson.

After walking a block, a black crow flew across his path and commanded him, [You should follow me].

"No! You can't talk! Stop it!" He dropped the pill bottle and held his ears. "You are just a dumb bird."

The bird cocked his head. [Freddy doesn't love you. Only I love you.]

Cud stared at the black-feathered God, now perched above a shop window. "Why? Why? I don't understand what is going on!"

The crow cawed, [You need to leave now].

"What?"

Red and blue flashing lights reflected off the buildings in the near darkness; he turned toward the source. A squad car arrived down the street in front of the pharmacy. The pharmacy shopkeeper pointed his way. A police officer yelled "Stop!" and jogged toward him.

Instead of running, he put his arms high in the air. "Yes, yes, I'm stopping! I need you to call my grandson!"

But as the officer approached, a pink haze filled the air; when his eyes came back into focus, the man's face was now a large cookie.

As the officer grabbed and wrenched his wrists, Cud ignored the pain and whispered, "You look delicious. What flavor are you? Chocolate chip?

Let me lick you!"

Shoved forward, he chided the cookie, "Don't be a naughty cookie! I know your kind! Let go of me! LET GO! We are USEFUL!"

Out of the corner of his eye—as the officer pushed him into the backseat of the vehicle—he noticed a flash of red hair near a shop window across the street.

After that, the rest was just a haze of delirium.

* * *

Stumpy's eyes felt like dry sand, and the stale air in the backpack was not good. Plus, all the yelling and crowds made him long for the quietude of his palm tree. He had to get out. He slid his head sideways to peer out the tiny opening in the canvas.

[Can we go home now? Yum time?]

His tall foreheaded friend wasn't paying attention.

A zipper would not stand in his way. He'd fought worse enemies like Green Tail and been victorious, as any Iguana King would. He clawed at the metal, [slash] [slash] [zzz] inching the zipper downward until he was free. The plastic seat next to Merv was empty, and he scrambled up. He nudged his friend's arm with his snout. [Yum?] [Leave now?]

The man shook his head and then pointed wildly at the muddy field and running horses; his friend jumped, shouted, his hat tumbled off his head, he bent to pick it up. His eyes glued forward in a kind of trance.

Stumpy slitted his eyes. It wasn't fitting for the Iguana King to be ignored.

He ambled back down to the concrete floor and snuck down the row, beneath the seats and under strangers' legs, to check out his environment. Surely, there were some treats or some cool vegetation to be found.

A mound of discarded, white crunchy popcorn presented itself. He slid out his forked tongue to touch it, but it delivered no cheesy goodness. Only the taste of paper and sand. Plus, the odor of human urine was strong in this place.

He continued his quest. Avoiding human feet, keeping to the dark spaces. A glint of metal gave excitement and hope. In a crevice of the concrete, he detected an item of potential value to his friend. He chomped at it, but found no purchase. He scraped at it with his claw, working it loose, bringing it to the surface. It wasn't a bottle cap; those were no good for trade. No, this item was smooth, yellow and heavy. Like other successful treasures. Possibly something worthy of a cheese puff...or maybe four.

Stumpy gripped it in his mouth and made the journey back through the maze of concrete and feet, following his own scent and that of his friend. Once back on the seat next to the creased-face man, he poked the metal item into his friend's hairy tan arm. [Good? Yum?]

A vocalization of pleasure emanated from his partner. Plus, a loving finger stroke along his dorsal crests.

The man did not produce food, but scooped him up and placed him back in the sack.

But this time, Stumpy knew his confinement was temporary.

Something big was going to happen.

Something good.

And his belly would be full again.

* * *

~Fifteen minutes earlier ~

The sun reappeared after the rain, with a rainbow shimmered in the distance behind the adjacent office building and parking garages. Rosalie turned the outside door handle of the camper quietly, in case Harold was still sleeping. She didn't yet have a plan on how to get him back to the hospital without revealing her identity or without folks asking nosey questions. But he was safe now, and that was all she could manage at the moment.

The camper was empty. Her bedding was folded neatly. The note on the counter was lucid.

Perhaps the old man just needed a nap to clear his head?

Problem solved.

Still, he had been so far gone. It made little sense.

But she had other things to worry about. Like collecting recyclables under cover of evening darkness so she could redeem them for cash, allowing the purchase of a replacement canister of propane for her camp stove.

Rosie grabbed an empty trash bag from her cupboard and headed out again toward the beach. Lots of aluminum cans there. Tomorrow was pickup day, but she would beat them to the booty. As she rounded the corner, red flashing lights startled her and she ducked into a vacant shop's recessed doorway. Just a few feet away, Harold shouted, insisting on licking the cop's face. Which meant he wasn't remotely okay after all.

Surely the officer would see Harold's hospital wristband and return him safely.

She crept closer, staying in the shadows, just to make sure.

Unfortunately, she discovered no sign of his pink wristband.

Maybe she just needed to walk up and politely tell the police to take him back to the hospital. Again, she dreaded all the ensuing questions. Questions were a killer.

Her mental gymnastics continued. The officer put Harold in the back of the vehicle.

The policeman radioed dispatch; something about bringing the old man to the station. After he shut Harold into the back of the car, the officer walked back to discuss something with a civilian; jotting down notes.

If they put Harold in a cell, the other inmates would do worse things than Terry. She understood prison life. Like the time Big Nancy made her rub the soles of her sweaty wart-ridden feet. No, she resolved, she had to do *something*.

With a dash and duck-walk around the police car, she lifted the door release.

"Harold," she whispered, "Come with me. Now."

"Hey, I remember you."

"Great. Come on."

"We are going to the cookie factory. The man said so."

"No, Harold."

The cop's head swiveled in her direction and she crouched lower. "Just follow me," she hissed. "Please."

"My head hurts."

"I'll take you to the doctor, I promise." In her soul, she made the same promise. She would take whatever risks to ensure he returned to the hospital.

"Okay," Harold slid across the bench seat, his hands in zip-tie cuffs in front of him. "I don't like these." He looked at his wrists.

She pulled her trusty multi-tool from her shorts pocket. "Pay attention. When I count to three, we're going to run, like in a race, to that corner. Do what I say, all right?" She flipped open the knife and sliced through his plastic cuffs.

He nodded, and she helped him out of the car, holding onto his right arm.

"Hey! You!" the cop yelled.

Oh, shit! "Run, Harold! Go!"

"Yes, I enjoy running! Weee!" He took off toward the corner, as she had instructed.

But instead of running with him, Rosie knew she needed to distract the officer if Harold were to have any chance of escape. She slammed the back door, walked around the vehicle and shouted, "Leave the poor guy alone!" For good measure, she spat at the ground in his direction.

The officer pulled a zip tie from his belt. "Miss, I'm arresting you for interfering."

"Officer, Harold is mentally ill. He belongs at Princewood Hospital."

He grabbed her wrist, but she kept her eyes locked on his in defiance.

"And you know this *how*?"

She struggled to break free, but his grip was too strong. She explained, "He had a medical bracelet earlier. Just call the hospital. Surely they've alerted the authorities that he's gone missing."

Harold stood fifty feet away at the corner. "Miss, can I lick his face now?"

She yelled, "Stop asking that!" To the cop, she said, "Do you get the picture now?"

The officer, with nametag Chadwick, released her arm. "Fine. I'll call them. First, I'm going to get him. Don't move or I *will* arrest you, understand?"

She exhaled, "Yes, sir, I understand."

With bated breath, she froze in place as the officer crossed the distance to the old man. In the shadows, she could see their outlines from the dim light of the business neon signs. A moment later, she heard the officer's cries and a skirmish.

"Hold still...stop! Ow! Motherf..."

The cop swung his baton in the air.

Harold whimpered and fell to the sidewalk. He didn't get up.

Rosalie ignored the cop's warning, now seeing red. She ran up.

"What the hell did you do?"

Officer Chadwick radioed for backup, giving the street names of the intersection. He clicked off the receiver. "I told you to stay. He fucking bit my nose. I'm fucking bleeding. He'll be fine. Now stand back or you'll be next.

Harold rolled on the ground, shifting to his side.

Rosie shouted, "You could have killed him!"

The officer leaned over Harold. "Stay down." He kicked the old man in the back and lifted his baton.

Panic coursed through Rosie. Without thinking, she grabbed the officer's taser from his waist belt and hit him in the side, the clicking of electricity mixed with the officer's cry of agony. But she didn't let up. Pressing the charge into his back, he crumpled to the ground inches from Harold, writhing; he curled into a ball.

Rosie threw the taser down the sidewalk, several feet away. She leaned over the cop, "Pick on someone your own size, asshole."

Now they really needed to get out of Dodge.

She reached down to take Harold's arm. "Can you walk? We need to go."

As they shuffled at the old man's pace, he said, "I'm sorry. I'm not useful."

If they could just around the next corner, there could be a way out. They just had to keep moving.

"Harry, let's just get through this night."

The blare of sirens seemed to come from all directions. But she knew the one place the cops would never look.

And it was just below their feet.

Chapter 14

Johnnie gripped the handles of the rented blue vespa, driving around the blocks closest to the hospital at first, then widening his search with each pass, looking for signs of Cud. The sun had set, but the humidity was still thick, like warm pea soup.

A park, roughly two blocks long, came into view. But what caught his attention was an older man with familiar looking white hair sleeping on a wood-slat bench. Johnnie parked and went to investigate. Drawing near, the man was clearly not Cud, and in fact, was an old woman.

Unfortunately, the woman must have sensed him hovering. She startled and yelled, "Rapist! Asshole! Get away from me!" She reached under the bench and retrieved a thick branch; she used it like a club against his midsection, despite his attempt to back away. She kept on him, hitting and spitting. "Pervert!"

His knee felt the brunt of her attack and he tried to ward off the weapon and stop the assault. "Lady! I was just looking for my friend."

She hocked a loogie that hit his cheek and then grabbed the crotch of her loose dress. "You want to feel my flabby coochie, you nasty piece of shit?"

All he could do was run. Run with a sore knee and his dislocated shoulder. Every foot plant shot pain through his joints, but he couldn't stop. Hobbling at the fastest pace he could muster, a beer bottle flew past him and shattered on the sidewalk, sounding like an evil door chime. A second bottle hit him between his shoulder blades, which stung and almost brought him down. A few steps ahead, he thought, if he just kept going, he'd reach the scooter. His only escape.

The street light he'd parked under was at full glow as he jumped on the seat and fiddled with the ignition key.

After a few sputters, the scooter came to life. Gunning it, he entered traffic, cutting off a red sports car, causing the driver to swerve and almost hit the curb.

The driver honked and screamed, "Dickhead!"

Johnnie couldn't resist giving a middle finger to the driver as he turned at the next light.

After a couple of blocks, the adrenaline that had inflamed his face and neck eased, allowing him to concentrate on his breathing. Still, he couldn't think straight while driving in circles.

Instinctively, he drove east toward the beach for a time-out. If he was being honest with himself, he had no ideas of where to look next.

He parked at the beach and stomped through the loose sand; his flip-flops flinging sand every which way. The waves crashed with a fury, mimicking his roiling self-loathing.

Who could he call? Certainly not Jackson. And Robin wasn't talking to him. Dottie always had good ideas, but would blab about his failure to everyone. Greta was acting weird. Surely, if he could just see her, maybe Greta would explain what was bothering her.

The hotel hosting the conference wasn't far. He sat on the sand, a foot from the water line. The breeze off the ocean felt welcome, literally cooling his heels. In the night sky, the green glow of city lights muted the stars; yet their presence made him feel even more insignificant.

He texted Greta. "Can I see you?" Refusing to exhale, he waited breathlessly for her response.

She responded:

"I'm busy."

There were no emojis. And Greta loved emoji; she often threw in random ones just to confuse him as a silly inside joke. But right now, not even a smiley face or a heart or a wink.

He texted back, "It won't take long," adding a smiley face which looked odd given the context, but he didn't know the emoji to convey his mix of fear, love and confusion.

"Don't bother."

His heart froze. Her answer rang like a death knell through his soul;

devastating all his hopes for happiness. Exhaling sharply through his nose, the only reply he could think of was, "Why?"

Three dots fluttered on his screen, showed she was typing... and he waited. A few seconds later, the dots ceased. Then they oscillated again. But after a minute, she sent no reply.

He texted, "Please tell me what I did. Whatever it is, I'm sorry."

No response. He waited another five minutes. The ocean waves rolled in closer and he scrambled back another five feet to avoid getting soaked.

In the night sky above, the blink of an airplane seemed to mock him. This could have been a beautiful romantic night in a vibrant city, the waves drumming like music, a cool breeze through his hair. He and Greta should be walking on the beach, hand in hand, bare feet, exchanging sweet kisses. He envisioned her chatting about her conference; him tickling her when she wasn't looking.

But no. Instead, he was alone.

Alone with his mistakes, feeling like human garbage for losing Cud and Stumpy and being punished by Greta for some mysterious reason.

It wasn't right, and it wasn't fair.

Why did the universe hate him? Where was his turn at happiness?

He dusted himself off and stomped back through the sand toward his scooter, determined to find Greta and get the answer he deserved.

A few minutes later, he parked on the street next to the hotel, his scooter diagonal next to a fire hydrant. Parking rules were the least of his concern. Johnnie stalked across the lobby, following signs for the conference hall.

The lobby was teeming with librarians, chatting in a collective roar, all wearing similar lanyards with nametags, holding book bags, some balancing small plates of food. A sign in the corner by the staircase pointed to the evening reception.

Greta had mentioned wanting to attend the reception, so he headed that way. At the double doors to a large hall, he spotted her red hair easily. She was in a conversation with a short brunette in the buffet line.

It was *his turn* to be angry. He cut through the crowd and disregarded the line of people waiting. He tapped her on the shoulder. "Greta, why are you treating me like this?" As he heard these words come out, he knew they were aggressive, but he would not keep apologizing. Not until he received a straight answer.

Her eyes widened and she inadvertently dropped pasta from her plate onto the carpeted floor. "What are you doing here?"

"I need to know if you are breaking up with me. Just tell me."

All conversation within a ten-foot radius around them quieted. Strangers' eyes burned on him like death rays and he realized he had shouted that last part. In a whisper, he said, "So?"

The brunette with dark eye makeup next to Greta stepped between them. "You should leave."

"I'll leave when I get an answer." The adult part of his brain knew this wouldn't end well. The reptilian part didn't care, seething with anguish and rage.

Greta's steel-gray eyes locked on his. "You're making a scene. Come with me."

He followed her, his eyes watery, not really able to see where they were headed. He kept his gaze either on the floor or on the back of her head as they wove through the crowd; they left the main hall and headed to a remote hallway by the rest rooms.

Now face to face, she crossed her arms and curled in her shoulders, becoming smaller before his eyes. "I know about the Goddess."

This was not the answer he expected. He wiped his eyes. "What are you talking about?"

Her body was rigid, and she shook her head. "I know *everything*. I read your diary."

His diary? His mind blanked. He barely recalled what he wrote in it most of the time. But it likely contained some of his fascination with the tall, sleek, and elusive blonde. "Wait. No. Greta...I love *you*."

"Stop lying. God, I'm such an idiot."

"No, I really do." He tried to take her hand, but she wasn't having it.

The hurt in her eyes were unmistakable. Whatever he had written about the Goddess had to be extraordinarily bad.

"Mildred Johansen, right? Your dream woman? You fucking write about her every three pages. Just leave me alone. Go be with her."

He rubbed his temples, trying to think of how to make amends. "No. Geez. She doesn't even know I exist."

Greta's open-mouthed expression instantly alerted him to his mistake. *The absolute worst thing he could have said.*

She scowled, "Right, so I'm *what*? A consolation prize? I found your stupid bar of soap. Fuck you, Johnnie Crosswell."

Greta pushed past him and he knew better than to chase her. Through the lobby, she headed to an elevator and stepped inside. The steel doors closed with a finality that made him want to vomit.

Bringing the Irish Spring soap was next-level dumb, when, in fact, he hadn't fantasized about the statuesque blonde in all the days he'd been with Greta.

This made him wonder: *If the Goddess gave him the time of day, would he ditch Greta?* He didn't think so. But he wasn't exactly sure; just like no one is sure what they would do if they won the lottery or what *exactly* they would say if they met Bruce Springsteen at a dive bar. Still, his uncertainty meant that Greta was probably right and deserved better.

It was clear he had done the thing he most feared. He'd hurt Greta.

Johnnie knew his *real fantasy* didn't involve the Goddess. It was believing he could have a normal relationship with his shitty brain and inability to say and do the right things.

His phone rang. It was Doctor Phillips. He sent it to voice mail.

It was now nine at night and Cud had been missing for several hours now.

The good doctor texted, asking him to call her right away.

He needed to do *one fucking thing* right for a change. But it didn't involve calling back his therapist. Finding Cud was all that mattered.

Another text came in from Jackson:

> "What in blazes did I tell you? Where is he? I will end you if anything happens to Pawpaw."

In a flash of thought, Johnnie considered finding the nearest tall building and jumping head first from the roof.

But he was no quitter. If it took all night, he'd find Cud.

Because that is what best friends do.

Chapter 15

Merv caressed the stack of hundreds with his thumb as he reclined behind the wheel of the aging Kia—the air conditioner blowing at full blast and spewing small bits of ice. Finally, his luck had turned. Stumpy had called the winner in the last three races at Merryknoll Downs, including a twenty-to-one longshot that paid him ten large. Now he had more than enough to pay back Bisbee. More than enough to keep his veneers intact.

He'd received ten voice mails from his bookie over the last eight hours, each with a threat of violence more ominous than the last. In the last message, Bisbee growled, "You'd *better* send a picture now to your momma so she can remember your face, 'cause I'm gonna rip out your pretty brown eyes and shove 'em up your…"

Merv could take a hint. He took a snapshot of the cash and sent it on, promising to wire the money in the morning, with a little extra for his trouble.

Bisbee texted back. "We'll see, muthafucka."

With the crisis averted, Merv could focus on other basic needs. His stomach rumbled. What he really craved now was rest and relaxation, with good food and cold drinks in the company of some hot Latina women.

An electronic billboard flashed an advertisement for Garcia's Rib Shanty & Beach Bar, with five-dollar margaritas on Sundays.

And today was Sunday.

A sign literally from above.

"Stumpy, you like margaritas? They're vegan, right?"

The iguana was asleep, perhaps exhausted from the day's excitement.

Merv considered returning his green partner back to Johnnie's mansion.

Now that he was flush with cash, he no longer needed his good luck charm to steal from beachgoers. Still, he thought it would be selfish to leave Stumpy out of the night's festivities.

"You enjoy the company of hot babes, right, Stumpy?"

The iguana slitted his eyes towards him, then turned around to bury his face in the crease of the passenger seat.

"I knew it!"

Merv pulled away from race track parking lot and drove three miles up the road to Garcia's. The parking lot was nearly full, with dozens of young men and women milling about, waiting in a line about fifty-people long.

He parked, retrieved Stumpy, placed the iguana on his shoulder, then donned his fedora, tilting it rakishly to the side. "It's show time," he whispered as he strutted to the entrance, ignoring the waiting patrons.

A guy with a clipboard glanced up at him and pointed half-heartedly to the end of the line.

Merv continued his forward progress and greeted him. "I'm the entertainment. Magic Merv and Stumpy the Psychic Iguana."

The man with the clipboard, wearing an oversized Hawaiian shirt with a beard separated into four skinny braids, looked up. "What? We don't have no magician. Sometimes we have bands or guitarists. Get lost."

"I'm here to change that. Who's the manager?"

"That would be Jayne Garcia. Do you have an appointment?"

"No. But I was in the neighborhood and I'm not gonna stay. Just let me chat with Ms. Garcia for five minutes." He spread his fingers to amplify his word. "Scout's honor." Merv smiled broadly with his eyes, feigning innocence. "I mean, who could resist this handsome guy?" He placed his hand on Stumpy's back and stroked his side.

"Yeah, he's pretty cool. Can I pet him?"

"Sure, man."

Clipboard guy ran his index finger over Stumpy's head. "I always wanted a reptile as a pet. I once knew a guy that had a boa constrictor, but it got too big and he had to get rid of it."

"Iguanas are really great. This guy is the smartest I've ever met."

"Go on in. Five minutes."

"Thanks man."

The host stepped to the side to let Merv pass, but simultaneously spoke into his headset saying, "Tell Jayne there's a guy with an iguana that wants to talk to her."

Merv hadn't actually intended to speak to the owner. All of this was just a ruse to bypass the line. He scurried into the venue.

The restaurant was dim, lit with string lights, with gray wood walls and a typical mishmash of decorations like old license plates, fishing gear, pig-themed slogans, and photos of celebrities that had visited. At the far end of the building, past the bar, the space opened to a sandy lot that was a poor imitation of a beach, as it was far from the ocean. Patrons chattering, kitchen noise, and Jimmy Buffett music created an invigorating scene, but Stumpy dug his talons into his shoulder in distress. It hurt like hell. "Ow!"

He headed to the bar and placed Stumpy on the wood top, holding him down to keep him from running.

"Hey, nice shirt. Looks like one of you isn't a Parrot Head," said the woman behind the bar. She had flowing black hair, shiny magenta lipstick, and wore a body-hugging black-and-white striped tank dress that made Merv's heart race.

"What? No. I love Jimmie."

"I mean your friend here." She leaned on the bar and lowered her face to gaze at Stumpy. In a soft baby-talk tone, she said, "You don't like all this noise, do you sweetie?" She chuckled and straightened to address Merv. "He's cute. I'm Jayne, the owner. And *you* are?"

Caught red handed. But he was so struck by her curves and high cheekbones, he took a chance and flirted, "In love."

"Ha! Sorry fella. What's your name?" She fished in a cooler behind the bar and pulled out two amber bottles.

"Merv."

"And what is your act again?" Jayne removed the caps from the beer bottles with such a fluid motion, Merv was impressed, and a touch aroused.

"Well, you caught me. I just wanted to get inside. It's been a long day out in the sun and I'm parched."

"So...your iguana isn't psychic? I must say, I was looking forward to having my fortune told." She gave Merv a wink and handed him a beer.

"He sure seems psychic. We won a ton of money today at the races and Stumpy picked most of the horses."

"Hmm. A talented little guy." She tossed back her hair and brought the brown bottle to her lips in a way that Merv found extremely sexy.

Merv chuckled. "Believe me, you don't know the half of it. He's got talent for miles."

"Oh really? Tell me more."

"How about I show you instead?" He pulled a gold cufflink from his pocket. The cufflink Stumpy had found at the horse track just minutes ago. "Do you have any grapes or fruit or anything?"

Jayne picked up a chunk of pineapple from an assortment of beverage fixings behind the bar. "Will this do?"

"Yes. Great. Is there somewhere less crowded we could go? I need some space for this trick."

"Sure, follow me." She picked up both their bottles and headed away from the bar.

He clutched Stumpy around his middle and followed Jayne around the bar, back through the kitchen, and out a side door to a portion of the beach 'patio' with three wood picnic tables. The twenty-by-thirty-foot area was separated from the public side by some tall, cheap bamboo fencing.

"We usually reserve this area for the staff or friends," she said.

"Cool. Okay. I'm going to put Stumpy down over here." He placed Stumpy in a corner. "Make sure he doesn't look."

Jayne giggled. "What is this?"

Merv jogged to the other corner of the rectangular space and dropped the gold cuff link on the ground, and strode back.

"Now what?"

Merv grinned. "Watch." He turned to Stumpy and dangled the pineapple slice above the iguana's head. "Stumpy, fetch."

The iguana whipped its head side-to-side, then sauntered along the bamboo fence. Ten seconds later, Stumpy raced to the opposite corner, picked up the golden nugget in his jaw, and waddled back to Merv and dropped it at his feet.

"Oh my God!" Jayne said. "He plays fetch?"

"Only with jewelry and wallets."

"Wait, you taught him this?"

"Yep." Merv dropped the fruit to Stumpy, who devoured it in two undulations of his gullet.

Jayne sat at the picnic table and pulled a joint from her cleavage. Giving him a knowing look, she asked, "Hmm. You are an interesting guy. I never meet anyone interesting. Want to get high?" She lit the end of the blunt with a tea candle at the center of the table.

"Sure! Hey, can we get some ribs also?" He sat down next to her.

She took a puff and then handed him the joint. "Fantastic idea. Stay here. I'm going to call some friends and have some refreshments sent in. Make it a party."

"I love parties."

Before she left, she turned and snatched Merv's hat off his head and put it on. "I like this."

"You can keep it. It looks great on you."

She slid her index finger over his nose. "What happened to you? Were you in a fight?"

"Oh. A guy punched me at the airport. Sheesh."

Jayne bent and brushed her lips on the tip of his nose. "Poor baby. We'll have fun tonight. You'll see."

As she leaned over, Merv got a good look at her cleavage as her long, wild hair brushed his cheeks. *Maybe he would get laid tonight, creating a perfect trifecta of amazing good luck.* First getting Stumpy back; second, winning all the money necessary to pay back Bisbee; and three, ending the night in the arms of a mysterious dark-haired beauty.

He admired the outline of her buttocks under her tight dress and the sway of her hips as she walked away.

Stumpy placed his foot on Merv's sneaker and looked up expectantly. "Hey, she likes us."

[Of course she does.]

"Thanks, fella. I couldn't have done any of this without you."

[Yum time?]

"Yum time for both of us! Boo-yah! I'll see if we can get you more treats." He picked up Stumpy and placed him in the center of the table. Merv poured a small pool of beer in front of him. "Come on, celebrate!"

Stumpy flitted his tongue on the frothy liquid; in no time, his green friend fell asleep.

* * *

The party comprised himself, Jayne, Jayne's cousin Lorenzo, her best friend Gloria, and her business partner, Elias. For two hours, they drank and smoked, ate enough ribs to kill three pigs, told dirty stories, and played spin the bottle.

He didn't enjoy kissing Lorenzo, even though it was more of a peck. And when Gloria's bottle spin landed on him, she kissed him with full-on tongue down his throat, so aggressively he gagged and collapsed to get air. Everyone giggled at that one. But despite the weird kissing game, he hadn't enjoyed himself like this in ages. Slowly, the party devolved into a make-out session, fueled by more weed, with Gloria, Elias and Lorenzo in a three-way huddle of heavy petting, leaving Jayne and him alone on the sand a few yards away.

Jayne pressed herself against him, sucking on his neck like a teenager trying to give a hickey. Merv closed his eyes, feeling his way, running his hands under her dress to caress her inner thighs. He didn't care if the others looked. He wanted her right then with a primal urge that suspended all decorum; his loins were on fire. But Merv waited until she gave him the right signals.

"I want you," he whispered.

She placed her hand down his shorts. "Ooh. Pappi. You got the stuff." He felt like he could come just from the stroke of her palm.

He groaned. "Can we go somewhere more private?"

She unzipped his shorts. "No, daddy. Right here. Right now." She called over her shoulder. "Gloria, don't you look now. We need some...privacy." Jayne hitched up her skirt and tugged off her thong.

Merv took that as a sign to unleash his boner from the prison of his tighty-whities.

Jayne slipped on top of him and it felt so good. He would never last at this rate. But he didn't care. *So close now. So close. Yes! Yes! This was happening.* The veins in his neck felt as if they'd explode, along with the rest of him.

Part of his brain registered that she wasn't Kemper. Not even remotely alike. *Would he ever make love with Kemper in front of strangers at bar?* Probably not. No, with his skinny pale boss, they'd have decent, respectable, sweet love-making in a proper bed, with dim candlelight and no reggae music. Without drugs, without a crowd, without sand up his asshole; at least, given the chance. Right now, with Jayne, the night was all about getting the release he so needed.

Jayne tilted her head back and shouted above the calypso music, "Make me come, you wild ranger. Harder. Give it harder, Pappi! Mmm, YES!"

And then time slowed down, and he stopped thrusting, because something was *definitely not right*.

Gloria, Elias and Lorenzo came into view, staring down at him. Elias held up Merv's shorts and pulled the stack of hundreds from the pocket, breaking into a wide grin.

Lorenzo held Stumpy by his short tail, swinging him slowly like a pendulum. His distressed green companion scratched at the air like he was drowning in a pool.

All three were laughing.

Laughing at him.

Waves of alarm broke him from his drug and sex-induced haze. Merv tossed Jayne to the side and pulled up his underwear to the sound of even louder mocking laughter.

Gloria took the money from Elias and began twirling around, stripping off bills and throwing them in the air, giggling like a little kid, singing, "Whoop, whoop".

Merv scrambled up from the ground; sand flew from his hands as he pointed to Stumpy. "STOP! Dude! Leave him alone!" He burst into a run at Lorenzo.

Lorenzo stopped swinging Stumpy and dropped the reptile from a height of three feet.

Merv tackled Lorenzo like a line-backer, their bodies falling hard. He gained the upper hand and landed a full-knuckled punch across Lorenzo's chin, relishing the pain in his hand. Feeling as if he'd won, Merv let up a mere moment until Lorenzo tossed a handful of sand at his eyes, blinding him. Merv threw his fists, some landing on flesh, others just air. Grappling for any advantage, he found Lorenzo's mouth. His opponent chomped down on his thumb. Merv retaliated in the most fitting way he could think of; he scooped a heaping amount sand and shoved it in the dude's mouth. Now hearing Lorenzo gag, Merv rolled to the side, extracted himself and wiped his eyes. Lorenzo gagged and spat, pawing at his tongue.

All of Merv's instincts told him to finish the guy and stomp on his neck to break his windpipe. Instead, he kicked more sand on Lorenzo's face and torso. "Fucking asshole. No one messes with Stumpy. You HEAR?" He grabbed his shorts and shoved his legs through the openings. To the rest of the gawking crew, he sneered, "I want ALL my money back, understand?"

Jayne and Gloria stopped giggling and silently hunted down and gathered the scattered bills. Elias, who seemed to be comatose, plopped on the ground cross-legged and mumbled, "Sorry, man. Don't be such a buzzkill."

Merv's face continued to burn as he gingerly retrieved the very agitated Stumpy and cradled him like an infant. He crooned to his small friend, "I'm sorry. We'll get out of here right away."

Gloria handed Merv the money, now a crinkled and messy pile instead of the once smooth, crisp brick. She said, "We were just playin' with y'all. Come on, have another beer with us. I have some coke, too." Gloria punctuated this with a sly smile and a wiggle of her shoulders.

Merv shook his head. "No. We're leaving." He approached Jayne, who looked like she had lost her best friend.

Mascara ran down her cheeks as she whispered, "I'm sorry, Magic Merv. We get a little crazy sometimes." She handed him his hat back.

Instantly, he felt like a schmuck. Even though he still believed they were entirely in the wrong. "Hey, you keep the hat."

She reached up and pecked him on the cheek.

Lorenzo was still prone on the ground; still spitting out sand and cursing. "Hey, someone get me some fucking water!"

Merv sorted through his cash, pulled out a hundred-dollar bill, and handed it to Jayne. "For any inconvenience." He nodded toward the sandy-mouthed asshole.

She hugged the hat to her stomach and nodded back. "Come back and see me sometime. I promise, just the two of us."

"I don't think I'll be back." With this final statement, he carried Stumpy back through the kitchen and out a different side-door to the outside. He stroked the iguana's head, trying to make amends.

With Stumpy's interests at heart, he knew where to go next. They drove to an actual beach out on the southern tip of beautiful Key Biscayne. Parked in the dark public lot with few other vehicles, Merv shut off the engine and turned to his buddy. "We'll sleep here tonight. Take the first flight home, okay?"

The iguana was asleep and didn't reply.

Merv reclined his seat and cracked the windows four inches to feel the warm breeze. On his phone, he pulled up the St. John National Park website to his favorite page; a picture of Kemper, kneeling next to a little girl with braids, with a caption that read, "Ranger Kemper Snow gives a wildlife talk to a local first grade class."

Even with her uniform masking her slender figure and her flat cap shielding most of her face, she radiated with a goodness that was so missing from his own life. He planted a kiss on his thumb and caressed the image, whispering, "I love you."

In his thoughts, he knew he would never be worthy of her. Tonight's debauchery was the only proof needed. Tears formed in the corner of his eyes, wondering if he could ever change.

The scratchy sand wadded up his butt crack made it uncomfortable to sit in the car, no less sleep. He considered whether to use the beach shower to wash himself clean. *But no, he deserved the red-hot irritation of his bung-hole as a reminder of his bad choices.* A sort of self-flagellation to force the changes he needed.

"Goodnight, Stumpy," Merv whispered as he closed his eyes. He hummed the tune One Enchanted Evening from the musical South Pacific, imagining himself and Kemper slow-dancing on the sand.

In his mind, Merv could swear he heard Stumpy reply—clear as day and in a stern Australian accent—*If you don't shut the fuck up, I'll slash your face off.*

He opened his eyes; Stumpy was still asleep and hadn't moved an inch.

Maybe he was just hearing things or losing his mind.

Or he had a concussion from his fight with that loser, Lorenzo.

The iguana was right.

Time for sleep.

Tomorrow was the first day of the rest of his life.

And Merv vowed to make it better than the last.

Chapter 16

The Home Design and Remodeling Show at the Miami Convention Center last year resulted in a treasure trove of useful items. Rosie always relished diving through the Center's dumpsters after a show, because there would be all kinds of swag and plastic banners, and sometimes aluminum framing, useful to Miami's homeless population. She had a stash of over two hundred ball-point pens for her trouble.

At the moment, she praised the Gods for her keyring mini-flashlight, with the Ace Hardware logo, because the sewer was as dark as a crypt.

It wasn't an actual sewer. Not yet. Because the city hadn't yet connected this line to any water sources. The system was still under construction. At five-feet in diameter, this main trunk line was still open on both ends, running a half-mile north-south. It wasn't the best orientation to reach the hospital, but it provided the necessary cover to elude the police.

The old man held her hand as they walked through the spooky space, ducking their heads in the cramped concrete tube, following the weak light cast in front of them.

"It's not much further," she said.

A familiar-looking round lump a few feet ahead caught Rosie's attention. As they drew closer, she flashed her light on the object. Glowing yellow eyes turned her way.

The raccoon, chewing on a dead squirrel, seemed irked by their presence and stared at them with black eyes. Yet, they had no choice but to continue forward.

She slowed, taking measured steps toward the frozen animal. It bared its teeth.

A case of rabies would be a fitting end to this crazy day, she thought.

Rosie yelled, "Get out!" The sound echoed through the long space. She let go of Harold's hand and waved at the demon.

The striped tailed, oversized rodent ran towards her.

Shit.

In her pocket, she retrieved her knife and opened the blade. "Stand back, Harold."

With precision, she kicked the oncoming beast in its face; for this was not the first time she'd tangled with its kind within the mean, darkened corners of Miami. It retreated, shook its mangy head, and came at her again.

A persistent little bugger.

"Don't make me kill you," she whispered. She kicked it again, but it avoided much of the blow, attaching its teeth to her ankle. She yelped from the pain that felt like a vise. There could be no mercy now. Rosie plunged the blade into its skull and twisted. The animal went limp.

Her ankle hurt like fuck-all. But they had to keep moving. She nudged the limp furball to the side and grabbed Harold's arm. "Come on. We need to keep going."

Rosie contemplated her previous escapades through city sewers. How the leader of the prison break, a woman called Tank, had been close behind her when the explosion occurred five years ago. Tank's large frame crashed over her, protecting her from the full blast of the fireball. Rosie had lost a molar in the fall onto the concrete, but considered herself lucky to escape with only patches of second-degree burns on her face.

It was a hard lesson in the dangers of confined spaces. A pamphlet she'd read from the trash of the Miami Firefighters Convention explained it all. Flammable gases often sought low spaces and concentrated there. Sadly, the woman with the lighter, she couldn't remember her name now, had been one of the nicer inmates.

A few minutes later, they emerged from the other end of the tube, which terminated inside an empty construction site surrounded by a chain-link fence. The neon lights across the street brought a sense of relief. One of her allies was close by.

They crossed the street and headed to the back door of the lively establishment. The sign read, *Performers Only*, yet she knocked anyway.

A tall, broad-shouldered woman, wearing lingerie and a sequin cow-boy hat, answered the door.

"Hello, sweet cheeks, what can I do for you?"

"Hey, could you tell Monica that Rosie is here?"

"Come on in. She's getting dressed."

Rosie kept a firm hold of Harold's hand and they navigated the room, lined with lockers, costumes, and makeup stations. The song, *It's Raining Men*, played at a distance; amplified every time someone opened the door.

Harold said, "I like this music." He swished his hips.

"We need bus money. Follow me. Don't touch anything. Queens HATE it when you touch their stuff."

Harold picked up a powder puff and brought it to his mouth.

She snatched it. "You can't eat that."

He whined, "I want my cookie."

The woman in the cowboy hat took the puff from Rosie. "Honey, we *all* want our cookie." She called out, "Monica! Visitors!"

A short, dark-skinned, bald-headed woman wearing a red business suit appeared from behind a wall. It took a second of recognition before she beamed, "Rosie! What brings you here, girlfriend?" She winked at Harold and turned her attention back to Rose. "Goodness, I haven't seen you in ages. You should see my new routine. It SLAYS!"

Monica waved to her other coworkers. "Rosie here kept me fed for months when I was on the streets doing crack. I'd be dead twice over if this angel hadn't come along."

Despite the compliment, Rosie did not welcome the attention. "Hey, can we talk in private?" She whispered, "Stop using my real name."

"Oh, right." Monica looked sheepish. "Sorry. Come back this way." She strutted to a rear alcove. "Hey, is that blood on your shoes? Are you in trouble? Did you kill someone?"

They followed their host to a dressing table. Rosie sat Harold on a red-velvet tufted stool. "Monica, I need to get this guy back to the hospital. Do you have ten bucks for bus fare?"

"Shoot! What happened to him?" Monica reached into a toiletries bag and removed three cotton balls; she applied rubbing alcohol to them. "Don't tell me...did fuck-head Terrence get a hold of him?"

"No, a fucking cop."

Monica dabbed the abrasion on Harold's forehead with the disinfectant. "Is that why you have the blood on your sneakers? Did you cut that pig mother-fucker?"

"No. A raccoon lunged at us."

"Ha! Look at you go. Sure," She tossed the dirty cotton into the trashcan and then pulled a folded fifty-dollar bill from her cleavage. "Take this. Are you hungry? I think there might be some leftover Chinese takeout."

"Thanks. Maybe next time. We need to go."

"Well, don't be a stranger. Come back tomorrow night. You have to see my new persona. I'm playing JK Rowling—I know, boo hiss and all that— but with a giant dildo stapled to my ass, and Gabby over there throws sheep's blood on me. It's messy as hell," she gestured in a wide circle, her red nails gleaming, "but avant-garde as fuck. The crowds go BANANAS for it."

Rosie laughed. "I might. Hey, one more favor. Can I borrow one of your wigs? Just in case?"

Monica grinned, "I always hoped you'd go blonde. Here," she snatched a shoulder-length blunt-cut wig from a Styrofoam bust. "Keep it."

They said their goodbyes. Not long after, Rosie and Harold finished their trek to the closest bus stop. The act of sitting reminded Rosie of how badly her feet ached.

Finally, she felt like she could breathe again. No one was chasing them. Soon she would complete her good deed and go back to her regular life, at least as regular as possible given her circumstances.

Her new friend leaned his head on her shoulder and snored.

She carefully donned the wig, tucking in loose strands of her reddish-gray hair, trying not to disrupt the poor man's sleep. The fake nylon hair probably looked terrible, but she needed the disguise now more than ever.

A bus approached down the dark street; its electronic sign read *City Center*.

She placed her hand on Harold's and whispered, "I'll get you there. I promise."

* * *

Rosie counted only four more stops until their bus reached Princewood Hospital. Harold was awake, staring out the window. She noticed a crumpled napkin in his hand, with some ink that looked like writing.

"Harold, what is that?"

He gazed at the wad. "I don't remember."

She took it and smoothed it between her palm and thigh. "Who is

Gertie?"

"Who?"

"This phone number. Is this a relative?"

Harold just blinked.

"I bet she is worried sick about you. Do you mind if I call her?"

He just shrugged.

The prefix on the number looked odd. Definitely not a Miami area code. She didn't have many minutes left on her pre-paid phone plan, but decided this person had to be important. It was nearly ten o'clock at night, yet a woman's voice picked up on the second ring.

"Hello?"

"Hi, you don't know me, but I'm with Harold Nome. Do you know him?"

"Sorry, no. I don't know anyone named Harold."

"Old guy, white hair, had a wrist-band for Princewood?"

"Oh, MY LORD! You found him!"

"Um, yes. I'm taking him back now." She checked her watch. "We should arrive in about ten to fifteen minutes."

"THANK YOU! How is he? Who is this?"

Rosie froze. She obviously couldn't give her name. In a panic, she hung up. *Shit.*

She wondered whether she would need a new phone and how much it would cost. Doing good deeds always involved some sort of financial setback. *When would she ever learn?* Her phone was as useful as an ankle monitor to someone like her.

At the next traffic light, the bus paused in front of an electronics shop. Flat screen televisions of all sizes and price points filled the front window. But what caught Rosie's attention was the news headline, "Insane billionaire missing in Miami." The scrolling text explained the elusive mogul, Cudlow Loughton, had escaped from the hospital. His son had put up a five-thousand-dollar reward. A picture of a somewhat younger and more polished Harold filled the inset picture.

She looked at Harold.

Then looked at the screen.

The bus pulled away, eliminating any possibility of learning more.

Five-thousand dollars! She could buy enough propane, bottled water and food for a year!

As the bus advanced closer to their destination, she concluded rewards were for people with actual identities that lived in the real world. Not fugitives like herself.

No, she would get Harold to the hospital, pass him on to the first employee she came across, and high-tail it out of there before anyone noticed her.

It was the only fucking way.

* * *

Johnnie continued riding the blue scooter around Miami, trying not to think about his breakup with Greta. Still, her every word hung on his mind. *Maybe he was better off living the rest of his life alone. Or maybe he could get a dog.* Questions circled his thoughts, including how in hell he would find Cud. Was it possible that Cud came to his senses and went back to the house? But if Cud was better, surely, he would have called. No, he concluded, something bad must have happened. And he needed some expert help.

After checking the map on his phone, he headed to the closest homeless shelter, the Miami Rescue Mission. The folks there would know where to look.

The street in front of the building was dark and quiet. A uniformed officer stood by the door.

He parked his scooter and did a smell test of the pits of his t-shirt. He didn't want the organizers to think he was homeless. But it had been hours since his morning shower and his hair was matted from his helmet and there were dead flies on his neck.

Johnnie wiped down his neck and shirt with his hands, attempting to pass for normal, and nodded politely at the police officer. The front door led to a breezeway with a check-in table. The man didn't look up and only said, "Name?"

With a measured, respectful tone, Johnnie said, "Good evening. I'm looking for a friend of mine. Could you tell me if he is here?"

"What is the name?"

"Um, well, he might not know his name. He's about 5-foot-ten, white hair, very thin."

"Sir, we only keep records by names."

"Right. Um…could I look around? My friend escaped from the hospital. He's been having mental issues."

"Do you have a picture?"

Johnnie bit his lip. "No, I'm afraid not."

"I'm sorry. We like to give our residents their privacy. You can understand we don't let outsiders wander around bothering them." The man waved his hand in the air in a meandering fashion.

"I won't say a word. I promise."

Desk guy nodded to the policeman. "Sorry, I'm going to have to ask you to leave."

"Fuck!"

The officer put his hand on his hilt, "You heard him."

"Fine. But, for argument's sake, where would you look for a homeless man?"

The man at the desk grimaced, "Try Eleventh Street…the underpasses. Just head due south from here. But if I were you, I'd wait until daybreak."

"Thank you." Johnnie exited the building, got to his scooter, and pulled up a map on his phone.

It wasn't a far ride, less than a mile. In no time, he found the first encampment; about a dozen tents, some domed camping types, and some makeshift shelters made from pallets and tarps. Chain-link fence bordered the encampment. Broken bottles and cardboard littered the area.

Johnnie parked his scooter, left his helmet on the seat, and braced himself. Entering this area was probably a foolish thing to do. Three men sat outside the tent closest to the break in the fence. They glared at him like sharks detecting fresh blood in the water.

He ducked through the fence and waved to the three as he approached, and kept his hands out to show he meant no harm. "Hi." The bare dirt reeked of urine.

"Wha you want, mo-fucka?" The tallest and heaviest of them, with a cross tattooed across his forehead, addressed him with a scowl.

"I'm looking for someone."

The smallest of the three, a bald-headed wrinkled man, wearing mashed-up grocery bags like a shirt, hurled a rock at him. "Let's get 'im!"

All three erupted from their sitting position, and five others burst from their shelters, running at him.

One of them yelled, "Dibs on his shoes and teeth!" Another yelled, "Fuck his shoes, I want his ride."

They cut off the exit in the fence behind him. In a heartbeat, he was surrounded.

He picked up a rock, not sure it would help, given they outnumbered him eight to one.

"Ha! Check out this pussy and his pet rock."

The man with the forehead tattoo seemed to be the leader, because he announced with authority, "I'm gonna break his skull."

Johnnie couldn't resist. "Too late."

He chuckled. "Ha! Give me your wallet and your phone."

"No." He scanned for a route of escape.

"What? You want to die?"

"Maybe."

"Damn, fucker. Have it your way."

His large opponent picked up a broken bottle, took a large step forward, and twisted it with a flourish toward his face.

Johnnie considered his defense, and was ready to kick the guy in the nuts, when a siren pierced their ears, coming towards them.

They all turned to look. Two police cars sped in their direction.

The homeless men scurried to their tents and closed the flaps.

With a sigh of relief, Johnnie ducked through the fence and jumped on his scooter.

The police cars continued on, clearly heading to a different destination or trouble spot.

Johnnie headed east toward safer, more populated, and well-lit areas. A vibration in his front pocket alerted him to an incoming call. Johnnie stopped near to an office building and answered.

It was Jackson.

"Hi. I haven't found him yet...I'm so sorry."

"John, Ms. Brown just called me. An anonymous caller just said she's returning Pawpaw to the hospital. Get over there now!"

"Will do. I'm on it." He didn't even think to say goodbye, choosing to end the call and drive off.

Finally, some good news.

He didn't believe in prayer, but in his heart, he prayed that Cud was okay. His thoughts wandered, wondering if Darla's recent interest in religion gave her peace. And maybe he was an asshole for trashing her beliefs. Still, he believed more in Karma than an all-knowing God or suppressed alien spirits.

At least Karma implied a cosmic balance of justice that made sense to him…where he had some control over his fate.

Even if that same Karma was kicking him in the balls at the moment.

As he motored on, the neon sign for the hospital came into view between the majestic palms.

Turning the corner and up the half-ellipse driveway to the front entrance, Johnnie couldn't believe the sight in front of him.

And it made his blood boil.

Chapter 17

Just like their favorite nightly quiz show, Johnnie created a mental list of potential answers:

- *Five news vans blocking the hospital entrance.*
- *Floodlights brighter than a thousand suns.*
- *Reporters and camera-operators elbowing each other for better positions.*
- *A throng of on-lookers with cardboard signs that read 'Save Cudlow'.*

All answers to the question: "What is a press-conference hosted by a slimy, rotund fuck-tard?"

At the center of the action, a short, tubby man—wearing a cheap-looking suit with a loosely knotted tie—boomed into a microphone from a narrow podium, "What has happened here today is a TRAVESTY! My client, the only son of Cudlow Loughton, is asking for the public's help to locate his father before it is TOO LATE! The reward of five-thousand-dollars will go to anyone who brings him back alive; but MIND YOU, to receive the reward, you must contact my colleagues at Norton and Murfree, Associates at Law, and DO NOT bring him back here, to this DEPLORABLE institution, that has CAUSED this tragedy. AGAIN, please, if you find Mr. Cudlow Loughton, bring him to Norton and Murfree DIRECTLY. Otherwise, NO reward."

Reporters snapped pictures of the barking sleazeball and asked questions in unison, trying to shout over each other.

"Mr. Greaves, do you think Cudlow is still alive?"

"What is the nature of his mental illness?"

"Greaves! Are the rumors true? Are you suing the hospital?"

A voice cried out from the crowd, "Let me through. I have Cudlow right here!"

Johnnie craned his neck.

A man in a black-leather biker outfit held the arm of a white-haired person. "Here he is." They approached Greaves.

The lawyer shook his head. "No! For the LAST TIME! Stop bringing me random old folks! What the fuck is wrong with you people? Fucking Miami."

Johnnie peered at the live footage from the news camera nearest him, and clearly the person being presented was not Cudlow…and not even a man. In fact, the gray-haired, skinny person looked remarkably like the woman from the park who had bashed him in the legs two-hours prior.

Greaves continued, "My client Elson plans to bring Cudlow back to his native England, where he will get the BEST care that money can buy. And yes, I plan to sue Princewood Hospital and his doctors into OBLIVION."

England? Did Jackson know? Or was Jackson in on this?

Johnnie worked his way to the rear of the crowd, scanning for the mystery woman and Cudlow.

Roughly two-hundred feet away, near the bus stop, he saw two figures walking toward the entrance. The gait of the man was unmistakable. *It was Cudlow!*

He jogged towards them.

The two paused. The woman took something off her head, something fluffy, and placed it on Cudlow's head.

"Hey! I'm Johnnie. Cudlow's best friend."

The woman, who seemed to be about Cudlow's age of seventy-five, shook as if startled and turned her face away. "Here, take him. And the reward."

"No, I'm not sending him into that side-show. Why is he wearing a wig?"

She stopped in her tracks and spun. "He's sick. He needs the hospital. I risked a lot to get him here tonight." The woman faced him; her eyes angry. The skin on her cheek and forehead looked odd, like crumpled paper; but maybe it was just shadows, he thought.

"You don't understand."

"Look, Johnnie…" The woman looked confused, peering at him with her head tilted, alternating sides and squinting. "Your name is John?"

"Yes, John Crosswell. I've known Cud for four years. He lives on the beach in St. John, where I work."

She touched his arm. "Cross…"

He recoiled, hating when strangers touched him. "Ma'am, thank you for bringing him back. But that guy up there? The lawyer? He represents Cud's evil son, Elson, who plans to lock him away for the rest of his life. Don't worry about it. I'll take it from here."

Flood lights blasted them, hurting Johnnie's eyes.

The horde of reporters came at them like locusts, buzzing and leaping, but carrying more camera equipment.

Johnnie said, "We need to get out of here. Now!"

The red-haired woman grabbed Cud's arm. "Where?"

"I DON'T KNOW! YOU DECIDE!"

"Fine. Follow me."

The three took off running, although Johnnie's knee still hurt from his previous injuries. His run was more like a hobble as he tried to keep up with Cud and the woman. They headed down the hospital driveway toward the main road. In the excitement, Cud's wig flew off and landed on the pavement. Johnnie decided a wig would never help them, and didn't stop to retrieve it.

The red-haired lady headed across the street. She ran into the middle of the road toward a fast-moving city bus, showing no sign of fear or hesitation.

The bus, with a sign that read 'No Service', slammed on its brakes with a nerve-shattering metallic screech. Johnnie held his breath, anticipating a bloody impact. Defying all laws of physics, the thirteen-ton vehicle stopped in time, merely two feet from the daring older woman.

Still unfazed and acting as a human shield, she yelled, "John, get him on this bus!"

Johnnie took Cud's arm, limped to the closed door, and banged on it with his fist. [BANG] [BANG]

The driver opened the door. "This is an unauthorized stop."

He stuck his middle finger at the man and climbed the two steps. "Authorize this!"

Once on board, the woman said to the driver, "Thank you, sir. Just drop us off a few blocks east if you can."

The driver just shook his head and floored the accelerator. "I saw those paparazzi. Who are you folks, the Beatles?"

All three took seats near the front. Johnnie growled, "Worse."

"I saw the news." He gestured his head toward Cud. "How is Mr. Loughton doing?"

Johnnie said, "Not good."

"My name is Craig. You aren't kidnapping him, right?"

"No. I don't think so," the woman said. "I'm...I'm Daisy. John here is Cudlow's good friend. I'm not exactly sure what's going on, to tell the truth."

Johnnie said, "Nice to meet you Daisy."

Craig shook his head and muttered. "White people."

John sighed. "Hey, we just need to hide for a few hours. Until the court verdict in the morning."

Daisy said, "Craig, could you drop us off near the science museum?"

"Sure, no problem."

They drove in silence for the next few blocks.

Johnnie did not know why she chose that location. But it was better than any idea he could come up with.

* * *

~Seven hours earlier~

Dr. Lou finished a video session with a patient and turned her attention back to her computer. An email had arrived from the Law Offices of Richard Greaves, Esquire, with a subject line of Cudlow Loughton.

As of three o'clock that afternoon, Greaves asserted she was officially removed as Mr. Loughton's lead physician and asked her to transfer any medical files to their paralegal. While the threatening letter from Greaves looked official, it didn't reference any court orders.

She forwarded the email to Jackson, asking what he made of it.

Meanwhile, another email alerted her that the hospital posted Harold's lab results to the on-line portal as promised. Lou assumed it wouldn't hurt to look.

The lab report was twenty pages long, with numeric results from complete blood counts, lipid panels, a metabolic panel, and some very specific bacterial and viral tests.

Cudlow's white cell count was high, meaning possible infection. Every parameter was within normal ranges as she scanned the first ten pages. On the last page, the word 'positive' next to the RT-PCR (reverse transcription polymerase chain reaction) urine test gave her hope.

It didn't explain all of Cudlow's illness, but certainly could contribute to it. Inflammation of the brain could manifest itself in unusual ways. She'd have to contact the CDC and obtain some mono-clonal antibodies to treat Cudlow; if, in fact, she was still his doctor. At the very least, she could advise Mr. Loughton's new doctor on viable treatment.

She called the attending nurse at Princewood.

On the tenth ring, an out of breath woman answered. "This is Naomi."

"Hello, this is Dr. Phillips. How is Mr. Nome?"

"Oh! Um…I can't talk right now. Bye…"

"Wait! Don't hang up!"

"Just call the hospital administrator, Velma Spencer. Bye."

She looked at her phone. The call was over.

The last time someone at a hospital hung up on her like that, she found out later that the patient had died. More than died. Specifically, they had swallowed an entire bottle of opioids that had been smuggled into the hospital.

Lou pushed aside her frustration and dialed Velma.

"Velma, what's going on? Is Mr. Nome all right?"

"Lou, we have a code green."

"No!"

"I'm very sorry. We alerted the police and are continuing to search the hospital."

"Vel, I just reviewed his test results. They point to viral encephalitis. Maybe he has some other issues, but he needs medical intervention right away."

"I understand. We're doing all we can."

The ominous email from the lawyer nagged at her. Lou asked, "Has a lawyer named Richard Greaves contacted you?"

"Yes. And you?"

"He says I'm off the case."

"Well, our in-house lawyer looked him up. Apparently, Mr. Greaves is notorious for dirty tricks. I spoke with Jackson. He told us Greaves is bluffing. There's a court hearing tomorrow morning in the Bahamas to settle the matter."

"Thanks, good to know. Call me the second you locate Cudlow… I mean Harold."

She ended the call and next called Jackson.

"Hello Dr. Phillips, how is my grandfather?"

"Hi Jackson, I have his lab results. Did the hospital call you?"

"No, I just touched down."

"Oh. Well, I have some good news and some bad news."

She relayed to him that Cudlow was missing and her suspicion that a virus was contributing to his grandfather's mental incapacity.

After absorbing the information, Jackson said, "Johnnie was supposed to stay at his bedside. I put him in charge! Bollocks! I knew it was a big mistake."

"I'm sure the hospital will find him."

"If I could, I'd come right back, but I have the court hearing in the morning. I'll be meeting with lawyers most of the evening to prepare."

"No, you do what you have to do. I'll write up my findings and send them to you in the next two hours."

When the call with Jackson was over, she called Johnnie.

After two rings, it went to voicemail.

Leaving a message was probably futile, but she did it anyway. "John, I've reviewed Mr. Loughton's test results. If you find him, please call me right away. It's vitally important he returns to the hospital."

Her girlfriend, Ann, popped into her office. "Hey, I overheard. What happened?"

Lou rubbed her temples and wheeled towards her. "They lost Mr. Loughton."

"Lost him? At the hospital?"

"Yes. Somehow, I just knew this case would turn into something…"

"Something what?"

"Anytime Johnnie's involved…I hate to say this, things go haywire."

"Why do you keep him as a patient, then?" Ann leaned against the door.

Lou rolled past her, into the living room. "I often ask myself that."

"No, seriously."

Lou boosted herself with her muscled arms, twisting to flop onto the L-shaped sectional. With both hands, she lifted her left leg and brought it onto the sofa, then repeated with the other. "Some of us made it out of the military without limbs. Others lost much more. Johnnie's memories were almost entirely wiped after being shot in the head. Can you imagine if I had come home from Iraq and didn't remember you?"

Ann joined her on the sofa and squeezed her hand. With a smile she said, "I'd *make* you remember."

She chuckled, "Yes, I guess you would."

"But that doesn't answer my question.

Lou bit her lower lip. "Johnnie went through a few doctors before he found me. I know he's not the easiest patient. But he's come a long way. I mean, sure, he has setbacks now and then, but he's making genuine progress. He came here with a *girlfriend*! He's finally putting himself out there, socializing in ways he hadn't before."

"Maybe he's an experiment to you?"

"Jesus, Ann, we are ALL experiments...full of hormones, stress, inadequacies and past trauma, all reacting to challenges and making choices in different ways. That's why I went into psychiatry. Human beings are fascinating! And the brain has resilience in ways we are still learning about."

"But you have plenty of clients. Too many if you ask me."

Lou locked eyes with Ann. "I keep Johnnie as a client because I care about him, even with his flaws."

Ann leaned over to nestle under Lou's arm. "Hmm. Well, that is very noble of you, doctor. But please think about cutting back your office hours. You keep promising."

Lou kissed the top of Ann's head. "Kid, I promise I'll *think* about it."

Ann raised her head and wrinkled her nose. "That is a *lousy* non-committal promise."

Lou grinned and playfully rubbed Ann's hip. "I suppose it is. Hey, I don't have any appointments for the rest of the day. How about an early cocktail and bubble-bath?"

Ann's pout turned to a smile. "Sure, babe. Race you there!"

Lou beamed at their inside joke as Ann bounded off the sofa. Logistically, it would take Lou another five minutes to join her. However, she relished knowing both the bath water and Ann would be warm and ready for her arrival. And life didn't get much better than that.

Chapter 18

The bus vibrated over the uneven pavement. With the interior lights off, Johnnie felt safe, as if no one could ever find them. But at the same time, he knew that wasn't true.

Seated behind the driver, he pivoted his legs into the aisle and clapped Cud's shoulder.

"How are you doing, buddy?"

"Johnnie, I'm glad you are here." Cud put his hand on Johnnie's knee.

"Yes! You know who I am?"

"Of course. But why are we on a bus?"

"Do you know where we are?"

"No. My head hurts like the dickens."

As the street lights swept across the windows, he saw a lump on Cud's forehead. "What happened to your head? Did you fall?"

Daisy, who had been looking out the window, turned to him. "We had a run-in with the police."

"Oh, no. Thank you for finding him." Johnnie wrinkled his brow. "Where *did* you find him, anyway?"

"He was wandering around."

"Well, thank you, Daisy. I'm sorry you got mixed up with this. You don't have to stay…"

The driver, Craig, barked, "Duck! Police!"

Seconds later, as they bent with their heads low, red and blue lights reflected off the ceiling and dissipated not long after, indicating the police had passed them.

"All clear."

[Brrrnnng…da da da dum…da da da dum…] Johnnie's phone rang, causing him to cringe with recognition. He didn't have to look at the incoming number to know it was Dr. Lou.

His finger hovered over the decline icon, but he gritted his teeth and hit accept.

"Hi Lou."

"I just saw you on the news! What's going on?"

"That stinkin' lawyer wants to take Cud. We had to run."

"Didn't you get my message? He has a virus. Get him back there NOW!"

"No fuckin' way. It's a trap. Whose side are you on, anyway?"

After a loud huffing noise, Lou said, "I'm on *Cudlow's* side. He needs to be in the hospital. *Any* hospital. Just tell me where you are. I'll come get you."

"No!" He stabbed the red icon to end the call. "Fuck!"

Daisy said, "You know, they can track you on that thing."

"Thing…my phone?"

"Yes! It has GPS. With all the cell towers around here, they'll have pinpoint accuracy. You should get rid of it."

"I can't. It has all my contacts in it. I can't remember phone numbers to save my life. Jumping Johosephat! It reminds me of a thousand things throughout the day, like when to take my pills or pay my rent. It's the closest I have to a real brain."

Daisy shook her head, "I understand, but—" Her phone rang.

He asked, "Who is it?"

She pulled the phone from her pocket and stared at it, "I don't know…no one ever calls me."

"Don't answer it!"

She hit accept and said, "Hello?"

On her phone's speaker, a British accent said, "This is Jackson Loughton. You had called Miss Brown earlier—"

Johnnie lunged at her phone and ripped it from her grasp. He took the phone to his side window and chucked it outside.

"Hey!"

He slammed the window shut. "We can't trust anyone."

Daisy snarled, "You owe me a phone, son."

"Fine." He faced forward; his arms crossed. A twinge of déjà vu made him freeze…it was as if he had heard the cadence of Daisy's voice before.

The way she said *son*. But not able to place it, he shrugged it off.

After three seconds of silence, his phone rang again, but this time the ringtone was the tune of "MMMBop", his sister's least favorite song and his way of needling her.

He debated whether to answer. As a Senator, his sister Robin had resources and contacts to help them. But she was pretty much a straight arrow and was likely *extremely* pissed at him.

Johnnie weighed these pros and cons. With only twenty-dollars of cash on him, he needed some resources. "Hi, Sis."

"Johnnie! Jackson and Dr. Lou both called me. They said you were on television…running away from the hospital with Cudlow! What the hell?"

In a sing-song manner, he said, "I'm fine, how are you?"

"Goddamnit! Don't be a butt-head!"

Johnnie chuckled. "Are you going to help or what?"

"Help? I have no fucking idea what the fuck is going on!"

"I'm saving Cud from that asshole lawyer."

"Lou says you hung up on her."

"She'll get over it. We need a place to lie low. Are you helping or not?"

"Return him to the hospital right now or I'm giving your location to the police."

Johnnie froze. He always forgot that Robin could see his location on the tracking app they both subscribed to.

Daisy whispered, "What is Robin saying?"

He wrinkled his brows at Daisy, "How do you know…?"

Robin yelled into the phone, "Well? I need your answer now!"

Johnnie whispered to Daisy, "She has my location."

Daisy scrambled over Cudlow and grabbed Johnnie's phone. She stormed to the rear of the bus, opened a rear window, and tossed his phone outside. "Now we're even!" Bracing herself in the aisle with a hand on the nearest seat back, she amplified her voice toward Craig the driver, "How long until we get there?"

Over his shoulder, he called, "Two more blocks."

She returned to the front of the bus and sat behind Cudlow. "When we get there, we need to move fast. Follow me and stick to the shadows, okay?"

Johnnie sighed. "Why are we going to the science museum?"

She whispered, "We aren't. Well, yes, but not exactly. You'll see."

"Oh." Johnnie pondered what that meant.

Cudlow stared straight ahead and announced, "I once donated a million dollars to the British Museum."

This was a fairly lucid remark, which made Johnnie's heart race with hope. He tilted his head to inspect Cud's face. "That's great! What else do you remember?"

Cud blinked, "I...I can't..."

"That's okay, buddy." He nodded, swallowing hard. "I understand more than you know."

* * *

They thanked Craig heartily as they exited the bus, but their goodbye was swift. Rosalie took Cudlow's arm. In a soothing voice, she told him, "We're going somewhere safe for the night."

Cud nodded. "Thank you. I'm sorry to be such a bother."

She beamed. "No bother at all. Come on."

They walked across a lawn, without making a sound, toward the closed museum. The area was bounded by the park, the bay, and a highway. The entrance was through the park, which was lit by tall posts with futuristic flat circular lights.

Instead of heading to the front entrance to their left, she waved to Johnnie to follow.

He whispered, "Where are we going?"

"Shh. Just follow me." She continued down the path, toward the adjacent art museum and the water's edge.

The hiding spot was one Rosie had inherited from a former sixteen-year-old runaway, who later moved back home to their parent's place in Mississippi. It was a very intriguing spot that offered secure, indoor sleeping accommodations, as long as the museum was closed and vacant, which it normally was between ten at night and six in the morning.

She took a left around the back of the museum, along the waterfront, and headed under the bridge. Cars traveling overhead caused booming sounds amplified by the steel girders and concrete abutment. No matter how long she lived, she knew the thunder of cars and trucks overhead would always make her feel the same dread deep within her bones; feeling as if the bridge would collapse unexpectedly, crushing her to death. Which is why she rarely visited this hidey-hole.

Rosie scrambled up a few feet from the base of the sloping concrete to reach her target: a two-foot by two-foot steel door with a padlock.

Johnnie stood below with Cudlow. "Where does that lead?"

"You'll see." She fished out her pocket knife and pulled out the metal hook attachment, which she had filed down to the right dimensions. Picking locks was a valuable skill she had learned in prison. In fact, a certain commercial-brand, brass-cylinder padlock was so easy to pick, she could do it without looking. And that skill came in handy, given the darkness of the underpass at night. Just insert the thin metal shaft behind the middle number and press. *Voila!* They were in.

She opened the panel door. "Come on, but be careful. There are rungs to the bottom."

Johnnie shook his head. "Isn't this breaking and entering?"

Rosie slid through the opening feet first, to get her footing, then held onto the top rung, her back slightly twisted to see him. "Jumping Jesus, are you kidding me?"

"Fine. Forget I asked."

"Good. Send Harold…I mean Cudlow first. I'll make sure he doesn't fall."

After they reached the concrete floor, eight feet below the opening, Rosie looked Johnnie in the eye. "This is an electrical vault. Don't let our friend touch anything, understand? He's been trying to eat anything that looks like a cookie."

He nodded.

She led them through the narrow rectangular tunnel. Heavy cables and some thinner fiber-optic lines ran along the wall like bundles of rainbow spaghetti. Several paces later, another metal door, regularly sized and this time unlocked, came into view. "Through here."

Rosie wondered what Johnnie's reaction would be. It was such a cool place. The museum's Van De Graaff generators for their electricity show could release a million volts. To handle their power loads, the museum had a dedicated underground vault with immense transformers, capacitors, and computers. And even more interestingly, the electricians had created their own hidden 'chill-out' spot in an adjacent empty room, complete with a microwave, comfy brown leather recliners and a television.

She pushed open this last door, flipped a wall-switch to flood the space with overhead light, and said, "Ta da!"

Johnnie rubbed his eyes and walked past her into the center of the space.

"Whoa!"

Cudlow wandered in and locked his eyes on the nearest recliner.

"Take whichever one you want."

Johnnie wandered the roughly twelve by twenty-foot room, then pointed to the microwave. "Is there any food here?"

"I hid some cans of chili here a few months ago."

"Cud, are you hungry, buddy?"

Cudlow curled up in the first recliner and said, "Night-night."

"Sleep sounds good to me too." She yawned and stretched her arms. "We have to get out by six, just to be on the safe side."

The recliners were arranged in a semicircle, all facing the television. Johnnie picked the one next to Cud and used the arm release to recline to full extent. Rosie flicked off the overhead light. Now the only light sources were the blue numbers showing the time on the microwave, and a green glow from the computer banks in the next room. The hum of the computers sounded like a white-noise machine and instantly the adrenaline rush subsided. She took the remaining empty chair, wiggling her aching hips to settle in. "Goodnight, John."

In the dark, Johnnie whispered, "Daisy, why are you helping us?"

She couldn't tell him the truth. *Not now. Not ever.* "I help all kinds of people."

"No, I mean, not like this, right? Don't you have a family to get home to?"

She stared at the tall ceiling, with its rough concrete and metal conduit. "I don't have a family anymore."

"I'm sorry to hear that."

Trying to change the subject, and genuinely interested, she whispered, "What about you? Are you married? Any kids?"

He let out a prolonged sigh. "I'm divorced. And my girlfriend just broke up with me tonight."

"Do you want to talk about it?"

"I'm such an idiot. Greta is the best person I know, and I fucked up big."

"I was married once. When my husband left me, I did all kinds of destructive things. I lied. Stole. Bought expensive things. Anything to make me feel something different than the pure rage that burned inside."

"Ha," he chuckled darkly. "I know all about rage."

Rosie heard the self-loathing in John's voice. "Well, you can't be all bad.

You're risking everything to help your friend."

"I think this is my fault."

"How so?"

"I got Cud mixed up in one of my half-witted schemes a few weeks ago and introduced him to my landlady. He fell in love with Gertie and went off the deep end when it didn't work out. If only… if I hadn't introduced them, he would still be happy, living on the beach without a care. God, he used to be the happiest person. And I fucked him over."

"Not everything in this world is your fault. Love is a mysterious thing. And you can't make someone love you. They either do or they don't." *And sometimes*, she thought, *letting them go feels worse than death*. But she couldn't tell him this. Instead, she asked, "Tell me…do you love Greta?"

The silence was palpable, making Rosie wonder if she'd hit a nerve.

John's voice cracked. "I think I do. Because I feel like I can't fucking breathe."

She continued to look at the dark ceiling, afraid to face him, afraid to see him crying. Because she knew how he would hate that.

"John, I've learned a few things in this life. As someone who's lost everyone she's ever loved…" Despite trying to offer a motherly, calming tone, her bottom lip quivered and her eyes watered, "What matters is getting up every day and being there for others. To give the love in your heart, even if it is never returned." Rosie wiped her runny nose with the back of her hand. "Because it's the only goddamned thing that works."

Chapter 19

Johnnie startled to the sound of clatter, yet he did not know what time it was in the windowless space. Across the dark room, he detected Cud standing, struggling with something in his hands.

As his eyes came into focus, Cud was clearly banging on a can of food with a fork, unsuccessfully.

Cud muttered, "Blimey."

"Hey, how are you feeling?" Johnnie said with a yawn, bringing his recliner to an upright position.

"Oh, did I wake you? I was trying to make breakfast." He held up a can.

Johnnie put on his glasses. *Baked beans, gross.* The other recliner was empty. "Um, where's Daisy?

"Who?" Cud put down the can.

"The woman who brought us here. Daisy. Reddish hair, about your age I think."

Cud stroked his chin. "Yes, I think I recall. I remember her fighting a raccoon. She's a tough lady!"

Johnnie furrowed his brow. "You seem...better. What else do you remember?"

"I had some very agonizing headaches. And I remember being in the hospital. Tell me, why did we run away last night?"

Johnnie erupted from his chair, crossed the room, and hugged his friend. "Cud! It's really you!" His bear hug turned into a gentle embrace as he could feel all the bones in friend's back, and he didn't want to crush him.

"Now, now. Don't make a fuss. Of course, I'm me. But why are we in a science museum? I did a little exploring while you were asleep. Is this one of those interesting sleep-away excursions?"

He let Cud go and noticed the time on the microwave. Five-forty-five. "Hey, we need to get out before they open. Come on."

"Fine, but I was wondering if I could borrow your phone and call Jackson. I'm sure he's worried."

"We can't call him, even if I had my phone. We don't have much time. Let's put this place back the way we found it." He put the other recliners back into their upright positions and rearranged the lumbar pillows.

Cudlow returned the can and fork back to the shelf above the microwave. "Johnnie, why are you so upset?"

"Upset? You think I'm upset?" Johnnie's voice traveled higher with sarcasm. "What, you think I'd be upset trying to keep my best friend from eternal doom?"

"Doom? Pish-posh. Let's just go home."

"Home? Ha! The whole fucking city is looking for you. Follow me. I'll explain over breakfast."

They wound their way back through the utility tunnel and up the rungs to the hatch outside. Once out from underneath the bridge, the sun's rays were blinding. It was going to be another unbearably hot July day.

Cud asked, "Where now?"

Johnnie pulled his wallet from his back pocket. It had a single twenty-dollar bill and his debit card. But knowing how easy it was for law enforcement to track ATM transactions, he couldn't risk getting more cash. "Are you okay with walking? I know a place about a half-mile south of here."

Cud nodded. "Smashing. And then you'll tell me what's been going on these last few days?"

"Yes."

They walked parallel to the water until they reached the only diner Johnnie could remember; the same one he and Darla visited yesterday.

Guided to a familiar booth by the hostess, Johnnie whispered to Cud, "You should take this seat." He motioned to the one where Cud would face away from the other patrons.

"I'll do whatever you ask, as long as I can have some hot tea and some French toast with bangers…or how you say, sausage." Cud smiled and gave a wink.

"Deal." Johnnie recognized that smile. It was as if Cud was the old Cud, living on the beach, without a care. Happy with an effusiveness that gave Johnnie hope about humanity; which was a tall order most days.

Cud picked up the porpoise-shaped salt and pepper shakers and made them swim in the air, leaping while saying, "Whee!" Then he made them kiss. [Mwah mwah] "Oh, these are delightful!"

Their waiter took their order a moment later. Johnnie ordered only corn flakes with milk to stretch their funds.

After some much needed bathroom breaks and receiving their food, they ate quietly until mid-way through their meal.

Cudlow whispered, "Tell me what happened."

"Your son, Elwood…El-fart…whatever…is trying to put you away and steal your company."

"No!"

"Yep." Johnnie slurped the excess milk from his cereal, not wanting to waste a drop.

"And where is Jackson?"

"He's in the Bahamas, at a court hearing this morning to try to stop him."

"Oh, the poor thing." Cudlow lowered his head and closed his eyes. "Bollocks."

"Hey, why does your son hate you so much?"

"I…don't want to talk about it."

"You never told me about your life before."

"Before?"

"You know."

"John," Cudlow knit his eyebrows, revealing a scowl Johnnie had never seen before. "We are friends. I value our friendship. But I've considered our friendship has been predicated on…well, the notion that we don't have to get into each other's business." He picked up the pale white porpoise salt shaker again and pretended it was eating his waffles.

"Oh."

"Don't look at me like that. I'm just a private person. That's all."

"That's all?" Johnnie huffed. "I lost my girlfriend, Stumpy, and my scooter trying to help you. And I don't deserve a simple explanation? Cud, don't be an asshole."

Cudlow put the salt shaker back and pushed away his plate. "I didn't ask you…"

"Yeah? Well, it's too late for that. Come on. We can't stay here."

"Don't be cross."

Johnnie shook his head in disgust, took the check and strode to the cashier, handed over the twenty and said, "Give the change to the server." He pushed open the glass door, with the bell above chiming, and stood in the parking lot, wondering where to go next.

Cud rushed up next to him. "I'm going to find a phone and call Gertie."

All the stress of the last twenty-four hours bubbled up like a volcano and Johnnie couldn't contain his exasperation any longer. "Gertie BROKE UP with you! Can't you FUCKING TAKE A HINT?"

Cud's eyes watered, turning a deep cyan blue. "No. Take it back!"

"She left you at the altar! She said NO! Get it through your thick skull!" He stabbed two fingers at his own skull for emphasis.

"No…that's not right. She loves me. She loves me." Cud walked in tight circles, mumbling, "…loves me. Has to love me… has to…"

Johnnie took cleansing breaths, trying not to be a complete jerk, because Cud was clearly taking this badly. "Stop. I'm sorry. Greta left me, too. I didn't mean…"

Yet, Cud didn't make eye contact. He wandered away, with no clear direction, weaving back and forth through the diner's parking lot, mumbling, "No…no…no."

He chased after him and grabbed his shoulders. "Buddy, I said I'm sorry."

But his friend was no longer there. The glassy look in his eyes had returned.

"Oh, fuck." Johnnie beat his forehead with his palm. "Cud, don't do this. Come back. Please!"

Cud turned catatonic before his eyes.

Johnnie shuffled Cud over to a bench in the shade facing the water.

Out of money, allies, and hope, he now knew why the universe was punishing him.

His next decision could be crucial.

And he'd have to lose his pride and do the right thing.

* * *

~Thirty minutes earlier ~

The sun was shining and the sky was cloudless. Yet the air in the tin can was stuffy and his tail still ached from the previous evening's assault.

169

Tall-face, still asleep next to him, was of no use.

Needing a satisfied stomach, Stumpy scrambled up and inched himself through the window opening, down the side of the hot metal to the black pavement.

The cool morning breeze rippled through his crests, and it was time to seek sustenance.

But this beach was different. Hard surfaces. Little shade. Two sleek palms surrounded by a desert of warm sand.

Humans were scattered on brightly colored beach blankets, smelling of lotion.

A silvery glint caught his attention. A man slipped a loop off his wrist.

This strange place didn't offer the refuge of vegetation to dart in and out unseen. This would be a daring challenge. Still, he ambled toward the water, parallel to his intended prey, considering an angle of attack.

A young human, of one-third size, called out and cooed at him, pointing with a chubby finger. Unsure of its intentions, he froze.

The child tittered and waddled towards him.

Smelling the air, he sensed a yummy offering. The young one had a banana and offered a piece, arm outstretched.

Irresistible. He ambled toward the delicious fruit, rolling his head side to side to better take in the situation and prospects for harm.

Moving closer…closer. All seemed well.

A scream.

An adult protector grabbed the child's hand and dragged it away with admonishment.

His banana prize was lost.

The sound of rain took his attention. A human was showering under a roofed structure.

Stumpy changed direction and moved toward the shady puddles, now with a full-bodied thirst. Lapping the cool liquid and bathing his stomach felt refreshing.

Still, he longed to return home and sit atop his favorite palm. To preside over his kingdom where he knew all and ruled all.

Would Green-tail take over his domain during his absence? That could not happen. He would fight and claw and decimate the long-tailed foe once and for all. If he ever returned.

But his home would not be complete without Johnnie and the old man.

The Merv-man was nice, but could never replace his true friends. The serene, lush beach he called home and his friends were all that mattered.

There was only one way to get through to Merv.

And he would beat him at his own game.

* * *

Merv squinted at the sun. Stretching his back in the cramped car sent shocks of pain throughout his body. He inspected his face in the flip-down visor. His nose was still black and blue, but now decorated with dark circles under his eyes that had sprouted overnight. The ache of the other bruises throughout his body, mostly on his sides, reminded him of the brawl last night. His victory normally would have aroused a sense of satisfaction; yet in the bright light of day, the harsh reality of his short-comings left him saddened.

His flight didn't leave for another four hours, yet he felt the urge to move on from the beach parking lot.

"Hey pal, ready to head out?" He glanced to his right, realizing he was speaking to an empty seat smeared with a wad of gray-green iguana dung instead of Stumpy.

"Stumpy, are you in the back?"

He scanned the vehicle.

Oh, no.

The window he had left open provided an ample gap, wide enough for the intrepid iguana to escape.

Merv donned his sunglasses and exited the vehicle. A few other cars had joined his in the lot since the night before. A twenty-something dude with a crew cut was removing his wetsuit next to a Jeep two spaces down.

"Hey, um, have you seen an iguana around here?"

The guy sat on his bumper and motioned to his right. "Yeah, over in the shower. Scared the shit out of me."

"Thanks." Merv jogged over to the cinderblock structure with open sides. Sure enough, Stumpy was sitting in a puddle left by the shower. He sighed with relief. "Man, I thought I lost you."

Stumpy looked up and cocked his head. [You should take a shower. You stink.]

"Yeah, good idea. I probably don't want to smell up the plane. Stay here." He put a hand out to signal 'halt,' unsure if Stumpy would truly understand.

He returned two minutes later with his bathing suit and a travel-size dandruff shampoo bottle. But Stumpy was gone. Weighing his options, he decided to take a shower first and then finding his leathery friend.

In the men's bathroom, he switched into his Speedo. In the hazy mirror above the porcelain sink, his body looked like a Rorschach test with large blotches of red and dark purple. The largest spot, across his ribs, looked like a red panda. Checking his undercarriage, he knew he should have waxed before he left St. John, because the small bathing suit was not giving enough coverage. He stuffed his stray pubic hairs beneath the Lycra as best as possible.

Out at the shower, the chilly water attacked his skin like ice pellets, causing him to shriek like a wounded cat. But he adjusted to the temperature after a few seconds. On the plus side, despite his injuries, he loved running his hands over his washboard abs and formidable biceps—the payoff of his daily one hundred sit-ups and push-ups. At fifty, he knew he was still an Adonis.

He slicked back his wet hair and washed it, letting the suds run down his face, squeezing his eyes shut. It was refreshing to wipe the grime and sand off his body, and he thought this day could be a rebirth or a new start. *Live clean and fly right,* he thought. *Pure in body and soul...*

Pressure on his foot startled him. He wiped his eyes and looked down. Stumpy had returned and placed his front foot on his.

[Yum time?]

"Hey, don't run off like that! I'll be done soon." He turned his attention back to removing the suds across his chest.

A heavy gold watch landed on his foot.

He picked it up.

A Rolex!

"Stumpy, did you...?"

No one ever expects to be punched in the head. And when they are, time slows down within those milliseconds before you hit the ground.

To Merv, it felt like an explosion on the back of his skull, followed by intense pain radiating down his neck, with the feeling of weightlessness during his free-fall and the bewildering thought of '*What the fuck happened?*'.

Slamming into the concrete wall, with its protruding faucet handles plunging into his collarbone, brought the passage of time back into perspective as he continued his uncontrolled descent.

A man wearing far too many thick gold chains around his neck hovered. "I should call the cops."

Merv didn't know what to say. Water from the shower head rained down on his cringing shape. He couldn't make out the man's facial expression precisely, but he imagined this guy wasn't playing around. "Dude, I never met this iguana before in my life! I was just standing here. What? You want to arrest a reptile?"

The guy picked up his watch and slid it over his hairy wrist. "I don't want to see you back here ever…you got it, peanut dick?"

Merv touched his forehead and found thick blood. "No, I'll never come back."

The angry man walked off, yet Merv sat on the wet concrete for a full minute before attempting to right himself.

Stumpy waddled up and nudged him on his calf. [Yum time?]

"You could have gotten us killed."

The iguana bobbed up and down, enthused.

"It's not funny."

Stumpy slitted his eyes and walked away.

"Not so fast!" He pushed himself off the ground and grabbed Stumpy's stubby tail. "Come on, I'll get us breakfast." Merv picked up Stumpy and cradled him like a football while grabbing his clothes and sneakers with his free hand.

As he walked back to his car, he whispered, "No more stealing…until we get home. Deal?"

Stumpy blinked twice.

Merv detected what he considered a sly smile on the reptile's face.

"Stumpy, did you do that…?"

He wanted to say, 'on purpose', but just hearing himself, he knew it couldn't be true.

Merv sat his friend on the passenger seat and chuckled.

"Yeah, I guess I deserved that."

Chapter 20

Johnnie waved his hand in front of Cud's face. "Buddy? Say something."
No response.

Some divine intervention was needed if they were to get to Lou's, because her apartment was over two miles away and he couldn't carry Cud that distance.

With no phone and no money for a cab, he was faced with almost no good options. Even if they could get a cab and assuming Lou would pay the driver, there was a high possibility that the driver would 'out' them for the reward.

He considered asking a stranger if he could use their phone. Yet, he hadn't memorized Lou's number, which meant he'd have to log into his email to find it. Lou's number and address were also in his journal, but that was at the rental house and he didn't have that address either. It all felt hopeless.

A lime-green Kia pulled into the lot.

Johnnie took notice of this vehicle because an iguana had its head poking out the passenger-side window.

Could it really be?

He trained his eyes on the green car as it pulled into a vacant spot near the diner's entrance, in a handicapped spot. The tall man with the egregiously garish shirt who exited the vehicle looked very familiar.

Johnnie patted Cudlow on the shoulder and said, "Stay here."

Cud didn't respond, remaining like a tree rooted to the ground, keeping his unblinking gaze on some distant spot on the horizon.

Johnnie jogged up to Merv. "What the hell are you doing here? And why is Stumpy with you?"

Merv's eyes bulged, "Whoa! Johnnie...I...um...I was looking for you."

"Bullshit."

"Um...what are *you* doing here?"

His mind blanked as he considered where to start the weird tale, but he had more pressing matters. "Shut up. I need your phone and a ride."

"No way. I'm starving." He pulled on the entrance door.

Johnnie slammed it shut. "Cudlow needs us. Come on." He pulled on Merv's arm.

Merv shouted, "You aren't the boss of me. Settle down!"

Johnnie sized up his co-worker's face, wondering why it was so messed up. "What happened to you?"

"I was in a few altercations and my head is splitting...which is why I'm going to get some GODDAMNED COFFEE first!"

He had no time for this shit. "Just give me your keys."

"Fuck no."

Johnnie sighed. He didn't want to fight Merv, but he would if he had to. "Okay, then give me twenty bucks for a cab."

Merv's eyes lowered onto a newspaper vending box by the front door. "Wait...is that? Jesus, a five-thousand-dollar reward for bringing in Cudlow?"

The newspaper showed Cud's picture with the headline, "Family Seeking Fugitive Billionaire."

"Yeah, but we can't give him back."

"Hold on. Did you kidnap him? That's some cold shady shit."

"NO! It's complicated."

Merv looked around. "Where's your girlfriend Greta?"

"What do you care?" Johnnie sorely wanted to bust Merv's already purple nose, but he knew that wouldn't help Cud. "Fuck it. I need your help. Be the good guy for once."

Merv's eyes brightened, as if he had an epiphany. "You know what, Johnnie boy? Yes. I will help. Merv is at your service."

"Seriously?" In his head, he knew it had to be some kind of sick joke or sarcasm.

"Yeah. I'm not a complete dick-head."

"Hmpf! Had me fooled. Come on, help me get Cud into your car. He's stiff as a fucking board."

After much difficultly folding Cud into the back seat, and some sleuthing through Johnnie's email on Merv's phone to find the address, they were on their way north towards Lou's apartment.

Johnnie, Cudlow, Merv and Stumpy entered the lobby. The doorman gave them a stern look. "Fellows, do you live here?"

Johnnie handed Stumpy over to Merv. "No. Could you ring Dr. Phillips in apartment 2801 for us?

"Is she expecting you?"

"Not exactly. Tell her Johnnie is here with…Harold."

The four of them waited in the glassed-in modern lobby for about three minutes until Lou came rolling out of the elevator, wearing a blue bathrobe over white silky pajamas. "John, thank goodness. How is Harold? I'll call an ambulance to take him back to Princewood."

Johnnie put his hands on Cud's shoulders. "No…no way."

"I'm his doctor. It's not up to you."

"Fine, then we'll just leave and never come back."

Lou sighed. "He has an infection. Do you want me to show you the lab results?"

"No. He was completely fine this morning…until…"

"Until what?"

Residents of the building walked by, giving them stares. Heat rose to his neck with the fear someone would recognize them. "Can we talk upstairs?"

"Yes, but the reptile stays down here."

Merv nodded. "Go on. We'll wait."

"Thanks, Merv." As he uttered these words, Johnnie realized he couldn't remember a time when he thanked Merv for anything. For an instant, he wondered if he was in a bad dream, like that Inception movie. And if that were the case, perhaps he could take control and tweak the narrative with his thoughts to cure Cud and get Greta back. *Create the perfect happy ending…*

Lou shook her head, "Johnnie, are you coming?"

He snapped out of his daydream. "Yes, coming."

A couple of minutes later, Johnnie escorted Cudlow into Lou's apartment. He'd only seen portions of her place during their video sessions, but it was grander and more impressive in person. It looked like it was professionally staged with its pristine white furniture and modern art.

A woman came out of door to his right and rushed toward them. "Lou, who are they? Wait…Johnnie?"

Johnnie grinned. "Hi Ann. Sorry for the intrusion."

"Oh my God, is that Cudlow Loughton?"

Lou nodded, "Ann, babe, could you give us some privacy?"

"Sure, I was going to head to the store, anyway. Text me when the coast is clear." She slung a worn leather cross-body bag over herself and kissed Lou on the head. In an instant, she was out the door.

Lou gestured toward Cud, "When was the last time he spoke?"

"About half an hour ago. It's like he's frozen solid."

"Get him to the sofa and tell me everything."

After Johnnie got Cud settled, he explained how Cudlow was so lucid and happy during breakfast.

"And then what happened?"

Johnnie wanted to lie and say 'nothing'. But Cud's life was on the line, so he swallowed hard and winced, "I yelled at him."

"Why?"

"He was talking as if he and Gertie were still a couple. I got angry. Probably because Greta broke up with me last night. I wasn't thinking clearly."

"She did?"

"Yes, but that doesn't matter right now. See, I told Cud that Gertie didn't love him anymore and to get it through his skull. And he went crazy…walking in circles like a zombie, muttering…and then his lights went out."

Lou scratched her head, "Interesting."

"REALLY? That's all you have to say?"

"It would help if I could run more tests at the hospital."

"Jumping Jesus! Shut up about the stinking tests and shit. The problem is his breakup. Even *I* know that. Fuck, all you doctors ever want to do is run tests and hand out pills!"

"That's not what I'm proposing."

"Look, he has some real mental heartbreak shit going on and you need to fix him."

Lou slammed her hand on her armrest, "Johnnie, I know you care about Cudlow, but there is no magic wand up my sleeve. Stay here. I'm going to get dressed and find my medical bag. I want to listen to his heart and take his blood pressure. Okay?"

Johnnie grumbled, "Sure. But don't call the police or the hospital."

"I wouldn't do that. I don't lie to you, remember?"

He remembered. Their honesty pact was the backbone of her rules for continued therapy, although he knew he often failed in this respect.

After Lou rolled out of sight, Johnnie picked up a magazine about photography from the coffee table and skimmed through the pictures. The wildlife scenes were magical. An article showcased Ann's work with the Nature Conservancy. A picture of a rare albino wombat sleeping with her cubs was stunning.

Out of the corner of his eye, Cudlow rose abruptly and walked in a straight line toward the glass sliding door to the balcony.

"Hey buddy, where are you going?"

"Gully told me I can fly."

Johnnie looked up and saw two seagulls sitting on the metal balcony railing outside. "Who? What are you talking about?"

Cudlow opened the door and stepped onto the balcony. Lou's apartment was on the 28th floor, with ocean views. A gust of warm air blew inside, rustling the pages of his magazine and causing the curtains to flap.

Cud placed his hand on the railing and leaned over. The birds scattered.

"No! Cud! DON'T!" He raced after him and grabbed the back of his shirt, pulling him roughly to the balcony floor and safety. "Are you trying to kill yourself?" This was a rhetorical question because he didn't want to know the true answer. "Please, snap out of this."

Cudlow, sitting in the corner against the building, brought his knees to his chest and stared straight ahead. "She doesn't love me." His voice was less manic now.

"Buddy, I'm sorry. I didn't mean what I said before."

His white-haired friend wrapped his arms over his head and sobbed.

"No, don't cry. It will all be fine. I promise."

"You don't understand. Freddy told me…so many times…I didn't listen."

"You mean Gertie, right?"

"I never listened."

"Tell me what's wrong." He sat next to Cud and rubbed his back.

In between sobs and sniffles, Cud said, "I can't live with it…I don't deserve to be here. My head hurts."

Johnnie shook his head. "Stop. You're scaring me. You are my best friend. Let me help."

Cudlow looked up, his eyes red and moist. "You asked why Elson hates me. The truth is, I hate myself more than he ever could." He got to his feet and lunged for the railing again.

Johnnie grabbed Cud around his middle. "No! If you go, I go." Deep inside, he meant it.

Lou appeared in the doorway, still in her bathrobe, but her hair damp. "Cudlow, let's talk. Please come inside."

Cudlow collapsed on the ground again, becoming completely limp in Johnnie's arms. "I'm so ashamed."

Johnnie cradled Cud, ensuring he had a tight grip, and turned his head to Lou. "Can you leave us for a moment? It will be okay. I promise."

Lou shook her head, "Johnnie, you aren't trained for this."

"Trust me. Give us just *one* minute."

The doctor's eyes bored into his and he could see the fear behind them. And Lou never showed fear in all the time he'd known her.

She said, "If you are not back inside in sixty seconds, I'm calling the police."

Johnnie nodded. "Deal."

Once Lou rolled away from the door opening, he spoke softly to Cud, "Someone wise told me you can't make someone love you…the only thing you can do is give the love in your heart and be there for others. Believe me, I've had so many days where I wanted to jump off a fucking roof." The truth of that statement hit him like a panic attack, making his throat tighten and each breath more difficult. But he persisted, trying to fend off his own breakdown. "Cud, I know I've never said this before… but I need you. You are my best friend. And you've saved me more times than you'll ever know."

"I…I have?"

"Yes. Well, both you and Stumpy. You've shown me that there is joy in life, even when I can't feel it."

Through his sniffles, Cud said, "I expect your progress has more to do with Stumpy."

Cud's attempt at black humor caused Johnnie to smile. He ribbed him back, "Yeah, well, he tells better jokes."

Cudlow chuckled, then continued to sob quietly. Yet Johnnie knew that the sound of his sorrow was different. Instead of tears of dark despair, these were tears and shudders with hope mixed in. And this was evidence enough to know that his friend might truly find his way back after all.

Chapter 21

Jackson straightened his suit jacket and brushed lint from his sleeve. The Magistrate's courtroom in Nassau was warm, despite the circulation of the wicker ceiling fans and the early morning hour.

He bent to his left and whispered to Mama Loughton. "Thank you for coming. I was surprised you agreed to help. Pawpaw told me once you were angry with him when he left the company—that you disowned him."

The wizened old woman in the wheelchair didn't look up from her knitting; she added rows to an already oversized cream-colored chunky-blanket that covered her entire lower half. "Cudlow is too sensitive. I may have called him a horse's ass when he told me he was leaving the company. But what do I care about money at my age, when I can't even take a dump by myself?"

"Shh! The others will hear."

Mama Loughton smirked and stuck out her tongue.

Jackson sighed and glanced across the aisle toward the plaintiff's table.

He whispered to Felicity to his right. "Who is that ghastly man? The one with the cystic acne? Is that the same…?"

She whispered back, "Richard Greaves. As I was leaving the ladies' room with your great-grandmother, he pounced on me to introduce himself. He's your father's lawyer."

"Is father coming?"

"No. Elson plans to speak to the judge by video conference." She pointed to a large LED flat-screen on a cart to the left of Greaves.

"Hmm." Jackson regarded Mama Loughton, sitting to his left. The hump on her back gave her a snail's shape. Her glasses were as thick as French

Macarons. "Grandmother, aren't you warm with that lap blanket?"

She glanced his way but kept knitting. In a tone far above a respectful whisper, she replied, "I'm fine. When is this motherfucker getting started? I'm missing The View."

"Shhh. You shouldn't use that language here. Please."

"I'm a hundred years old. Don't tell me how to talk."

"I'm only saying, the judge might not like it."

"When she gets to be my age, she can tell me what to do."

Jackson tried to work out the math of that one, but chose not to argue.

The human dung beetle named Greaves slithered over, his wide scuffed dress shoes squeaking on the terrazzo floor. "Jackson, I don't think we've met. Richard Greaves." He extended a glistening palm.

Jackson refused the handshake. "I know who you are."

"Sonny boy, you've done a great job these years, at least as best as someone your age could be expected to. But it's time for the grownups to handle the family business, understand?"

"I will never hand over Loughton Enterprises to my rotten father."

"Whoa. Why so bitter? You've got a golden opportunity here. He's prepared to keep you on as Chief Operations Officer. Let you run the day to day. You should take the deal now, while your daddy is feeling generous."

"Fuck you and fuck him."

"Sorry, hey, don't say I didn't try to be cordial," he smirked. As he sauntered back over to his table, he pulled some tissues from his suit pocket to mop his brow. But a used Q-Tip, covered in bright orange wax, fell out of his pocket and bounced on the floor, unnoticed by the grotesque human blob.

The room came to order as the Chief Magistrate entered. She wore a royal blue robe, plus the traditional Colonial curly wig—in the shape of a rectangle—on top of her braided black chignon. The bailiff called, "Rise for her honor, Judge Maxine Bastian."

Judge Bastian instructed everyone to sit, proceeding to review some papers in front of her. The silence in the air was thick.

Greaves raised his hand. "Judge, may I begin—"

"Sir, I have not called on you yet. You will *know* when I call on you to *speak*, because I will call your name, Mr. Greaves."

Judge Bastian looked up from her dais and darted her eyes toward Jackson's side of the room. "Ms. Felicity Jones, I take it that this is your first time before my court?"

"Yes, Judge."

"And I presume the woman to your left is Mrs. Camille Loughton, Mr. Cudlow Loughton's biological mother?"

"Yes, Judge."

"How old is Mrs. Loughton again?"

"One hundred, your Honor."

Mama Loughton put down her knitting needles and croaked, "I'm right here! Don't act like I'm not here."

The judge ignored the outburst. "And you purport she should act as Mr. Loughton's temporary guardian?"

Across the aisle, Greaves cleared his throat. "AHEM! Judge, that is precisely our point—"

Judge Bastian pointed her finger. "Sir, if you interrupt one more time, I will place you in contempt of court."

Mama added, "You tell 'em sister!"

Felicity nodded. "Although Mr. Elson Loughton, Cudlow's son, is technically next of kin, we believe his mother, Camille Loughton, has Cudlow's best interests at heart. A judge in Miami has already granted her a temporary guardianship for seventy-two hours to allow doctors to assess his condition."

The judge went back to reading. "Loughton Enterprises is currently managed by Jackson Loughton?"

Jackson spoke, "Yes, your Honor. That's me."

"Hmm-mm." She furrowed her brow. "And where is the plaintiff, Mr. Elson Loughton?"

Greaves glowered. "Is it my turn now?" His sarcasm was punctuated by a nasal whine.

"Yes, Mr. Greaves. Is your client present?"

"Given the urgency of this matter, he couldn't arrange for travel from London to be here today, but we've arranged with the bailiff to set up a video conference."

"Well, get him on. What are you waiting for?"

After some fiddling with the remote, Elson's face appeared on the screen.

From the angle, Jackson couldn't see his father well, but could hear him clearly.

The judge continued, "Mr. Elson Loughton, I read the petition and watched the video that accompanied it. Your father appears quite ill. So, I understand that this is an urgent matter. What I don't understand—please help me here—is why you are asking this court to turn over a billion-dollar company to your control, when clearly, your father had you removed from the business a decade ago."

Greaves interjected, "I can clear that up."

"I *didn't ask* you." She shot him a look that would make any man's balls shrivel.

Elson replied as if reading a prepared script, "My father's mental health has been questionable for a very long time. I believe he removed me from the company at the earliest stages of his illness...a rash incoherent move. Which only amplifies why I must take control. By his own words, my son Jackson informed me how Cudlow worked around the clock recently for a month, adding to his poor health. Clearly, running the business has contributed to the further decline of his mental health."

Jackson couldn't believe his ears. *Only his evil father would sink so low.*

Judge Bastian turned to Felicity. "I read the letter from Doctor Louisa Phillips of Miami, Florida. She confirms Mr. Loughton's mental issues. Does she have a diagnosis yet?"

"Yes, Ma'am. Very preliminary." She held up a piece of paper. "It is her assertion that Mr. Loughton—Cudlow—has brain swelling from a Zika infection. An infection he likely received during his recent trip to the Galapagos. It should be fully treatable. I have a copy of the lab results."

The judge looked over her glasses. "When did Dr. Phillips learn this?"

"Late last night. May I approach?"

Greaves yelled, "May we BOTH approach? Why is this the first time we are hearing this? I smell deceit!" He waved his arms in the air and stomped his foot in mock outrage.

Mama Loughton perked up and said, "HA! You smell your own shitty farts! PEE-YEW!"

Jackson smiled. He offered his hand to Mama and whispered, "Well done." She gave his hand a squeeze in solidarity.

The judge banged her gavel. [BANG] "Mrs. Loughton, I won't have any of your outbursts either."

Mama waved, "Fine. I'm leaving." She placed her aluminum knitting needles on her lap and used the joystick to engage her electric wheelchair. Reversing from the table, she then surged forward, navigating down the side aisle. A guard at the back of the room opened the heavy wood door for her.

Before she left, she announced, "That short asshole stunk up the hallway before. Worse'n wild pig excrement, I tell ya. Hey, Elson! Grandpa Albert asked me to give you a warning. Knock off this shit or he'll send Margaret Thatcher to haunt you AND your dead rodents!"

A group of reporters sitting in the back of the room broke out in roaring laughter. One of them followed Mama outside the room.

Judge Bastian banged her gavel. [BANG BANG BANG] "SILENCE!" The room quieted. "Bailiff, hand me the lab results from Ms. Jones."

After reading it, she asked Felicity, "Where is Mr. Loughton right now?"

Jackson's heart raced. Cudlow was still missing, which didn't enhance their case.

"Your honor?" Jackson raised his hand.

"Yes? Stand up."

Jackson smoothed his tie and stood, unsure of whether to make direct eye contact. "My grandfather is missing. He evaded the security at the hospital in Miami. I'm sure my father will tell you it is all my fault. And perhaps it is. It was my decision to take him there. I take full responsibility."

"Tell me, young man, *why* don't you want your father Elson to have medical proxy?"

Jackson glanced at Felicity for guidance.

She nodded and whispered, "It's okay. Just speak from your heart."

He took a deep breath, feeling as if he had already lost. "Your honor, my father is a bitter man. He has told me many times that he hates paw…I mean grandfather. I worry he'll act in retaliation, choosing to keep him confined with no effort for treatment."

"I see. And do you have any proof of this intention?"

He thought hard. "Not precisely. But if father truly cared, he'd leave the company out of this."

"Thank you. Please sit. I'm not a family counselor, nor do I choose to be. I'll issue my ruling in one hour. Adjourned."

She gaveled out and erupted from her chair with a flourish of her blue robe. Before the bailiff could get out the words, "All rise," she had exited through the rear door.

Felicity put her hand on Jackson's shoulder. "Don't worry. You did fine."

Everyone filed out of the room and into the hallway.

They found Mama Loughton talking with a reporter down the hall by the water fountain. The last thing Jackson needed. *Hadn't they been through enough airing of the family's dirty laundry?*

Felicity tapped the reporter on the shoulder. "Leave her alone. Now!"

The reporter, a young man with a goatee, grinned. "Mrs. Loughton has been entertaining me with her stories. She was just telling me about how she met Cudlow's father, Albert, during World War II. Fascinating. And she still sees his ghost."

Jackson loosened his tie, unable to contain his decorum any longer. He raised a fist at the reporter and yelled, "Bugger off!"

The reporter put away his notepad and nodded. "Nice talking with you, Camille." He smiled and walked away.

An awful smell wafted through the hall. Jackson couldn't place it. Something between raw sewage and roasted nuts. *Did his grandmother need a new Depends?*

The answer became obvious. Sure enough, Greaves was waddling towards them. "Hey, did you see the news last night? Cudlow was kidnapped by that loser, the St. Johnnie Killer! Saw it with my own eyes. Wowee! Maybe poor ol' Cudlow will end up as a corpse on Miami beach. Ha! Better luck next time, kiddo."

Jackson couldn't take it any longer. "Fuck off, Greaves."

Mama Loughton wheeled toward the skeevy lawyer. From a slot on the side of her wheelchair, she pulled out her bent-wood cane and smacked Greaves across the kneecaps. [WHACK] "Get out, you verminous creep!" She whacked him again on his shoulder for good measure.

"Ow! I'll sue you for battery! Stop!" Greaves backed away a few feet and rubbed his shins.

"Ha! You can't put me in prison! I'm a centenarian! Hee, hee!" Mama accelerated towards him, waving her wooden cane. "Come back! I'll give you such a wup'n!"

Greaves fled through the hallway. No passersby, nor any law enforcement, offered the screaming lawyer any aid or intervention.

Felicity said, "Let's get coffee and come back. They'll call when the judge has a verdict."

Jackson chuckled, "We should wait for Mama Loughton."

"I have some calls to make. Meet me at the café around the corner. I'll save us a table."

"Will do."

Jackson waited in the hallway, hoping Mama Loughton would return soon. He checked his phone. Dr. Phillips had emailed a few minutes earlier, stating she still hadn't been able to get through to Johnnie.

Five minutes later, Mama came around the corner, her cane broken into two pieces on her lap. "Jackson, we can go now." She inspected the splintered wood. "Darn it. I'm out of superglue."

"I'll buy you another. What did you do?"

"I chased that rat two blocks. Told him what for. But then I got chest pains."

"Oh, Grannie, are you okay?"

"I'm fine. Just over-did it. Look! See? He's still here."

"Who?" He scanned the empty space.

"My Albert! Right over there."

Jackson wasn't falling for her usual trick. "Grannie, I need to ask you something. Why does father hate Pawpaw so deeply?"

She sighed and wiped sweat from her forehead. "It's warm in here, isn't it?"

"Yes, it is. Please tell me. I can't take it anymore."

She leaned in close. "It's not really my place. I try not to get involved but given the situation, it's about time you knew." Camille whispered, "Don't tell Cudlow I said anything, promise?"

"I promise." He crossed his heart.

"Your grandmother, Winnifred, she had hidden letters. Love letters from an old beau…a man she'd dated at college before she met Cudlow. Well, one day, about six months into Winnie's cancer treatment, your father came to visit and offered to make space in her room for her new hospital bed. Elson moved a dresser and found a box full of letters. Being a nosy sort, he read them. See, the thing was, Winnie was corresponding with her old flame for several years, until she was diagnosed. She wrote about leaving Cudlow and how she didn't love him anymore." Camille put her hand on his. "I mean, who could blame her? Cudlow was a workaholic and overall cold fish back then."

"Oh no!"

"Oh yes! And when she passed, Elson threw this secret in Cudlow's face at the funeral. Blamed him for Winnie's death and her unhappy life." Mama Loughton lifted the broken pieces of her cane and adjusted her lap blanket beneath. "Of course, Cudlow was blindsided…devastated. That's why he ran away. I thought he'd be gone for a couple of months. You know," she waved her hand in a circular motion, "to grieve and work out his feelings. Then, after a year, I thought, maybe Cudlow was happier away from the business and enjoying retirement. Well…you know the rest."

"My father is a bleeding asshole."

"Oh, yes, he can be a righteous prick. But he deeply loved his monther Winnifred. They were thick as thieves, those two. When Elson was growing up, Cudlow said those two watched old movies or played cards for hours most weekends, often without him. Jackson, if you had seen the sorrow in Elson's eyes…I imagine he said those terrible things to your grandfather out of grief." She gave a weak smile. "Problem is, sometimes you say a thing and it can never be unsaid."

Jackson recalled how Grandmaw Winnie taught him how to play Hearts when he was nine; she had a light in her face and hid cards up her sleeve to play jokes on him. She had a way of teasing in such a playfully absurd way…hoping to be discovered…making amends with a hug or tickle. The times he visited Grandmaw were some of the happiest of his childhood. With this new information, he understood how his father would have loved her as much as everyone else did…perhaps more so. "Do you think they'll ever reconcile?"

"Dear-heart, what matters is your life. Don't make the same mistakes. Find someone to love and never let them go. Just like me and Albert. He visits me every day." Her shoulders slumped, and she dropped the halves of the cane, causing a clamor on the hard floor.

"Grannie, are you feeling all right?"

She squinted behind her thick lenses. "Albert is coming closer. He says Cudlow will be fine now. And…I have to go."

"Come on, stop playing Grannie."

She pointed a gnarled finger down the hall. "There, in the circle of light. So handsome…"

Jackson swung his head, arching his neck higher. "There is no…"

When he reset his gaze on Mama Loughton, her face hung down at an unnatural angle, with a stillness in both her eyes and her hands only found in the deceased.

Was she gone? He lifted her chin. "Grannie! Come now! Are you all right? Grannie!"

He leapt off the bench and raced down the hall to the security desk. "Quick, I need an ambulance. My grandmother is ill."

The security guard called for medical help and jogged back to the scene with Jackson.

Five minutes later, in the ambulance, the medics pronounced Mama Loughton dead.

Chapter 22

Jackson's phone rang while he was in the hospital mortuary. *It was Felicity*. He had to take it.

Without the usual pleasantries, she got to the point, "The judge gave her ruling at ten-thirty."

"What happened?" He paced in a wide circle, staring at the polished floor. The anticipation and cool air of the basement morgue sent a chill down his spine. "Did father win?"

"She's holding her final ruling in abeyance for thirty-days, pending further evaluation of Cudlow's health. Assuming he surfaces again."

"That's good, right?"

"Yes, we'll live to fight another day. Greaves was gloating earlier over the news of Camille's death; but he was quite cross when he heard the judge's order."

He stopped pacing. "So…who has medical proxy until then?"

"You do."

Jackson exhaled with relief. A text message popped up on his phone. "Hold on…oh thank God. Dr. Phillips just texted that Pawpaw is at her place with Johnnie."

"That's wonderful news. Call me later."

"Absolutely." He ended the call with Felicity and called the doctor. "How is he?"

"He wants to tell you himself. I'll put him on."

He waited until he heard his grandfather's voice.

"Jackson, I'm so sorry. I know I made you worry and caused such trouble for you. I hope you can forgive me."

"Paw, you sound better. How are you feeling?"

"I feel like myself at the moment. Doctor Phillips has a treatment plan laid out. And I want to go home."

"Home...where?"

"To Nassau. The good doctor here has arranged for an excellent physician to care for me at the hospital there."

"I can't wait to see you."

"The thing is, besides treating the infection, I have a bit of work to do...on myself. I'll need some time away to process everything in a safe setting."

"Yes, I understand. Take as much time as you need." Jackson grimaced. "I don't want to add to your burden, but I have some sad news. Camille passed away."

After a long pause, Cudlow said, "I expect she's with my father now."

Jackson smiled. "It seems as if he never left her."

"Yes. She always claimed to see his ghost. You need to find a love like that and stop worrying about an old fart like me."

"That's what she said."

"Ha! I'll be home soon. I love you, Jackson."

Hearing his grandfather's laugh made his spirit soar. "I love you, too."

* * *

Two hours later, after retrieving their luggage from the rental house in Miami, Johnnie, Cudlow, Merv and Stumpy boarded a private jet—courtesy of Loughton Enterprises. They planned to fly to the Bahamas first, leaving Cudlow with Jackson; the second part of the flight would deliver Johnnie, Merv and Stumpy to the airport on St. Thomas.

Cudlow and Johnnie took seats in the cabin's first row. Stumpy scrambled on top of the window ledge to enjoy the view. Merv stumbled to toward the rear of the cabin, complaining about wanting some quiet time and 'shut eye'.

After the plane reach its cruising altitude, Johnnie popped open a can of soda. "Cud, have you thought about your plans after the hospital and therapy?"

Cudlow reclined the back of his seat and intertwined his fingers across his chest. "Well, the first thing I need to do is ensure the company is safely within Jackson's ownership. But Felicity can handle most of that."

"No, I mean, where will you live?"

"Yes, I know what you meant. I'd like to continue living on St. John."

"What about Gertie?"

"I still love her. But I can…I will…let her go if that is her wish."

"When we got our luggage earlier at the house? I saw a note from Greta. She told me not to call her."

"How do you feel about that?"

Johnnie wasn't sure how long his heartache would last, but he was sure of one thing. "I just want her to be happy."

"Precisely. Just as I want Gertie to be happy." Cudlow turned his head toward the side window and stared at the clouds.

"Cud?"

"Yes?"

"When you come back to St. John…would you consider moving in with me?"

His white-haired friend looked at him quizzically. "Oh, please, you don't want that."

"I've thought about it many times. You shouldn't go back to the beach."

"Hmm. I'll tell you what. How about I stay with you temporarily— maybe a few weeks or months—until I sort out a more permanent option?"

Johnnie grinned. "I would like that. Thank you."

Cud's eyes sparkled with excitement. "I've been thinking about purchasing a small beach-front parcel and building a simple cottage with a thatched roof and a wide porch. Not much bigger than your current apartment. You know, one of those tiny homes that are so popular with the new generation. Something under the trees." Cudlow waved and pointed. "Over there, hand me your coaster. I'll sketch it for you."

From the back of the plane, Merv's snores erupted like a foghorn. [HONK…zzzz…HONK]

Cudlow giggled. "Poor Ranger Merv. I guess his broken nose means his little game caught up with him."

"Game?" Johnnie handed Cud his new damp coaster.

"Yes, the reason he absconded with Stumpy." Cud turned over the cardboard to the dry side and clicked his ballpoint pen to draw.

"Wait, what?"

"You know, how he supplements his income to cover his sports wagers. I've overheard him several times speaking with his bookie. Merv's luck is quite poor."

"Cud...I have no fucking idea what you're talking about."

Cudlow stopped drawing and met his eyes. "He's trained Stumpy to steal jewelry and wallets from the tourists in exchange for dried fruit and other snacks. I thought you knew..."

"Jumping Johosephat... are you shitting me?"

"I've seen their secret exchanges many times. He really should be more careful." He continued his cartoonish sketch. It was clear Cudlow would have failed architecture school.

"How long has this been going on? You should have told someone!"

Cud laughed, "Johnnie, you know this more than anyone...I don't get involved."

* * *

Johnnie and Stumpy arrived at the Cruz Bay ferry dock at two in the afternoon. Merv was on the same ferry, yet they parted ways and sat on opposite ends of the boat. There really wasn't anything left to say. Merv had made him swear not to tell their supervisor Kemper about the thievery. Johnnie said he couldn't promise that, because he was trying to be a more honest person.

"How about this?" Merv had said. "Only tell her if she asks you directly. I promise I won't steal anymore. Scouts honor."

Johnnie huffed, "What, were you a Boy Scout?"

"I made Eagle."

"Jumpin' Jesus. What the fuck happened to you?"

"Don't know exactly...I developed some bad habits. But I swear, I'll change."

That was the moment Johnnie didn't want to hear anymore of Merv's bullshit. Not that he considered himself to be completely pure of heart and mind. In fact, it would be completely hypocritical for him to look down on Merv and his failings. But he hated the fact that he enlisted Stumpy in his sordid scheme. "Fine. I won't say anything as long as you stay away from Stumpy. And we never talk about this again."

"Yes, absolutely. You got it, bro!"

Now, with his duffel over one shoulder and Stumpy on his other, Johnnie kept his gaze forward, disembarking from the ferry and following the throng of visitors down the pier.

His older sister, Robin—dressed in her white skirt suit and wearing navy pumps—stood waiting on the sidewalk for him. Her brown hair was in a messy bun and while she was objectively pretty, she had that familiar wrinkle between her eyebrows that conveyed almost perpetual annoyance with him.

When he reached her, he planted his feet apart and set his duffle on the ground. "Hey."

She tsked. "I can't believe you brought Stumpy with you again."

Her tone was a bit too judgmental for his taste. He gritted his teeth and counted to himself. "It was Cud's idea." With his right hand, he stroked the iguana on his shoulder.

Tourists passed by in clumps, chattering inane things like, "I saw this cute straw hat...it's beer-o'clock somewhere...I'm going to sue the airline...Is that a real iguana?" He'd learned the hard way never to make eye contact with strangers.

Robin dangled a key ring. "Jackson bought you a car. Dottie picked it up yesterday and brought it over from St. Thomas." She gestured to a shiny blue Jeep Compass parked on the street.

"Damn. Cool." He considered jogging over to inspect it, but that would be rude, so he stared at the ground.

Robin punched him in the shoulder. "Try not to kill anyone."

"Ha, ha. That was so funny I forgot to laugh." He rolled his eyes upward. "How is Cudlow?"

He crossed his arms and rocked back and forth on his heels. "He'll be in the hospital for a few weeks. I'm going to try to visit when I can. His mother's funeral will be held next weekend. I want to be there for him." Johnnie realized he was talking quickly, trying to stave off the real question between them.

Anxiety bubbled up in his throat as he waited for his sister's response.

With a tilt of her head and cutting tone, Robin asked, "So, are we talking again?"

And there it was—the elephant in the room. He wrung his hands. "Seems that way."

His response must have irked her, because she narrowed her eyes to slits. "Butthead." She threw the keys at him. "I'm going back to work. Call me when you're ready to apologize."

"No, wait. I'm sorry, sis." He placed Stumpy on the curb next to his duffel bag and knelt to retrieve the keys that had ricocheted off his chest. He hurried after his older sister and tapped her arm. "I really fucked up and I know I've been a jackass."

She huffed and swept stray hair from her eyes. "Damn straight." Her expression softened. "John, I hate to admit this, but I've missed you. And I'm sorry things didn't work out with Greta."

"Oh, for fuck's sake. HOW do you know that already?"

"Um, because Dottie works for me?"

"Shit. Right." He shook his head, although it made perfect sense.

"Come on, let's get out of the sun and grab a beer. Tell me all about it."

"I thought you had to get back to the office."

"I can make time."

They sauntered across the street to the Yellow Parrot and took seats at the bar. Mandy, the bar-keep, placed four cherries on a napkin and clucked her tongue. Johnnie sat Stumpy down on the bar top and the iguana scampered excitedly toward the fruity treat.

During the first beer, Johnnie relayed the story about the evening press conference with Greaves in front of the hospital and how they escaped to the museum.

Robin rested her chin on her palm. "That woman you were with—from the news footage—what was her name?"

He had to think about that one. "I can't remember. When we woke up the next morning, she was gone. I began to wonder if she was real."

"I know this will sound crazy, but she reminded me of mom."

The neurons in his gray matter sought more information, but he could only recall a flickering feeling of déjà vu when the woman said his name. "But mom died."

"Yes. The day after you came back from Afghanistan."

They sipped more beer. The alcohol gave him a rush at first. But now, working on his second beer, more depressed thoughts and self-pity took root. "I saw Darla."

"Holy shit. How did that go?"

"She said I had *always been* an asshole. Even before the accident. I mean, fuck. Maybe I'll never have a good relationship."

Stumpy wandered up and nudged his hand. He stroked the iguana's chin. "At least, not with a human." He hung his head and told Robin about Greta finding his diary and how he confronted her at the hotel. "She probably hates my living guts."

Robin tousled Johnnie's hair. A move signaling she was inebriated from her beer, because she wasn't usually so affectionate. "John, let me tell you this. No man is perfect. Most women know this…cause it's a frickin' fact. It sounds to me like you need to grovel. Grov-ELL. Apologize to Greta and keep apologizing. Then grovel some more. And if that doesn't work, I guess you'll have to let her go. But I hope she takes you back because I really like her."

Johnnie pushed his empty bottle away. "I really like her too."

His sister chuckled and shouted to the ceiling, "Fuck the Goddess! I bet she's a stuck-up royal bitch."

"Whoa, settle down. I think you've had enough to drink."

She laughed darkly, "Yeah, but not enough alcohol to get through the finance committee meeting at four."

"Let me walk you back." Johnnie settled the tab and left a generous tip for Mandy.

As Mandy scooped up the bills, Johnnie asked her if she could watch Stumpy and his bag for a few minutes. She just smiled with a nod and waved at him to go.

Johnnie helped Robin off her bar seat, ensuring she didn't topple over. Her slim, five-foot-two frame clearly didn't have enough body mass to handle two beers.

During the quarter-mile walk to the legislature annex building, he enjoyed listening to Robin complain about the futility of her next meeting while loopy and relaxed, unlike her usual high-strung, hyper-responsible self.

She waved her hands and mumbled, "Fucking appropriations committee is taking forever and, of course, their voice mail is always full. They won't answer one fucking question." She raised two middle fingers skyward for emphasis.

He felt like a schmuck, realizing he hadn't asked her about her personal life. "Hey, how are things with you and Arturo?"

Robin grinned. "A lady never tells."

"That good?"

"Yes, Art is amazing. He can compartmentalize all his work shit. You know how I'm always stressed? Artie can deal with drug overdoses, domestic disputes, and confront all kinds of heinous tragedy, and still come home, take off his uniform, and act as if he was playing with puppies all day long. Damn. I need to learn how to do that."

Johnnie laughed. "Yes, you need to chill sometimes."

"Oh, shut up, butthead. Although you'd appreciate how much fun I'm having with Dottie. She keeps trying to pry information about my relationship with Art. She's as subtle as a heart-attack. I can tell my silence is eating her up."

Johnnie looked up the sidewalk. *Speak of the devil.* Dottie was waiting at the Legislature entrance, as if she had ESP and predicted Robin's precise arrival time.

He wondered which one of Dot's spies had notified her of their movements. "Good afternoon, Dottie. She's all yours." He scanned the street for web cams.

Dot grinned and held open the door for Robin. "Nice to see you, Johnnie. Give my best to Cudlow and Jackson and tell them I'm praying for them."

Not believing in prayer himself, he imagined trying to pass on this message to Cud convincingly. However, to be polite, he just said, "I will."

After the two women entered the building, he remained glued to the sidewalk, knowing that the public library was just another two blocks up the street.

Every cell in his body wanted to run towards the library and begin the groveling process.

Johnnie counted on his fingers. The conference in Miami ended this afternoon and Greta wouldn't be back until late tonight.

But he couldn't fuck up another time.

He needed to write out a speech.

And it needed to be the most sincere and amazing apology in recorded history.

Chapter 23

The next afternoon, Johnnie finished work at three. All day long, he'd thought about what he would say to Greta and how he would say it. Now, faced with the actual mission just minutes away, his mind blanked.

All the impressive words he had strung together in his mind had vanished, like grains of dust blown away in a nuclear explosion. Intrinsically, he knew they would never come back.

He parked his new Jeep near the library, then climbed the steps toward the front door. Still in his park uniform and boots, he understood he had to avoid making a scene with Greta. Park Service rules required a certain decorum when wearing the uniform in public. A factor he hoped would benefit him.

Entering the building, the check-out desk was directly ahead. His nemesis, Ms. Teller—the elderly head librarian—looked up from her computer screen and gave him a look that could kill a small bird.

In his head, he recalled his sister's words. She had once said he was the bravest person she knew. Yet he wanted to run. He would rather face another Taliban fighter than Ms. Teller.

She smiled in a manner more like an evil grin, with blood red lipstick that oozed into the wrinkles above her lip. "Good afternoon, Mr. Crosswell."

"Good afternoon." He took off his cap and flipped up his sunglass lenses. "Is Ms. Hobbs in?"

Teller turned her attention back to her screen, in a manner so dismissive it stung. "Ms. Hobbs doesn't get off until five."

"So, she's here?"

"If this is a personal matter, I suggest you contact her after business hours."

He closed his eyes in frustration. His goal of *complete honesty in all things* was not meant to cover situations dealing with evil hags. "I have a question for her about a book."

"What is it? I'm sure I can answer it."

Shit.

He scanned the adjoining rooms. In the wing to the right, he saw a flash of red hair. Greta was standing beside a rolling cart, shelving books.

"I don't want to trouble you. Bye." Before Ms. Teller could protest, he strode through the arched entry, across the non-fiction section toward Greta. "Hey."

She glanced up from the book spine she'd been inspecting. Her head swiveled like she was an antelope spooked by a cheetah; Greta walked behind the book cart to create a barrier between them. "What are you doing here?" she whispered.

In a hushed tone, he said, "I wanted to make sure that you are okay and to apologize."

"I'm fine. You should leave."

"Can we talk later?"

Her eyes turned moist. "There isn't anything left to say." She hugged an oversized hard-cover book about the Napoleonic wars.

"That can't be true because I love you."

"Why…why should I believe you?"

Ms. Teller tapped him on the shoulder. "Mr. Crosswell, I thought I made it clear. I'm asking you to leave."

He spun, trying to maintain composure. In a quiet, measured tone, he responded, "Ms. Teller, this is none of your concern."

Teller's facial muscles clenched with fury. "This is MY LIBRARY. EVERYTHING that happens here is MY CONCERN. Greta, come with me please."

It was like a western show-down. No one wanted to flinch first. Greta placed the heavy book on the cart and crossed her arms. In a mirroring fashion, Teller placed her hands on her hips and jutted her pointed chin. He stood between them, knowing none of this would go well. A memory flashed through his head of a young Afghan farm boy trying to stop two goats from head-butting each other. It hadn't gone well.

Ms. Teller snorted, "Mr. Johnnie Crosswell, leave now or I'll call Chief Tobias."

She was referring to the head of the St. John police department; the only other person on the island who had tormented him at equal measure.

Greta said, "Really? He's done nothing wrong."

"I asked him to leave, and he's still standing here. It's called trespass."

It was time for him to step away and de-escalate. "Ms. Teller, you have a blessed day. Greta, I'm sorry I troubled you. Good day." He donned his cap, strode past Satan's sister and headed outside.

The heat of the sun's rays matched the temperature of his face. With his breath knocked out of him, he sat on the steps half-way down and bent his head.

Unable to move, he evaluated all the mistakes that just occurred and fought back the urge to cry or hit something.

How would he have the chance to grovel if he couldn't talk to her? Would Ms. Teller ban him from the library again? Was he an idiot to think he'd ever find true love?

Baking himself in the blazing afternoon sun wasn't the answer to any of these questions.

He pulled himself upright and dusted off the seat of his green cotton pants.

Greta jogged down the steps, "John."

"Greta, let me explain."

She gave him a guarded look. "You have one-minute."

He didn't have time to arrange his words. Inhaling deeply, he prepared for his unprepared speech.

"I love you and I know you don't believe it and sometimes I wonder if I can love anyone with my damaged head…and look, I know the goddess isn't real…not like a real person…more like a dumb idiotic fantasy…not fantasy…do you know what I'm saying? But I know now that love is about caring about someone…being there for them…and I want us to have that. Love means you can't take someone for granted…you have to show them. And you have to show the love inside your heart every day. I'm not perfect. I fuck up all the time. And you really deserve someone better. I only know that you've changed me…and I want to keep changing and become someone you might learn to love."

Johnnie inhaled to refill his depleted lungs. There were probably thirty more seconds on the artificial clock, but he left it there.

She cocked her head to the side and fixed her gaze beyond him. "Is that your car?"

He wiped his eyes and glanced back at the Jeep. "Yes, Jackson gave it to me. To replace the Flying Pig."

"Jackson had asked me what your favorite color was. I like it."

"Well? Is that all you have to say?"

She chewed on her fingernail and nodded. "Meet me at 5:30 at Mama Jo's."

He grinned so hard his face hurt. Mama Jo's restaurant was the location of their first date, which gave him hope. "Does that mean you forgive me?"

"Let's have dinner and figure it out."

"Yes, good idea."

She walked down the three steps toward him and gave him a peck on the cheek. In a whisper, she said, "You aren't as fucked-up as you think."

Johnnie stood transfixed as she turned and headed back up the steps to the library. "See you later, Ms. Khan."

Greta turned and squinted her eyes with her hand shading them. "Hey, how about...we just be *ourselves* from now on?"

He nodded. "Yes, I'd like that."

After she entered the building, he bounced down the steps with his chest feeling as light as a helium balloon.

Maybe this chapter would have a happy ending.

And he wouldn't need to wear Viking horns after all.

* * *

Elson finished his lecture and cleaned the whiteboard as his students filed out. His phone rang.

It was Greaves.

"Hello, Mr. Greaves."

"Hey Elliot, I just talked to your son, Jacko. He told me your old man is acting normal again."

"*My name* is Elson. So?"

"Well, look, I know you wanted to appeal, but I got other clients. My time is valuable. So, unless you want to pay me upfront, let's say, twenty-five G's to start, I've got to move on."

"No, but my father is insane. He's lived on a public beach for a decade.

Surely, the *right* judge will understand…"

"Hey, no hard feelings. We gave it all we had. See, my paralegals called around. The hospital he checked himself into? Well, a nurse there said Dudley was…"

"You mean, Cudlow."

"Yeah, Dudlow was cracking jokes and telling stories to the staff. The nurse said he was utterly delightful or some shit. Not cuckoo like before."

Elson huffed. "But, for all we know, it could be temporary."

"Yeah, so call me if he goes looney bird again. Bye now."

Before Elson could utter a word, the line went dead. "Hello? Hello? Bollocks."

The door to the lecture hall slammed.

Henrietta rushed towards him. She was wearing her pink bunny-slippers and a red tracksuit. "WANKER! You bastard! You don't think I read the papers?"

"Honeybun, what are you talking about?" He retreated behind the lectern for protection.

"You hired a lawyer? Tried to take back the company without telling me?"

"No…father was ill. I didn't think you cared."

She stalked towards him with her arm raised to strike. "Jackson called me. Told me everything."

"Since when do you listen to that traitor?"

"He wants us to be a family again. If you apologize."

"I'll do no such thing."

"Arsehole. You didn't even tell me that Camille died."

"I thought you wanted a divorce."

"You got that right. Well, I don't bloody care what you do, but I'm going to spend time with my boy and go to the funeral."

Elson stared at her. "Ha! You only want to ingratiate yourself with Jackson to latch onto his money."

She spat on him; a wad of white foamy spittle landed on his jacket collar. "You don't know how to love anyone but yourself. Jackson is a good kid and I've missed him. A mother needs her son. Get bent." Hen stormed out again, slamming the door behind her.

Elson smirked. Getting Henrietta out of his life was reward enough.

He opened his briefcase and removed the lid of the Tupperware container to gaze upon its contents. "You are my *real* friend, aren't you?"

The bloodied baby tawny owl he'd picked up in the street earlier stared at him with dull eyes.

Closing the lid, he stroked the container lovingly.

This new project would be his masterpiece and his new companion.

Deep inside, he felt he was evolving.

Like a god, bringing the dead back to life.

And no amount of money could make him feel more powerful.

ABOUT THE AUTHOR

DS Whitaker is a Virginia author who loves quirky, contemporary stories with oddball twists. Johnnie in Miami is the third book of the Johnnie Series.

Her debut novel, Antigenesis, was a finalist in the 2020 National Indie Excellence Awards. Johnnie Finds a Dead Body, book one of the Johnnie series, was a 2021 NIEA Finalist for comedy.

Follow her on Twitter at @ds_whitaker. To get updates about the next books in the Johnnie series, subscribe to her mailing list at www.dswhitaker.com.

Other works by DS Whitaker:

> Antigenesis
> Planet of the Creeps
> Shower of Lies
> Johnnie Finds a Dead Body (Book 1)
> Johnnie the Pirate King (Book 2)

The next book in the series, *Johnnie and the Tempest*, is planned for a Spring 2023 release.

Dear Reader!

While I have your attention,
please consider leaving a book
review on Amazon or Goodreads!

Thank You!